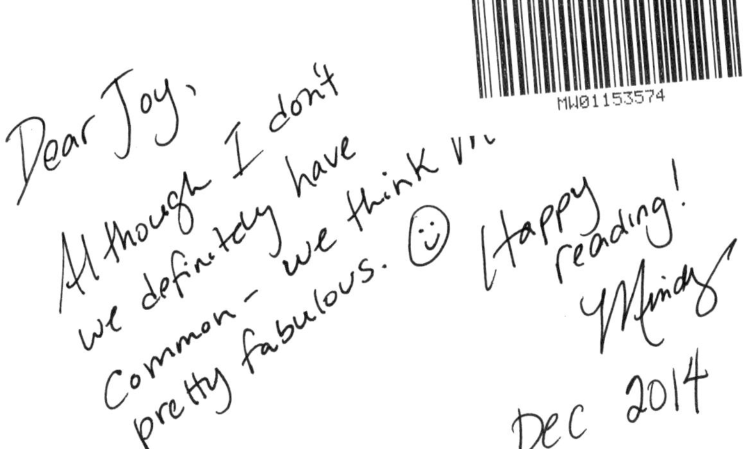

A Murder in Mount Moriah

Lindsay Harding Mystery, No. 1

Mindy Quigley

For Paul

Little Spot Publishing

http://littlespotforstories.com

Cover design by Genevieve LaVO Cosdon

Other novels in the Lindsay Harding series:

A Death in Duck

Chapter 1

Lindsay Harding watched her soldier—this man who shared her every interest, her every future goal—move across the body-strewn battlefield. He crouched and fired, moved behind a low earthen mound, and reloaded. She was close enough to see the delicate curve of his jaw with its downy fluff of beard. Yes, there was no doubt about it. Her soldier was swift, handsome, and courageous—and all of nineteen years old.

A nineteen-year-old Civil War reenactor. She, a thirty-year-old hospital chaplain and ordained minister with a mortgage and two degrees, was here at Mount Moriah, North Carolina's annual battle reenactment after having been "89% compatibility matched" with a teenager who spent his free time playing army in a Confederate uniform.

The subscription to the online dating site had been a birthday gift from her well-meaning friends. Almost instantly, she had received a "wink" from Doyle Hargreaves. Lindsay had not yet learned enough about internet dating to be wary of sunglasses or dim lighting or shots taken from a great distance. Nor had she understood the importance of absolute specificity when detailing the acceptable age range for your potential matches.

Lindsay and Doyle had arranged to meet at the entrance to the state park where the reenactment was held. By both temperament and training, Lindsay was a master of the art of maintaining a neutral expression when confronted with surprising revelations. When she first beheld Doyle's baby-pink cheeks and wispy facial hair, her brain might have been screaming "Cougar!", but her face remained a mask of Sphinx-like detachment. When Doyle responded to her polite inquiry about his profession with the statement that he was "finishing off some high school credits this summer so I can get my commercial truck driving license in the fall," however, she could only stare at him in goggle-eyed, slack-jawed horror. Doyle became defensive. "I was going to join the Marines, but I lost three toes in a lawnmower accident last year. Now they won't let me enlist."

"Sorry. It's not the trucking part. It's just that, well, you're still in high school."

He pouted. "I only gotta pass Señora Smolinski's Spanish class and then I get my diploma."

Lindsay bought him sarsaparilla, which seemed to appease him. As they wandered among the food stalls and the demonstrations of nineteenth-century arts and crafts, Doyle sipped his drink and chatted amiably. He told her about the battle he and his fellow reenactors were there to recreate, a small, unheralded skirmish that took place toward the war's end in March of 1865. Union and Confederate troops had fought on and off for almost three days to an inconclusive outcome, with the Union regiment stymied and the Rebs retreating in the middle of the night. In the Mount Moriah reenactment version, however, the battle would be confined to a large, open field and would be neatly condensed into the space of an hour and twenty minutes.

As Doyle spoke, Lindsay warmed to him. He was a nice guy. Handsome. Cheerful. He was very knowledgeable about the Civil War. Maybe the eleven-year age gap could be surmounted. Maybe they would look back at this meeting, years from now, grilling hot dogs in their backyard, little Doyle Jr. jumping through the lawn sprinkler, and laugh at the serendipity of it all.

Then Doyle told her about the button peeing.

She had expressed admiration for his uniform, a well-tailored jacket the color of butternut squash skin. He was delighted by her compliment. "Yeah, I buried the jacket in the yard for a couple of weeks to get it to look old and smell like dirt. And you gotta store the brass buttons in pee. Otherwise, they look too shiny."

"Pee?"

"Pee. You know, pee?" He had mimed an action that would have been better left un-mimed. "It makes 'em a little tarnished. They're more authentic that way." Doyle slurped the last of his sarsaparilla and tossed the paper cup in a garbage barrel. "Look, Lindsay, you seem really nice or whatever and your face and body are pretty good, but I don't think I can date a Christian minister. You see, I'm thinking about becoming a Zoroastrian."

"Uh-huh," she replied, nodding gravely. She was confused by the sudden conversational transition from urinating on your clothes to converting to an obscure Eastern religion. Before she could muster any kind of well-considered response, Doyle abruptly bid her goodbye and left to prepare for battle. Lindsay was left standing open-mouthed among the soldiers and belles.

Her cell phone began to ring. She pressed the green button to answer and was met by the sound of hysterical laughter.

"Shut up," Lindsay said.

"Can I come out now?" asked the caller.

"Yes, I think the date is officially over," Lindsay replied.

Lindsay's best friend, Rob Wu, emerged from behind a nearby stall that sold replicas of nineteenth-century ladies' undergarments. He was wiping tears of laughter from his cheek. "Oh man, Linds. That guy was so young he was an embryo." Rob was a slender and neatly manicured Taiwanese man, whose accent flipped back and forth between Chinese and Southern—sometimes within the same word. The chaplaincy supervisor and head of the Pastoral Service Department at the hospital where Lindsay worked, Rob spent as much time as he possibly could figuring out how to schedule her for back-to-back night shifts and then hiding from her wrath when the schedule was posted. He considered this pursuit both a hobby and a vocation.

"I knew I shouldn't have let you come. I'll never hear the end of this." Lindsay had asked Rob along for moral support in case she got stood up or her date turned out to be a total creep. She never would have brought him if she had known that he would be a witness to her humiliation at the hands of a teenager who pees on his clothes as a hobby.

"Seriously, why did you let that date go on for almost a half hour? What were you guys talking about all that time? Couldn't you have gotten rid of him earlier?" Rob asked.

Lindsay hung her head. "Actually, he was the one who ended it."

Rob grimaced and put a consoling arm around her. "Oh, Linds. What do you want to do now? Do you want to go home?"

"I might as well stay and watch the reenactment. We know lots of the guys out there, and don't usually get to see them in action. It might be fun. Besides, I've gone through a lot of waxing and buffing to get here today. I can't remember the last time I was this shiny and hairless."

They found a seat on the grass behind a yellow rope that demarcated the field of battle. By now, crowds of spectators had gathered and the artificial conflict was in full swing. The reenactors seemed to be drawn from all walks of life—everyone from diehards who arrived days beforehand and set up authentically Spartan bivouacs on the edges of the open fields to hobbyists who showed up for a couple of hours and strained to fasten their blue or gray uniforms over the twenty-first century swell of their beer bellies.

Lindsay surveyed the scene before her. Groups of Confederate and Union reenactors threw themselves into battle with the heedless zeal of lemmings hurling themselves into the sea. Doyle had moved out of the range of her vision, into the haze of cannon smoke. She looked up at the bright, almost pure-white sky, allowing herself to lapse into a kind of heat-induced meditation. She was grateful that at least Rob hadn't been standing close enough to overhear their conversation. No one ever had to know about Doyle's summer school classes or his lawnmower accident or his religious conversion. Her dreamy thoughts were punctuated by the thunder of the cannons and the war cries of the Rebs. Gradually the sounds changed. The canon fire died away, replaced by confused shouts and the wail of an ambulance siren.

"What happened?" Lindsay asked. Her gaze zeroed in on the field before her where an ambulance maneuvered over the ground, leaving waves of bewildered reenactors in its wake. Even the billowing smoke from the artillery seemed to get out of the vehicle's way.

"No clue," Rob replied. "Probably just some fatso reenactor passed out in all the excitement and heat."

The ambulance stopped at the farthest reach of the battlefield, out where the cleared land gave way to thick woods. Two paramedics hurried out and knelt over a soldier whose prone form was barely visible through the haze and confused movements of the reenactors. Lindsay strained to make out the details of the fallen body. She noted with relief that the injured reenactor was a large man, far too large to be Doyle or any of her reenactor friends.

"I don't know, Rob. Something's not right." The paramedics worked with a dreadful urgency that Lindsay had sometimes witnessed in the hospital's ER. The kind of urgency that gave her a sinking feeling in the pit of her stomach, knowing that she might soon have to break bad news to some unlucky family. A few frenzied moments later, the paramedics loaded the fallen man onto a stretcher, spirited him into the ambulance and drove away toward the main road.

All the soldiers had by now ceased fire and stood staring at one another. Their choreographed movements interrupted, they seemed to have forgotten their purpose. There were confused shouts and suddenly the onlookers who had been standing next to Lindsay broke through the perimeter rope and rushed onto the battlefield, checking to make sure that their husbands and sons were safe and accounted for. Lindsay and Rob found themselves propelled forward by the surging crowd. It felt for a moment as if a frenzied mob scene might erupt. Instead of a mass panic, though, the crowd began to slow and spread out. What ensued wasn't mayhem, but rather a fairly orderly process of wives and girlfriends gathering up their make-believe soldiers and forcibly leading them away.

Lindsay and Rob soon found themselves standing alone, about a dozen yards from where the fallen soldier had lain. The grass all around their feet was spattered with a rust-colored substance.

"What is that? Engine oil from the ambulance?" Rob asked, following her gaze.

Lindsay crouched down and touched her fingers to a place where the substance pooled on the parched grass. She gasped and jumped up, holding her hand out to Rob with a horrified expression. "It's blood."

"Jesus," Rob whispered, wiping Lindsay's hand on his shirt. "Hey, let's get out of here." He tipped his head toward three uniformed police officers moving quickly in their direction, carrying what appeared to be crime scene tape. Rob grabbed

Lindsay's hand and they maneuvered swiftly back into the crowd.

They made their way back to the stalls. Rob said, "I need a drink. I'm going to find a lemonade stand." Rob was famously teetotal. He had never so much as tasted anything stronger than black coffee.

"Honey, I'm gonna need something a lot stronger than lemonade," Lindsay said. "I'm going home to crawl into a nice, comfy bottle of wine." Might as well call it a day. After all, this had been the most successful date she had been on in recent memory. Best to quit while she was ahead.

Chapter 2

Two days later, Lindsay found herself eating breakfast in the cafeteria of Mount Moriah Hospital with Rob and their friend, Anna Melrose. Anna, an emergency room doctor, was tall and athletic, her tan skin set off nicely by her white doctor's coat and perfect white teeth. With light brown hair gathered into a loose ponytail, she looked like she would be as comfortable playing beach volleyball as mending broken limbs and bloody noses in the ER. Her good looks alone were enough to render her despicable in the eyes of most female hospital staffers. Worst of all, though, Mount Moriah was a Southern hospital, smack in the middle of North Carolina, and Anna Melrose had the audacity to be from Hoboken, New Jersey. She had a rotating cast of boyfriends—often older, sometimes married, always very handsome.

"I don't know how you can eat those," Rob flicked his fingers toward Anna's bran muffin. "I swear those muffins are made from wheat chaff and recycled newspapers."

"What can I say? My body is a temple," Anna countered.

"A temple, huh? Must be one of those pagan temples where they have obscene week-long orgies," Rob said.

"Oh, it's a pagan temple all right. A temple in which they sacrifice their enemies to dark and powerful gods." Anna took a huge bite of her muffin. Still chewing, she said, "Just ask my ex-husband." Anna paused and surveyed Rob's breakfast—a Tupperware container of chicken wings and a muffin from the commissary. "There is really no justice in this world. You and Lindsay both eat like twelve-year-olds at a slumber party and don't put on a pound. I even whisper the word 'Twinkie' and I have to spend two days in the gym."

Lindsay vaguely registered this smirch on her eating habits. Rather than defending herself, however, Lindsay merely sighed and began distractedly dragging her spoon through her bowl of Froot Loops.

"Lindsay, are you still depressed that things didn't work out on your neonatal soldier date?" Rob said. "You look terrible. I mean really, really awful."

"Aren't you sweet to be concerned about my well being," Lindsay said, flashing Rob a syrupy smile while simultaneously kicking his shin under the table. "But it's not because of Doyle. Doyle was top notch. In fact, I've decided that from now on, seven-toed, Zoroastrian teenagers are my type."

"What is it then? Seriously, you look like a hairball wearing a chaplain's coat," Rob said.

"As a matter of fact, I do feel like cat barf. I was up all night. A really nice guy passed away."

##

The events of the previous night seemed like a dream. At the beginning of her night shift, Lindsay had fallen into a fitful sleep in the hospital's tiny chaplain's bedroom. Around 1 a.m. she had been awaked by a page from the ICU. She had zombie-walked down the dimly lit hallway and up two flights of stairs passing through the main intensive care room, where the beds' occupants lay sleeping and still—a row of sarcophagi. At the end of the room, a little hall led to two private rooms. Lindsay knocked on one of the doors.

"Come in," a woman responded.

Lindsay opened the door. It took her eyes a moment to adjust to the fluorescent lights that blazed from the ceiling, illuminating vinyl seat coverings, laminate tables, and curtains that forged an unholy alliance between paisley and polyester. Vernon Young, a plump yet sturdy-looking black man in his early thirties, lay in bed, connected to an array of life-support machines and monitors. Kimberlee Young, his wife, looked up wearily from her sentry post at his bedside. She had an appealing chubbiness and freckles that dotted her pale white skin like confetti. Her eyes were red-rimmed and swollen. "Hey," Kimberlee sighed.

"Hey," Lindsay replied. Her natural inclination was to

follow this with, “How are you?” but years of chaplaincy training had driven that futile question out of her repertoire. Lindsay joined Kimberlee at Vernon’s bedside. “Would you like me to pray with you?”

“No!” Kimberlee held her hands in front of her as if she were warding off an onrushing mugger. She got herself in check and relaxed her posture slightly. “I mean, no, thank you. I mean, I don’t see how that’s gonna do him any good at this point.”

“The prayer doesn’t have to be for him. It can be a way of pausing to take it all in.” For two long days, Lindsay had shared Kimberlee’s bedside vigil. She had tried in vain several times to encourage Kimberlee to reflect and spend some quiet moments in her husband’s presence.

Once again, Kimberlee resisted. “I don’t need to pause. I’m fine.” The two women sat together in silence, watching the rise and fall of Vernon’s chest. Finally, Kimberlee stirred. “Did you see that Momma brought Vernon his favorite strawberry rhubarb pie?” Kimberlee gestured to the side table. An untouched pie topped with cross-hatched crust glistened under the fluorescent lights. “The man is in a coma, clinging to life, with an IV and a ventilator, and she bakes him a pie. I guess that’s her way of helping, but it’s so depressing for it to sit there like that. It’s such a waste.” She began to cry with a sudden force, as if a giant fist was squeezing the air from her lungs.

Lindsay patted Kimberlee’s shoulder and walked purposefully out the door. The squish-squish of Lindsay’s rubber-soled footsteps diminished as she moved further away down the hall. Her sudden departure silenced Kimberlee’s sobs. She sat staring in astonishment at Lindsay’s empty chair. After a minute or two, Lindsay’s quick steps could be heard advancing back toward the room. Lindsay entered and walked past Kimberlee to the side table, wielding a small, white plastic spork that she had acquired from the nurses’ station. Without saying a word, she plunged the spork into the pie and took a bite of the pink, gooey filling. “That’s the best damn pie I’ve ever eaten,” she said, her mouth stuffed with fruit and pastry. She offered a heaping sporkful to Kimberlee, who looked at her as if she had just squirted Easy Cheese on a communion wafer.

"Would your Vernon want you to sit there crying about a pie?" Lindsay asked. Kimberlee was dry-eyed now, but she continued to stare—silent and slack-jawed—at the chaplain. Lindsay raised her eyebrows expectantly and moved the pie-laden spork closer to Kimberlee. It seemed to hang in the air like a question mark. Finally, unable to hide the beginnings of a smile, Kimberlee held out her hand for the spork. The two women sat in silence, taking turns sporking pie.

##

Anna interrupted Lindsay's thoughts. "Oh. Did that guy die? Bummer. You were friends with his wife or something, right?"

"Not really. I knew her a little from high school. Her family owns Bullard's Bar-B-Q Buffet."

Rob said, "Wait. The guy who died. Are we talking about the black rebel soldier guy, Vernon Young? From the reenactment?"

"Uh-huh," Lindsay nodded. Her mind flashed back to the smoke-obscured scene the previous Saturday, the confused shouts, the fallen reenactor being loaded into the ambulance, the drips and smears of blood on the sun-parched grass.

"You worked on the guy in the ER, right?" Rob said to Anna.

"Yeah, I was on shift on the day of the commemoration last year, too. And the year before. We usually get our fair share of 'casualties'—you know, sun stroke, dehydration, overly enthusiastic 'soldiering' from these middle-aged reenactor types. But I think this guy had to be the first actual Civil War battle death since 1865.

"It was surreal," she continued. "A chubby black guy in a Confederate uniform rolls in on a gurney, and then this herd of loud, pudgy white people stream in saying they were his family."

"The police spent hours questioning all the guys at the reenactment after you left, Linds. They think the shooting was intentional," Rob said.

"Intentional?" Anna almost choked on a piece of bran muffin. She gulped some orange juice. "You've got to be kidding me. Why would someone murder him out there, surrounded by spectators and booths selling funnel cake and airbrushed t-shirts? It was probably an accident. Some Joe Six Pack probably loaded a real cartridge instead of a blank and capped his buddy."

"Rob's right," Lindsay said. "I can't understand it either, but I was in the room with Vernon's wife when the police told her. They're treating the death as suspicious. They've opened a murder investigation."

"There were dozens of soldiers involved in that reenactment. Not to mention all the people watching," Rob said. "And we're not talking about a bunch of rednecks who just like running around with guns and waving the rebel flag, either. Some of them are pillars of the community." He shook his head. "I sure hope the police have some good evidence to go on, because if it was murder, then half the people in the county are suspects."

Anna rolled her eyes. "'Half the people in the county are suspects'? You sound like Agatha Christie."

"Hey, I'm just trying to inject some color into the drab palette of your life," Rob said.

"Now you sound like an ad for paint."

Lindsay ignored their bickering and used her spoon to chase the last Froot Loop around her bowl. She thought back to her bedside vigil with Kimberlee Young. Lindsay had sat beside her until dawn, long after the unknown sniper's bullet had taken Vernon from the world. As she took her leave, Lindsay had said that she wished she could have known Vernon.

"Me, too, sugar," Kimberlee replied. "You would have loved him. Everyone did."

Now, as she thought back, Lindsay couldn't help but see the obvious lie in Kimberlee's statement. There was most definitely at least one person out there who did not love Vernon Young.

Chapter 3

Lindsay woke up in the early evening, just as the sun was beginning to dip behind the row of pine trees facing her living room windows. Whenever she came off a night shift, she spent the following afternoon dozing on the living room couch in her sweatpants. Somehow getting properly decked out in pajamas and climbing into bed seemed like an admission of defeat, but skipping sleep altogether seemed like unnecessary bravado. An afternoon couch nap struck the perfect balance.

Lindsay sat down in her small yellow kitchen, poured herself a bowl of Cocoa Puffs, and began flicking through her mail. The handwriting on an oversized, envelope caught her eye. It contained a card fronted by a cheerful cartoon drawing of a claw-footed bathtub filled with hippopotami. Inside, the message read, "Hippo Bathday!" The handwritten note below said:

Dear Lin-Lin,
Sorry this is a bit late. You know me—always busy busy busy! Things with me are good but I can't believe I'm old enough to have a 30 year old daughter!!! Ha ha! Now I'm gonna have to start lying about your age as well as my own. Ha ha!

I'll be passing your way in a couple weeks and I'd love to get together and catch up. I hope you had a nice birthday!!!
Xoxo,
Mom

There was a Glamour Shots-style four-by-six inch picture of Lindsay's mother tucked inside the card. Sarabelle Harding's image stared into the vague distance at the edge of the frame, avoiding Lindsay's gaze. Her blonde hair was styled into an attractive cascade of loose curls. Ice blue eyes sparkled from beneath copious false eyelashes. Some kind of gauzy filter had been applied; it erased years of hard living from Sarabelle's face. Lindsay wondered if, somewhere under that mountain of make-up and behind the photographer's tricks, Sarabelle retained her fine-boned beauty.

Lindsay examined the envelope. No return address. It had been at least a year since she'd heard from her mother—five or more since they last saw each other in person. A familiar hollowness gnawed at Lindsay's solar plexus. When Lindsay was six, her parents had been arrested for running a small-scale marijuana operation out of their modest brick house. They were each sentenced to five years in prison, and Lindsay was sent to live with her father's aged aunt on an island in North Carolina's Outer Banks.

The Outer Banks of Lindsay's childhood was nothing like the sunny holiday retreat that Spring Breakers and well-heeled beach house owners rhapsodize over. Until the mid-1980s, there was no real road connecting their small community with the mainland, or even with the adjacent island enclaves of Duck and Kitty Hawk. The scattered full-time residents numbered in the low hundreds; the nearest house with children was half a mile away from Lindsay's. The intrepid holidaymakers who ventured to Corolla in those early days were mostly middle-aged artists or fishermen, seeking solitude. On the rare occasions when they did make conversation with the locals, it was only to say how charmingly old-fashioned Corolla (they pronounced it 'Kah-roe-lah' like the Toyota Corolla) was, and that living on Bodie Island (they pronounced it 'Bow-dee' like the skier Bodie Miller) must be like taking a vacation all year round. The locals would snap back that *Kuh-raw-luh* and *Bah-dee* Island suited them just fine, thank you very much.

Lindsay and her great aunt—who she called Aunt Harding, never Aunt Patricia—shared a weather-beaten cottage near the northern tip of Bodie Island. Each morning, Aunt Harding would trek off down the sandy path to preside over the sorting and delivery of mail in the island's small post office. Lindsay would make her own way to the island's little school, or, during the summer holidays, spend the days beachcombing. She would find little treasures in the flotsam and keep them in her own secret mermaid's cave under the front porch steps. Her treasure trove contained everything from chunks of smooth green glass to the sun-bleached skull of a horse. Lindsay's bleak, windswept childhood had been punctuated by bimonthly visits to the Raleigh prisons that housed each of her parents. On Saturday mornings, she called on her mother at the North Carolina Correctional Institution for Women. At lunchtime, her grim-faced aunt drove her ten minutes down the road to the much-less-grandly-named Central Prison to eat sandwiches and Nutty Bars out of vending machines with her father.

After four years of model behavior and a jailhouse baptism, Lindsay's father was granted early release from prison and was eventually deemed fit to regain custody of his daughter. Her mother, meanwhile, had an extra year added to her sentence after getting herself involved in a jailhouse gambling ring. When Sarabelle was finally released, the damaged little family attempted to reconcile. Aunt Harding had kept up with the mortgage payments on their small brick ranch house in Mount Moriah, and the three of them returned to live in the now-marijuana-free space. They stalked around the place like caged lions: Lindsay's father, puffed up with his new-found sense of responsibility and his new-found religion; Lindsay's mother, with her furtive movements, still a prisoner in her own mind; and Lindsay herself, on the brink of adolescence, a sealed box of roiling emotions. The fragile union lasted eighteen months. Then, one February night, Sarabelle disappeared. Since that time, Sarabelle had haunted Lindsay's life like a ghost, floating in when it suited her and then vanishing with little trace.

With a sharp snap of her wrist, Lindsay tossed the card, the picture, and the envelope into the trash. She went to her bedroom to change into her running clothes. A moment later, she walked back into the kitchen and retrieved the card, standing it carefully in the kitchen windowsill. Surely Sarabelle remembering Lindsay's birthday meant something. And she was suggesting that they meet. Maybe she was finally ready to make amends. Lindsay looked at the cheerful hippos, their rotund little bodies distorted by slanting rays of late afternoon sunlight, and allowed herself the merest hint of a smile.

##

Lindsay's house stood at the frayed edge of Mount Moriah. The town itself nestled in a little valley among the rolling hills of the Piedmont, the area between North Carolina's coast and the Appalachians—a collection of buildings and houses orbiting the twin poles of the Mount Moriah Regional Hospital and the Walmart Superstore. There was little hustle and even less bustle. Lindsay lived beyond these orbits, out where the buildings trailed off into an ever thinner sprinkling of mobile homes and dilapidated farmhouses. Her little white house stood alone on an acre of land surrounded on all sides by tall pines and a thicket of dense undergrowth. She thought of it as her own little ship, sailing on a sea of solitude. Only the ship was badly in need of a paint job. And the ocean was mostly made of kudzu.

She stood on the front porch now performing some perfunctory stretches, in preparation for a run. Seven p.m. was the absolute earliest she would consider jogging this time of year. During the summer months, the air remained thick and humid well into the early evening—venture out any time before dusk and you'd feel more like you were swimming than running. The sun was low on the horizon, but there was still at least a good hour of daylight left.

Quickly gathering speed, Lindsay moved out of her neighborhood onto a tree-lined, two-lane road. Within a mile of her house, the houses gave way to tall pines, clay-lined creeks, and the low, rolling hills of the Carolina Piedmont. She passed the last outcropping of Mount Moriah's version of civilization—a trailer park optimistically called Malibu Village—and crossed the road toward the piece of scrubby pine forest known as the Richards Homestead.

The Homestead, once a profitable tobacco farm, had been gradually sold off over the years to housing developers. What remained was spread over 40 acres and bordered on one side by the interstate. The Richards family, who had made a small fortune in tobacco during the nineteenth century, had long since given up farming and moved into more hospitable surroundings. The land had lain fallow for as long as anyone could remember. The current Richardses lived in an 8-bedroom house in town. There was speculation that they would someday relocate to somewhere fashionable and exciting, like Winston-Salem, or France. But so far the family seemed content to revel in their status as the social and political royalty of their own little Central Carolina fiefdom.

Lindsay ducked through the wire fence next to the road, ignoring the *No Trespassing* signs, and picked up one of the old logging paths that crisscrossed the land. As she advanced through the trees, the air became cool and fragrant. The pine trees along the path bore strange scars and deformities, like veterans from some long-forgotten war.

Lulled by the warmth of the evening and the rhythm of her breathing, she almost didn't see the men at first. But there they were, up ahead, striding swiftly across the clearing—three men dressed in the summer uniforms of Southern white men, khaki pants and short-sleeved button down shirts. They stood very still, looking intently into the trees on the far side of their SUVs. In two years of jogging on these paths, this was the first time Lindsay had seen anyone out here. She stopped in her tracks, observing them almost in awe.

One of the three men walked to his gleaming SUV and retrieved a rifle from somewhere in the back. He crouched next to his vehicle, out of the range of Lindsay's vision. She wondered if they could be out-of-season poachers—a not uncommon occurrence on private forest land like this. She dismissed the thought quickly. They were far too brazen, and they were obviously not dressed for hunting. After a few moments, the report of the gun exploded through the heavy evening air. Lindsay involuntarily ducked, even though the shot was in the opposite direction of her. The men jumped up, whooping and high-fiving. They talked for a minute more and drove away in their separate, shiny SUVs, kicking up a dusty haze in their wake.

Lindsay remained still until the sound of the engines was replaced by the chirp of crickets. Out across the meadow, a lone firefly glowed in the amber twilight. When she was quite sure that they were gone, she ran swiftly across the clearing toward the spot that the shooter seemed to have been targeting. She walked along the tree line, peering into the rapidly darkening stretch of forest. There was a rustling from a clump of bushes that stood at the base of a gnarled tree. Her pulse quickened. She moved toward the bushes as if pulled along by an invisible rope. Under the cover of the trees, there was very little daylight left. She crept closer, trying to still her pounding heart. The rustling continued intermittently. She was now within yards of the movement's source.

Suddenly, as if it had been shot from a cannon, a small, dappled doe burst out of the thicket of bushes and sprinted straight at Lindsay. Lindsay dove sideways, her body slamming hard into the ground. The doe, too, zigzagged to avoid a collision. Lindsay scrambled around on the ground and eventually regained her footing, but by then the animal had disappeared into the darkness of the forest. Lindsay began to brush the dust off of her bare arms and legs. She stopped as her hands made contact with something sticky. Blood. It dotted her body like gruesome confetti. She followed the trail of blood with her eyes. Some of it led toward the bushes, some of it away, in the direction the injured animal had bolted. Lindsay shivered in spite of the oppressive heat. Those men had shot the deer without care or reason. Worse still, they hadn't had the compassion to finish the job. As quickly as she could, Lindsay turned around and ran home. As she ran, she tried to forget the terrible fear in the doe's eyes. She ran and ran, as the darkness swallowed up the daylight in ravenous gulps.

Chapter 4

When Lindsay arrived for her shift at the hospital the following day, Geneva Williams accosted her in the small, windowless office that, along with the sleeping room, made up the chaplains' quarters.

"Girl! I have found him! Don't you say no, because he is perfect."

Lindsay's co-worker wagged her finger forcefully to emphasize each phrase. Lindsay's stomach sank. Geneva, a sprightly black woman in her late sixties, was determined to find Lindsay a husband. Every time a new man joined the hospital's staff, Geneva would covertly investigate his marital status and his interests, all with an eye toward preventing Lindsay from ending up, as she put it, "A sorry old spinster living out your days with a dozen cats and sack full of knitting."

"I have married off three daughters and four sons," Geneva said. "All happy. Fifteen grandchildren. No divorces."

"I know. You've mentioned that. Frequently," Lindsay replied.

"I just want to make sure you heard me. One-hundred percent happy. Zero percent divorces. You cannot argue with statistics. Now then, sit down and let me tell you about your future husband."

Lindsay groaned, but obediently took a seat at one of the two compact, wooden desks that furnished the office. Although Geneva only stood 4' 11", she was a formidable woman. The daughter of sharecroppers, she'd put herself through teacher's college and taught second grade at the all-black school in New Albany, a larger town not far from Mount Moriah. After she married, she and her husband settled down to become the co-pastors of their own small evangelical ministry, The New Holiness Temple of Blessed Deliverance.

After her husband's death the previous year, Geneva had

ceded full-time pastoring to one of her daughters and decided that instead of retiring, she would shift her focus to ministering to the sick and the bereaved as a hospital chaplain. As the head of the pastoral services department at the hospital, Rob had previously instituted a policy that all full-time hospital chaplains and chaplain residents at Mount Moriah had to hold a graduate degree in theology, be ordained in a recognized denomination, and have interned in a hospital, prison, or hospice. Somehow, though, here was Geneva, a recently-minted chaplain resident, with only a K through 9 teaching certificate and the formidable force of her personality. Geneva was undergoing the intensive, self-analytical process of chaplaincy training called Clinical Pastoral Education, or CPE. She had finished the first unit, which allowed her to begin her residency, and she was still technically under the supervision of the more senior chaplains. This technicality, however, did nothing to diminish Geneva's unquestioned, vigorously self-promoted authority in matters of courtship and marriage.

"His name is Drew Checkoway," Geneva began. "Tall, dark, and handsome. He's a brain surgeon, girl! Which means smart. And rich. Thirty-five years old, never married, no kids. It doesn't happen every day that a quality man like this drops into our laps."

Lindsay couldn't deny the truth of this last statement. Although Mount Moriah's population had grown increasingly fluid and cosmopolitan in recent years, the arrival of a young, eligible man was still an occasion to be met with heightened interest. Clearly this guy was too good to be true. "Probably gay," Lindsay said.

"Don't you think that that was the first thing I checked up on? What am I? Some kind of amateur? Not gay, girl. You got to get yourself that man. Carpe Brain Surgeon. I already seen some of the nurses batting their little eyes at him. Drew Checkoway. Remember it because that's your future children's daddy's name."

"I'll be sure to look out for him."

"Do. Now I gotta go. Rob's been on me to write up an entry for my reflection journal. Wants me to reflect on my feelings about having to do a reflection journal. I swear the boy is trifling with me. Sometimes I have to pray to Jesus to help me restrain myself from whooping his little behind with a hickory switch. I really do. Maybe I'll write about that in my journal entry." As Geneva opened the door to leave, she turned her head back to look at Lindsay and said, "Mrs. Lindsay Checkoway. Even sounds good. Hope you aren't one of those women who keeps her name when she gets married. Can't stand that. Makes it too confusing to know who belongs with who. Mrs. Lindsay Checkoway, then." Geneva spoke these last words with such conviction that Lindsay felt sure that, in Geneva's mind at least, the future was as stone-solid as the Ten Commandments.

##

Lindsay didn't have to wait long to meet the much-heralded Dr. Drew Checkoway. A few hours into her shift, as she made her way up to the oncology unit to visit a patient, Lindsay ran into Anna in the hallway. While the two women were chatting, a tall man with sparkling green eyes approached them. His black hair was collected into a trendy configuration of stacks and spikes; his face sported a calculatedly rugged amount of stubble. The precision of his grooming, and particularly the deliberate semi-beardage, reminded Lindsay vaguely of George Michael's post-*Wham!* period. Lindsay's hackles were raised.

"Hello, Dr. Melrose," the man said, smiling broadly. It was a sweet smile, a bit lopsided. Lindsay cautiously lowered one hackle.

"Call me Anna, please. Dr. Melrose sounds old. And far more mature and responsible than I actually am."

"Well, Anna," he said, laughing, "I think I'm lost. This hospital is about half the size of the one I worked at in Chicago, but it's at least ten times as confusing. I was just walking down a hall that ended in a staircase that led up to a brick wall." Okay. He was charming and self-effacing. He glanced at Lindsay. Actually, she decided, he was more Greek god than 80s pop.

"Ah, yes," Anna said, oblivious to the movements of Lindsay's hackles. "That stairway used to lead to Pediatrics, but they tore it down when they built the new children's floor. Apparently, the staircase is holding up something important, and can't be demolished without taking half the building with it. Which way are you headed?"

"Allegedly there is an MRI machine on this floor, and allegedly I cannot miss it."

"I'll take you," Lindsay said, perhaps a little too eagerly. "I'm going that way."

"I'd better be getting back to the ER," Anna said. "There's probably an oozing sore or obstructed bowel down there with my name on it. I'll catch you guys later."

As they walked along the corridor, he extended his hand. "I don't think we've met. I'm Drew Checkoway."

She shook his hand. "Lindsay Harding. I'm one of the chaplains here."

"Oh! Someone told me about you."

Lindsay panicked, fearing that Geneva may have informed Drew of their imminent wedding.

"Yeah, one of the other doctors said I should always recommend that nervous patients talk to you before they have surgery, even if they're not religious, because you calm them down. I have to say, I didn't expect you to be so young. The community hospital I worked at in Chicago was in a mainly Catholic neighborhood, so the chaplains were usually old celibate dudes with black clothes and pot bellies. None of them looked like you, that's for sure."

Trying to ignore the flaming redness rising in her, Lindsay launched into a rambling chronicle of Mount Moriah Regional Medical Center's history. It had been founded as a small rural clinic just after the First World War. Up until the 1960s, it stayed essentially unchanged, delivering the county's babies and patching up the injured. That all changed in 1962, when the matriarch of the wealthy Richards family was stricken with bone cancer. The woman needed a lengthy, specialized course of treatment that the little clinic was unable to provide. After months of travelling back and forth for treatment, she finally died at a hospital in Boston, far from her home and family. Her husband became the benefactor of the new Mount Moriah Regional Medical Center and the family's large endowments had kept the hospital ticking ever since.

Lindsay finished her recitation just as they reached a large glass door marked *Magnetic Resonance Imaging.*

"Well, this is where you get off," she said. Normally, she wouldn't have even registered the double entendre, but somehow in Drew's presence, it seemed to hang in the air like an invitation. Lindsay blushed.

Drew didn't seem to notice her embarrassment; he was already peering through the glass door. "Thanks a lot. When I heard that Mount Moriah had a 12T MRI machine, I had to see it for myself. This morning, I saw the triple-filtration hemodialysis infuser and the laser-guided robotic laporoscopy device in the operating theater. And all the reconstructive surgeries here are planned using a 320-slice CT scanner, with 16-centimeter anatomical coverage!" He paused, noticing Lindsay's blank expression. "Sorry. I should've tested the waters first with a few discreet references to biomechanics before I unfurled the whole Über-nerd package."

Lindsay laughed. "It's great that you're so enthusiastic."

"That's why I took this job. My hospital in Chicago was so under-funded. I was tired of trying to perform brain surgeries using a spatula and a piece of fishing line. I can't get over the money that flows through this place."

"A century and a half of exploited labor and a whole lot of lung cancer will buy you some pretty cool gadgets," Lindsay said.

Drew raised an eyebrow.

"The Richardses, our generous benefactors, come from a long line of tobacco farmers and cigarette oligarchs. They were the 'R' in R&G American Cigarettes. The current generous benefactor, Silas Richards IV, sold his stake in the company and is now the distinguished state representative from the 64th District. The Richards family's money, plus Silas's political position, keeps the spigot of funding flowing freely to the hospital."

"A hospital funded by cigarette money. Like the mob building cathedrals in Sicily." Drew shrugged. "Well, I'd better get going. Hope to see you around again. If I ever find my way back to my office from here, that is."

Lindsay walked back down the hall and through the doors of the oncology ward. "Lindsay Checkoway," she whispered to herself. Geneva was right; it didn't sound half bad.

Chapter 5

As Lindsay walked out to the hospital parking lot after her shift that evening, Rob called her cell phone.

"What are you doing tonight? We're taking Old Joe to the Mex-itali."

The Mex-itali was the best Mexican restaurant in Mount Moriah. It was also the best Italian restaurant in Mount Moriah. It was also the only Mexican or Italian restaurant in Mount Moriah.

"I wish I could. You know how I love eating tacos marinara while listening to Joe Tatum's views on al-Qaeda's involvement in the moon landing conspiracy. But I have to stop in and see Kimberlee Young. You know, Vernon's wife? She's asked me to do the memorial service."

"Your life is just a nonstop party, Chaplain Harding. Let the good times roll!"

Lindsay walked toward her car, an ancient, electric blue Toyota Tercel. Twilight was just beginning to descend over the wide expanse of parking lot. Visiting hours were winding down and the lot was half empty. She could see a piece of folded paper tucked under the windshield wiper. Her first thought was that it was an advertisement. The local dry cleaning place was always papering parked cars with 2-for-1 deals. She idly plucked it from the windshield with one hand while fishing in her purse for her keys with the other hand. Rather than the glossy advertising paper she expected, though, she found herself holding a piece of lined notepaper. A bit of the edge was frayed where it had been torn from a spiral-bound notebook. She stopped rummaging in her purse and opened the folded sheet. In small, cramped handwriting, she read the message:

WE KNOW YOU GOT THE MONEY HONEY. WHEN THE TIME COMES NOBODY NEEDS TO GET HURT.

NOBODY EVEN NEEDS TO KNOW.

Lindsay had no idea what the note meant. She had no money. She could barely afford her monthly student loan payments. Even more than the strange content, though, it was the writing itself that unsettled her. It wasn't so much the implied threat. It was the way the words were etched so violently into the paper that in places they tore right through it.

With rising panic, Lindsay looked around her. At the edge of the parking lot, in the shadow of a tall tree, a lone man stood. He was tall and whip-thin, wearing a denim jacket despite the heat. He stared straight at her, unmoving. He raised his hand to light the cigarette that was perched on his lips. He was only about 30 feet from her, but Lindsay couldn't make out the details of his face. When he brought the lighter toward his mouth, she gave out an involuntary gasp. The light from the flame made his large, round eyes glitter an iridescent green, like the eyes of an insect. Lindsay and the stranger stared at each other for a long moment. He continued to smoke his cigarette, drawing the smoke deep into his lungs with each inhale. Lindsay didn't take her eyes off of him as she frantically rifled through her purse, still searching for her car keys. She found them at last, and, with trembling hands, unlocked the car door. She hurtled her body inside and locked the door behind her. She cranked the engine and peeled out of the parking lot, trying to put some clear distance between herself and the green-eyed stranger.

##

Lindsay was still shaken by the strange note and the man with the insect eyes as she pulled off the main road into the Youngs' neighborhood. She had briefly toyed with the idea of reporting the incident to the police, but she realized that, in fact, there was nothing to report. A bizarre unsigned note. A bug-eyed man who may well have just stepped into a shady spot for a smoke break. Creepy, yes. Criminal, no.

The Youngs' street—a block over from the high school that Kimberlee and Lindsay had attended—was filled with identical-looking houses, each fronted by a well-tended patch of lawn. Kimberlee lived in a modest two-story colonial that was painted the color of fresh-churned butter. Kimberlee answered the door smiling broadly. "Lord almighty! It's hotter than Matt Damon in a pair of tight jeans out here! Get yourself on into the air conditioning."

Lindsay was grateful for the cheerful greeting. It helped to banish the lingering unease brought about by the strange note. However, when she looked closer, she observed Kimberlee's vacant-eyed exuberance: tight smile, carefully styled hair, bright makeup. Her expression brought to mind dance music that continued to play long after everyone had left the party.

Kimberlee pulled Lindsay inside and gestured to the pink overstuffed leather sofa that took up the better part of the living room. "Have a seat. I'm so glad you could do this. Our family has never been real religious. Growing up, Sunday was our only day off from the restaurant, so we always went down to the lake or out to the movies. I guess pulled pork and sweetcorn fritters were our religion." She laughed feebly at her own joke. "I thought we should have some kind of preacher to do the service, though, to make it seem more, you know, official." She laughed again, a tinny, mirthless laugh. "Can I get you anything? Some sweet tea? My sisters came by this afternoon, and they brought some berry cobbler. Do you want a piece?"

"No, I'm all right, thanks."

"Have some fruit, then," Kimberlee said, extracting a fruit basket from among the vases of condolence flowers that covered the massive coffee table. "One of Vernon's reenactor friends sent this over."

"Thanks." Lindsay reluctantly took a small bunch of grapes. She knew from long experience that it was rare to escape the home of a fellow Southern woman without facing an artillery barrage of cakes, sandwiches, and sweet tea—the Southern version of iced tea that involved adding as much granulated sugar as the laws of physics and chemistry would allow to the beverage before chilling it. It was better to surrender as quickly as possible rather than risk the full hospitality assault. To resist was to invite confrontation with a cold ham and three kinds of pie. Plucking a grape from the bunch, Lindsay asked, "How is your family doing? I could see how close you all are when they came by to visit."

Kimberlee had three sisters and a brother. They all lived in the area, and they all worked, in one capacity or another, at the family's barbecue restaurant. Keith, at forty the eldest of the clan, was the general manager. Kimberlee's sisters, Kathilee, and the twins—Kristalene and Kennadine—were busy with their young children, but they found time to wait tables, bake pies, or deliver catering orders. Kimberlee's parents, Versa and Buford Bullard, did the lion's share of the cooking.

"I can't tell you how shocked everybody is. The restaurant has been closed since it happened. It's the first time I ever remember Momma and Daddy closing when it wasn't a Sunday or Christmas. They all loved Vernon. He didn't have any family of his own, really, just some cousins up in Philadelphia, so Momma and Daddy were like parents to him. And he was so good with all the little nieces and nephews. They just worshipped the ground he walked on. They can't believe their Uncle Vernon is gone."

"And you? How have you been holding up?"

"I think I'm okay. Or, I should probably say, I'm okay unless I think. If I can just manage to keep moving every minute for the rest of my life, I'll be fine." Kimberlee tried to laugh, but her voice cracked and the sound emerged as more of a squeak. "Speaking of which, let's get down to business. We'll have the memorial service and a luncheon in the atrium at the country club. Silas Richards arranged that for us. He and Vernon were buddies from the reenacting group. I've put together some songs and poems and things for the service." She picked up a small stack of papers and laid them out on the coffee table. "Vernon liked old-timey songs and poems. But I don't want any of those Jesus-y, 'everything is great now because you're up in heaven' hymns. Everything is not great and I want him here with me, not up on a cloud strumming on some golden harp. That's a giant crock of..." She caught herself and looked across at Lindsay. "No offense."

"None taken."

"It's just that if one more person tells me that Vernon is in a better place now, I'm gonna set my hair on fire. I'd rather keep the service light and fun. You'll be like an emcee," Kimberlee said brightly, as if she were asking Lindsay to read the announcements at the Rotary Club Fourth of July Picnic.

The diminished role Kimberlee envisioned for her did not bother Lindsay. In fact, she would have been greatly relieved not to have to try to think of profound words that would somehow encapsulate the grief and turmoil caused by Vernon's untimely and violent death. However, she felt compelled to press Kimberlee on the issue. She had seen too many bereft people try to rush through the grieving process. They would just keep patching the cracks in the concrete of their psyches until one day the weight of their loss would crash down and crush them.

"I agree that a celebration of life is appropriate," Lindsay said gently. "But I wonder whether you might want to slow down a little? Including prayer or meditation in the service, along with a nice eulogy, might give you and others a chance to engage with your loss."

Kimberlee threw Lindsay's words back at her. "I don't want to 'engage with my loss.' I want the whole thing to be uplifting. Like a party, without mentioning about the way he died. That's all just too ugly to talk about and my husband doesn't deserve a memorial with ugliness."

Lindsay decided to continue the conversation later; there was a steeliness in Kimberlee's expression that was going to be tough to break through. "The tone will be a reflection of the life he lived." Lindsay changed the subject. "Have you planned the burial yet?"

"No. The coroner still hasn't told me when they're going to release Vernon's body. Could be another week yet, and I'm not waiting on them. Whenever that comes, we'll just do something small. Just with the family."

Kimberlee paused and took Lindsay's hand. "I'm really glad that we are getting to know each other. Funny that we didn't socialize very much in high school. It's a real shame. I guess we moved in different circles."

"Yeah." Lindsay smiled. "You were popular and on homecoming court. My extracurricular activities were smoking and sulking under the baseball bleachers. Different circles."

"I don't know why you hung out with that crowd, honey. They were losers." Kimberlee paused for a moment noting

Lindsay's raised eyebrows. "Don't act like you don't know that. They didn't have one single thing going for them, bless their hearts. I always thought you were destined for better things. You had brains. And you were a lot better looking than the other girls in that group. Like Hunchback Heather or that Dracula girl. What was her name?"

"Julee Rae Janson," Lindsay said. "She dances at the Commodore's Lounge down by Statesville now, and I think that Dracula cape is part of her, um, act." Lindsay started peeling the skins from her grapes, piercing each one with her thumbnail and extracting the flesh inside. "I think my daddy being who he was had something to do with how I acted back then. And the whole thing with my parents. It wasn't exactly a recipe for social acceptance in a small-town school. I guess I identified more with the 'losers'. They didn't ask questions."

Before Kimberlee could reply, there was a sharp knock at the door.

Kimberlee leaned back and parted the vertical blinds on the window behind the couch with her fingers. She let out a startled little gasp. "Oh gosh. It's the police."

Chapter 6

Kimberlee walked quickly to the door, muttering half to Lindsay and half to herself. "My brain has up and removed itself from my head. I completely forgot they were sending someone around tonight." She fluffed her already-voluminous hair and arranged her heavily made-up features into a smile before opening the door. "Well knock me down with a feather! If it isn't Warren Satterwhite! Don't tell me that *you* are the police. Look at you, all handsome and grown." She let out an appreciative whistle. "Still skinnier than a snake on stilts, though. Look who it is, Lindsay. This is turning into a regular high school reunion!" A pale, red-haired man loped into the room. He was thin and slightly gangly, with even features and warm brown eyes. Kimberlee gestured to the couch. "I know you remember Lindsay Harding. You two knew each other back in the day, as I recall."

"Well this sure is a surprise!" Warren exclaimed. "When did you get back into town? You were living up in Columbus, right?"

Lindsay rose from the couch and hugged her old friend. "Yes, I was up North for a few years after I graduated from college. But I've been back in Mount Moriah for about two years now. Have you been here that whole time? I can't believe we haven't run into each other."

"I'm over in New Albany. I don't get over this way much and when I do, I'm afraid it's only for work. I work on violent crimes—thugs and drugs—so I tend not to see 'normal' people very regularly. At least not while they're still alive." A flush rose in his cheeks, highlighting a smattering of freckles. "Sorry, Kimberlee. I really am sorry about your loss."

"Of course, honey."

Lindsay registered a bizarre disconnect in Kimberlee's expression. For a moment, the lower half of Kimberlee's face was fixed into a polite smile. Her eyes, however, flashed like daggers.

Kimberlee cleared her throat. “So, is there any news on the investigation?”

“The SBI lab over down in Raleigh is still running some tests on all those reenacting guns we collected out there, but we haven’t turned up anything.”

“Why don’t you come in and sit down awhile? Lindsay here was just having some fruit. What can I get you? I’ve got cold chicken and berry cobbler. Do you want a sandwich? Some sweet tea?”

“I’m all right, thanks.”

“I’ll just make you up a little plate, then.”

Kimberlee flitted off to the kitchen. Hearing the clinking of cutlery and the opening of the fridge, Lindsay realized now how lucky she was to escape with only a fruit basket.

“It’s a real pleasant surprise to see you here, Lindsay. I didn’t know you and Kimberlee were friends.”

“I’ve run into her a few times over the years, but only in passing. I’m a chaplain at the hospital. Kimberlee called me up when they brought Vernon in, and I stayed with her while he was in a coma and when he passed away. Now I’m doing the memorial service.”

“A chaplain? I can’t believe nobody told me that! I guess it’s been a long time since I ran into anybody from the old crowd.”

“They probably wouldn’t remember me, anyway. You were the only jock who condescended to talk to me.”

“Condescended, hell! If it wasn’t for you, I never would have passed Trigonometry. And thank goodness I did pass. After I wrecked my elbow pitching senior year, all the big schools that had been dangling scholarship offers suddenly disappeared. Wofford was the only place that would have me, because I had halfway decent grades. Without a college education, I never could have made sergeant this fast. So I owe my whole career to Lindsay Harding, the math whiz!”

Lindsay rolled her eyes. “I’m sure all of your success as a police officer is down to the Trig homework I helped you with when we were sixteen.”

“Absolutely,” Warren said, nodding earnestly. “People

think police work is all clues and leads and suspects, but really, we solve a lot of cases with cosines and tangents. We plug all the variables into a special computer, do some calculations, and it spits out a list of suspects."

"Really?"

"Um, no," Warren said, laughing good-naturedly. "That would at least make things interesting. We get at most three murders a year, and usually the suspects are just obvious. Two guys argue over a girl in a bar. One of them ends up beaten to Jell-O salad with a tire iron. You search the other guy's car and find a bloody tire iron. Case closed. Every once in awhile, one comes my way that takes a little more proving—someone killed for the insurance money or something. A couple years ago, I had a woman try to put out a hit on her ex-husband over custody of their cockatoo. Ninety-nine percent of the time, though, it ain't exactly *CSI*. The real hard part is doing everything exactly by the book so the charges will stand up in court."

Kimberlee returned, bearing two plates laden with sandwiches, fried chicken, coleslaw, and pie.

"You looked hungry, Lindsay, so I brought you a little something." She took a seat on the pink leather La-Z-Boy chair opposite them. "Well, Warren, what is it you want to know?"

Chapter 7

"We just need to find out a little more about Vernon," Warren began, opening a small, spiral-bound notebook. "What he did, who his friends were. I know you already went over a lot of this with the Mount Moriah police, but there are still a few pieces missing. I wanted to talk to you more informal, you see, because we know each other from way back."

"All right, then. Shoot," Kimberlee said.

"Well, I'll start with an easy one. How did you and Vernon meet?"

Lindsay sensed an undercurrent of seriousness in Warren's tone that belied his friendly words. She suddenly felt out of place. "Should I leave you guys to hash through this?" she asked.

"No, honey," Kimberlee said. "Just sit yourself down and enjoy your food. I'm sure this won't take long." She turned to Warren and began an exhaustive retelling of her early courtship with Vernon, detailing everything from what Vernon wore when she first saw him ("…jean shorts and a light blue polo shirt and light blue is my favorite color so I knew that was a good sign…") to the pizza toppings on the first meal they shared ("…pepperoni with mushroom and extra cheese, and I said, 'That's my favorite, too,' and Vernon said…").

"How did you end up going to college in Boston, anyway?" Warren asked, trying to derail a blow-by-blow recounting of Kimberlee and Vernon's fourth date (…to a Red Sox game. We sat in the fifth row, behind the Sox's dugout, and Vernon caught a foul ball, which I still have around here somewhere if you want to see it…).

"It was a music conservatory. I got a scholarship for banjo performance. My sister Kathilee went there, too. Don't you remember? We used to play at school assemblies and stuff. The Bullard Banjettes?"

Warren flipped through his notes. "As a matter of fact, I

wanted to ask you about that very thing. Didn't you gals usually play at the reenactment?"

"Yes, sir. I was there every year for the past 13 years. Except for this one." Kimberlee paused. "I can't tell you how many times I've wanted to redo that day since it happened. Maybe if I had been there, I would have noticed something. Maybe I would have seen Vernon fall and made them check on him sooner." As she spoke these last words, Kimberlee's joviality rushed out of her. She sat for a moment, her hazel eyes suddenly the color of thunderclouds.

"Why didn't y'all play this year?" Warren pressed.

"Well, the Banjettes did play. All except me. We had a catering order to get out for that evening. Silas Richards's daughter's pre-engagement party? They're having the real engagement party in a couple of weeks out at the country club, so this was the pre-engagement one where all of them that are planning the real engagement party can get together. The groom is from New Albany. Morgan Partee? Maybe you know him? His daddy owns Partee Auto World? Anyway, Momma couldn't fix all the food and pack it up by herself so I stayed at the restaurant and helped her cook."

"It was your idea to stay behind?"

"I think it was Vernon who suggested it. Or maybe Momma," she said with a vague wave of her hand. "I can't rightly recall."

"Couldn't somebody else have helped your mother so that you could perform at the reenactment? You guys have some hired help out there, don't you?"

"Well, I suppose one of the guys that work in the kitchen could have stayed behind, but they all wanted to go out to the reenactment with their kids. They all have kids, you see, and that Civil War stuff is fun for them," Kimberlee replied.

"You didn't like watching the reenactments?"

"You've seen one, you've seen 'em all. I mean, I'm glad Vernon had a hobby that he enjoyed so much, but that was his thing, not mine."

"So you just worked at the restaurant all day with your mother?"

"Yes, I told you that already," Kimberlee said.

Lindsay was feeling increasingly uncomfortable as Warren's pretence of a friendly chat began to fall away. It was now clear that there was a deeper motive behind his visit. Warren also seemed to sense Kimberlee's darkening mood, and he changed his tack. He took a bite of fried chicken smacked his lips. "Now that is a beautiful piece of poultry. I swear the Bullards can do voodoo with a deep fryer." He settled himself back into the pink leather couch. "Now then, how did Vernon get interested in reenacting?"

"It was the movie *Glory*, really," said Kimberlee, brightening a little. "You know? The one with Morgan Freeman? Even in his history classes in college, Vernon had never heard that black soldiers played such a big part in the actual fighting of the war. He did some looking and next thing I knew he'd up and joined with the US Troops Colored Infantry Regiment in Massachusetts.

"Keith, my brother, is a big history buff, too. When we moved back here last year, he and Vernon thought it would be funny if Vernon switched to the other side. It was kind of a joke at first between them—a black rebel soldier. Vernon found out, though, that there were a few black guys who fought on the Confederate side. Slaves that went into battle alongside their masters and some free blacks who sided with the South for whatever reason. He and Keith signed up together to start reenacting with the local group here.

"A lot of the reenactors take on personas, you know. They pretend to be a specific person from history. Vernon's 'impression'—that's what their pretend self is called—was based on an actual guy from North Carolina, from Alamance county, in fact. A freed slave named Samuel Wilcox who kept a journal about his life. Vernon was researching every detail he could find about that man's life. I can't say I ever understood the appeal of any of it. Who wants to spend their free time reading some dusty old book? But he loved it. Every spare weekend, he'd pass hours in the library—finding out what Samuel Wilcox ate for breakfast on a Monday morning in 1862. That kind of thing. He spent so much time and money scouring eBay and all these specialized reenacting sites for the right kind of clothes to wear. And then going out to these events, or battles, or whatever you call them, every few months."

"Sounds like a serious hobby. He must have been pretty gung ho."

"Oh, he liked to be authentic, in terms of the history stuff and the clothes, but he wasn't really hardcore. Not compared to some others. His regiment was mostly farby guys."

"Farby?"

"Far be it from authentic. Farbs. That's what the real hardcore guys call guys like Vernon. The Hardcores sleep outside before the battles and spoon together in the dirt to keep warm. They go number two outside." She pursed her lips, clearly horrified. "They even starve themselves to look thin, like real soldiers. Vernon liked his indoor plumbing and he was most certainly never one for starving himself!"

Lindsay wondered if her erstwhile date, Doyle, might eventually become a Hardcore. Certainly peeing on your clothing must be some kind of gateway excretion. It was a slippery slope between that and al fresco pooping.

"Still, you said that his reenacting took up a lot of his time and money." Warren said.

"He did spend a fair amount of money on it, but I don't reckon it was any worse a hobby than golf or fishing."

"And money was not a problem for you guys?"

Kimberlee eyed him warily. Asking about another person's intimate marital finances was not a fitting thing to do in mixed company. A Southerner should know better. "We did all right."

Warren would not be bought off with this evasive half-reply. "How good is all right?"

Kimberlee frowned, regarding Warren as one might regard a child who takes off his pants at a church picnic. "Well, if you must know, we did quite well. When we moved back down here, Vernon worked for the city manager's office, with their databases. He had an idea, though, that Momma and Daddy could expand Bullard's catering business by doing fancy barbecues at people's houses. I remember he said that he wanted to 'bring down-home nostalgia food to the *Southern Living* crowd'. Momma and Daddy didn't cotton on at first, but they let him try it out. He printed up some fancy menus on real thick, shiny paper. They made Bullard's food sound like something from a French bistro. 'Pulled pork and vinegar sauce' became 'slow-smoked, fork-shredded shoulder of Carolina pork, served in cider *jus*'. Instead of using Styrofoam plates and paper napkins, he served the food on china and poured the sweet tea with crystal pitchers. It caught on faster than a deer tick on a dog's behind. After that first summer, he quit his job and started working full-time for Bullard's. Since then, the money's been good."

"Kimberlee, this question's real important. Was there anyone that didn't like Vernon? Any disagreements with any of the other reenactors?"

"Of course not," she said defensively. "Everyone loved him. He was a real nice and friendly person. They all were. We've had them over to the house for cookouts, for heaven's sake. All of them got along." She crossed her arms and turned toward Lindsay. "You know, this is just like TV. They always ask if the victim had any enemies. Why do police always ask that?" She turned back toward Warren and continued, "Wouldn't I have already told you right away if there was somebody I thought could have killed him?"

"I'm sure you would have. But sometimes it's not obvious. When people cast their minds back over things, after something has happened, sometimes it changes how you see things. Can you do that for me a second? Just think about the last few weeks and think if there was anything at all unusual. Did Vernon act strange? Any unusual phone calls at the house? Anything at all? Just close your eyes a minute and think on it."

Kimberlee frowned, but dutifully closed her eyes. She nodded her head slightly back and forth, as if she were watching the past play like a silent film across her mind. After a moment, she stopped and her eyes sprang open suddenly.

"You know, I almost don't want to say this, because I don't want to admit that you were right about the remembering, but I do remember something. I'm not going to say 'It's probably nothing,' because that's what they say on TV when they think of the thing that they didn't think of before. Vernon said that he'd read something in that diary—Samuel Wilcox's—that he said was going to be big. That a lot of people would be real interested. He was excited over it. More than excited, even. Agitated, is what I'd say. He didn't want to say too much about it right then, he said, because he wanted to look into it some more. I never really asked about his history stuff, because it was about as interesting to me as a tree made out of wood. I only remember it because of how he was acting."

"I don't suppose you have a copy of that diary?"

"I'm afraid not. It's a one-of-a-kind type of thing. They keep it in a special room down at the county library. Vernon had to go down there whenever he wanted to look at it."

"Did Vernon keep notes?"

"Not that I know of. I think he just read it."

Warren jotted a few things down in his notebook and then flicked the cover shut. "Well, I think that's about all for tonight. It was real nice to see you again, even under these circumstances. I hope we'll have some news for you real soon."

Lindsay looked down and noticed that Warren had eaten everything on his plate.

"You know, it's gotten awful late somehow," Kimberlee said, yawning. "Why don't we take care of all this memorial stuff tomorrow, Lindsay? Do you have some time? I don't want you driving home in the pitch darkness."

"That'd be fine. I can stop by in the afternoon, after work," Lindsay said. She was enormously grateful to be let off the hook, as she was already having trouble keeping her eyes open. Night shifts always threw off her body clock for days afterward. She rose to leave.

Warren stood as well, but then caught sight of the papers on the table upon which Kimberlee had printed the readings and songs for the memorial service. "*The Soldier's Last Battle*. That's one of my favorite poems. Did you print this out?"

"Yes, it's for the memorial service. I found it online somewhere and I remembered that Vernon had liked it."

"Would you mind if I took this? Can you print another copy for yourself?"

"Sure, be my guest."

"Thanks for the food. Make sure you call me if you think of anything else."

Chapter 8

Lindsay and Warren walked away from the Youngs' house into the twilit evening. The dissonant music of crickets and locusts filled the air. At the bottom of the Youngs' driveway, Lindsay turned toward Warren.

"I didn't want to ask inside because I didn't want to upset Kimberlee, but why do the police think that it's murder?" Lindsay thought back to yesterday's conversation with Anna and Rob. "Couldn't it just have been an accident? Maybe someone just used the real bullets instead of blanks?"

"Not likely. Right before any reenactment each company's officers do a safety check where they inspect all the weapons. Every guy who was out there swears that they did the check that day, and that nothing was out of the ordinary with any of the weapons. We collected all the guns that were used, just in case. The State Bureau of Investigation has already started doing ballistics comparisons to see if any of them could have fired the bullet that killed Vernon. But regardless of how those tests turn out, we have reason to believe someone had it in for Vernon."

"What reason?"

"I can't really talk about it."

"Oh, come on. We're old friends," Lindsay said. "Without me, you'd be nothing, remember?" Warren remained silent. Lindsay batted her eyes coquettishly. "Pretty please, with maple syrup on top?" Still no response from Warren. "This is my best Southern belle impression, Warren Satterwhite. I can't believe this doesn't have you eating out of my hand." She crossed her arms and frowned. "If you're waiting for me to flash my petticoat, it's not going to happen." Warren stayed mum, mirroring Lindsay's crossed arms and allowing only the slightest hint of a smile to creep across his face. Lindsay altered her tactics, putting her hands on her hips. "As a chaplain and a bone fide minister, I'm a professional secret keeper. It comes with the territory. You wouldn't believe some of the death bed confessions I've heard."

"Such as?"

Lindsay shrugged. "Now, I wouldn't be a very good secret keeper if I tattled that easy." Lindsay's coy smile melted into an earnest expression. "Honestly, you can tell me what you know about Vernon. I'm not just asking out of idle curiosity. I really like Kimberlee, and Vernon seems like he was a wonderful person. I want to understand why this happened to them."

Warren softened. "You would need to keep this totally secret, even from Kimberlee. Especially from Kimberlee."

"I am a woman of the cloth. Trust me." She held her hands in prayer position in front of her chest and cast her eyes piously up to the sky.

"A week or so before the shooting, Vernon came in to talk to one of the officers in Mount Moriah. He brought a note that contained some very specific threats against his life."

"Threats?"

He looked at her hard, his lips clenched in a narrow line. "The gist was that if his black self knew what was good for him, he'd better stop parading around with that white wife of his. There was something about his not being fit to wear the Confederate uniform."

"Why didn't Kimberlee mention that when you asked if anyone had a grudge against Vernon?"

"He never told her. He said he didn't want to worry her. Who knows, though? Maybe he didn't want to tell her because he thought she might have something to do with it."

She looked at him sternly. "I can't believe you're suggesting that Kimberlee would fake racist threats against her own husband."

"I hope not."

"Come on now, Warren, it's plain that she adored him. She lights up when she talks about him. How many wives, after almost ten years of marriage, can remember every detail of every date they went on with their husbands?"

"Look, your job is based on trust, mine is based on suspicion. I can't stop investigating somebody just because they're nice."

"Well then you should stop investigating somebody when they are obviously devastated by the death of their spouse," Lindsay huffed.

Warren shrugged his shoulders, "All I can say is that you'd be surprised what people are capable of when it comes to people they love."

"I think *you* would be surprised what people are capable of when it comes to people they love," Lindsay countered.

"You should consider yourself lucky that you get to see that side of people."

"I do." Lindsay frowned and began digging in her purse for her car keys. "Something bothers me about this threatening letter. If the police knew about these threats, why didn't they protect him at the reenactment?"

"Come on, Lindsay. We couldn't protect him out there. They hold the battle over a huge piece of land, and some of it is heavily wooded. We don't have that kind of manpower. We have eleven full-time officers, Mount Moriah has six. Most of them are patrol officers who spend their time handing out speeding tickets and busting kids for drinking Mad Dog down at the quarry. That's why the two departments are working this murder together now. Between the two forces, we have a total of three officers, myself included, that are experienced with criminal investigations. We're not the FBI. And we're definitely not the Secret Service. Besides, most threats like this don't amount to anything."

"So you just ignored it?" Lindsay said.

"Of course not. We took it real serious. For a mild-mannered guy like Vernon to get all worked up like that, we thought there might be something in it. We even put in a call to the FBI to see if there was anything cooking up among the white supremacist element around here. The FBI monitors activity among fringe groups, you know. They told us that everything seemed quiet—no reason to think the white robers and skinheads were up to anything out of the ordinary. Even still, we told Vernon not to go to the reenactment, or any other Civil War events for the time being. We told him just to lay low and watch his back until we could look into it some more. That seemed like the easiest row to hoe.

“We also offered to set something up where one of our patrolmen could drive by the house now and again and check things out, make sure he and Kimberlee were all right. He said okay, as long as we could do it without his wife finding out. Our guys circled their house a few times a day and never saw a thing.” He shook his head and let out a long exhalation. “I’d better be on my way. It was real nice to see you, Lindsay. I hope we don’t have to wait another 10 years to run into each other.”

Warren waved out the car window as he drove off down the street. Lindsay looked back at the Youngs’ house, its yellow paint glowing cheerfully under the street lights. The well-tended flower garden and tidy lawn gave off an aura of domestic tranquility. Inside, Lindsay could see Kimberlee moving from room to room, turning off the lights. For a moment, the sidewalk where Lindsay stood was plunged into semi-darkness. Then Lindsay watched as, one by one, Kimberlee turned all the lights back on. This task completed, Kimberlee began again, flicking off the switches as she moved through the rooms. Her movements cast shadows out unto the Young’s front lawn—the crisscrossing forms kaleidoscoped eerily across the darkened grass.

Chapter 9

At lunch the next day, Anna, Rob, and Lindsay shared their usual table in the hospital cafeteria. "You missed a great meal at the Mex-itali last night," Rob said to Lindsay.

"That place is an abomination. Lasagna should not be served with a side of refried beans. It's wrong on so many levels," Anna interjected.

"Your problem is that you can't put aside your preconceived gastronomical notions. Mex-itali is a pan-global fusion restaurant blending Old World and New. How else can you explain the delicate culinary synergy that is the Meatball Marinara Enchilada?" Rob asked, his eyes twinkling.

"You're right. There is no explanation," Anna replied dryly.

"How did your memorial preparation go?" Rob asked, turning to Lindsay.

"It went…weird. A cop from New Albany, in fact, a guy I know from high school, stopped by and asked Kimberlee a bunch of questions about Vernon. There was something kind of crafty going on. Like he was asking questions, but they weren't the real questions, if that makes any sense." She furrowed her brow. "Then Kimberlee force-fed me a plate of fried chicken and pie. I have to go over there again today to finish all the arrangements for the memorial service."

"Ugh, why are you doing a funeral?" Anna groaned. "Do you not get enough quality Grim Reaper time here? You basically spend eight hours a day talking to sick people or dying people or the families of sick, dying people. It's very morbid and unhealthy. I don't think you're seeing enough action in your romance department. Your priorities are out of whack. I'm a medical doctor, so I know."

"I agree that 'none whatsoever' is probably not enough action. I don't see my job as morbid, though. I'm basically a traveling companion, making people more comfortable on their journey through life."

"I could never do the work you do. Lots of days, I see death. But I never have to accept it. You know? I fight against it. The fight is quick and usually I win." Anna continued to poke at the remains of her salad. "God, I hate talking to the families. At least that's usually quick, too. 'I'm very sorry Mrs. Wilson. We did everything we could, blah blah blah.' Mrs. Wilson cries. I hug her. I nudge her toward the door or call one of you. I could never just sit still and hold hands and accept it all!" She pushed her chair back with a screech and lifted her tray. "Well now I'm cranky. I don't know why I am friends with you…you…co-pilots on Bereavement Airways. I'm going to find a nice, alive patient who needs their appendix out or a face full of stitches or something."

Rob and Lindsay watched Anna leave, and turned back to each other, smiling.

##

Lindsay and Rob's first encounter had nearly ended in a riot. They met at the small Christian college they both attended as undergraduates. The professor in their Intro to Modern Christianity class prompted the students to discuss the theological underpinnings of the Southern Baptist Convention's stance opposing women in the ministry. They were divided into two groups: Lindsay spoke for the group in favor of women ministers, Rob spoke for the case against. The two of them sat at the front of the class, while their professor, a mild-mannered Methodist who wore sandals and a ponytail, moderated the debate.

Rob had been raised in Taiwan, by devout evangelical Christian parents. He attended an American missionary school there and aspired to be a missionary himself. Lindsay had grown up with a similarly narrow exposure to religious diversity. In Mount Moriah, religion came in two flavors—black Protestant and white Protestant. She was, however, possessed of a strong anti-authoritarian streak, a trait that often revealed itself in her views on religion.

"In 1 Timothy, Paul wrote that, 'A woman should learn in quietness and full submission. I do not permit a woman to teach or to have authority over a man; she must be silent,'" was Rob's opening salvo. He laid his hands on the table in front of him as if to rest his case.

Lindsay was not cowed by his theatrical display of certainty. "Quoting scripture is just an excuse for not thinking about what you're saying. According to the Bible, the sun moves around the earth and the ocean is filled with sea monsters."

"That stuff is in the Old Testament," Rob replied. "The Old Testament may be more…poetic, but what the Apostle Paul wrote is pretty obviously meant to be literal and to be followed by anyone who calls themselves a Christian."

"You can't pick and choose which parts of the Bible to interpret literally and which to interpret metaphorically. Is it a rulebook or a guidebook? And you can't pretend that all Christians think the same way about this or any other issue."

"If you don't think the Bible is true, don't be a Christian. Go and find a copy of the dictionary. That's true, right? Worship that."

The class exploded with a level of pent-up idealism that can only be found in a room full of eighteen-year-olds; they were brimming with poorly-understood ideas and unchecked hormones. The students shouted at the debaters and at one another. Lindsay and Rob shouted louder. The two sides became more and more entrenched, with neither willing to give an inch of ground. Lindsay and Rob could now barely be heard above the din. Their professor stood and walked calmly over to Lindsay and Rob. He laid his hands briefly on the top of their heads. Then he walked up and down the aisles of the classroom, touching each student lightly on the head. It was as if he had discovered an invisible mute button. As he touched the students, their voices were stilled. When the room was finally silent, the professor said quietly, "Well, I think that's enough for today. Enthusiasm is always welcome in this classroom. And in the future, I know that you will find ways to express your enthusiasm that are respectful of your classmates' opinions."

By the end of the semester, Lindsay and Rob had taken their professor's advice to heart. They still disagreed about almost everything, but they both began to embrace the idea that silence and listening were sometimes a better way to be heard than shouting. Gradually, quietly, they became inseparable friends.

Chapter 10

At the end of her shift at the hospital that afternoon, Lindsay sat in the small chaplains' office, typing her case notes into the hospital's database. The ancient computer whirred like a spinning top and superheated the air all around it; its calefaction almost cancelled out the frigid air conditioning blasting from the ceiling vent.

Geneva entered the room and walked straight over to the scratched, wooden desk. She planted her small hands down and leaned in toward Lindsay. "Well?" she demanded. "Have you seen him?"

Lindsay nodded.

"And?"

"He's gorgeous."

"Ha!" Geneva triumphantly poked the air with her small, bony finger. "Just remember to name your first child Geneva. Genever if it's a boy."

"We've got a ways to go before we're thinking about kids' names."

"Don't you worry. He'll take notice of you. Nice girl like you. Polite. Christian. Nothing wrong with your face. Body neither, 'cept maybe too skinny." She leaned further forward and peered more closely at the frizzy curls that escaped Lindsay's ponytail. "Well, you got something strange going on with your hair, but that's okay. He'll see past that and that will prove that he's a man of integrity."

There was a knock at the door and Rob poked his head into the office. "Ready to go, Linds? I'll walk to the parking lot with you."

"Just one minute." Lindsay didn't take her eyes off the computer screen where a series of error messages notified her that the system memory was low. "I swear I'd be better off chiseling my notes into stone tablets. I think it's running Windows B.C.

You're the boss, Rob, can't you do something about this? Why doesn't any of the hospital's cash flow down here?"

"You know where pastoral services fall in the hospital pecking order—somewhere below landscaping. As long as that computer keeps limping along, they're not gonna replace it."

Rob greeted Geneva and perched himself on the corner of Lindsay's desk, swinging his legs and using his fingers to tap out an irregular beat on the desktop. "Stop fidgeting," Lindsay said irritably, still not looking at him. Rob instantly ceased all movement but began to hum softly to himself. His humming was dreadfully off-key, though Lindsay knew for a fact that he had near-perfect pitch. "You're such a child."

"My, my Reverend Harding. You should really try to hold yourself above such petty name calling," Rob admonished. He had always taken great joy in exercising his singular ability to needle Lindsay, and now that he was her supervisor, this joy increased ten-fold. Geneva simply rolled her eyes at them. As Lindsay finished the last of her paperwork, Geneva's pager began to vibrate. She held it up and looked at the code. "ER. Dang. That probably means a dead-on-arrival, talk to the grieving family thing. I was hoping for a nice, quiet shift."

Rob's needling, combined with the computer's inefficiency, had soured Lindsay's mood. "That's another thing. Why do we have to use pagers, anyway? In case we get an urgent call from 1987?"

Rob considered a moment. "You know what? I never thought about it. I guess there'd be no sense in calling us on a phone, because the message is always some version of: Get over here now! The only real questions are where to get to and who wants you there."

"Also, pagers are cheaper than cell phones. Hospital will spend $600 a week on flower arrangements for the lobby, but Heaven Almighty protect 'em if they spend a dime on us chaplains," Geneva said, rising from her chair.

Geneva moved toward the door, but Lindsay stopped her. "Hey, Geneva? Before you go, I need to ask your opinion."

"Girl, you know you don't need to ask. My opinions will be offered regularly and free of charge."

"You heard about the shooting last weekend at the reenactment? Vernon Young?"

Geneva nodded gravely. "It's about the only thing on the news."

"The main theory the police are working on right now is that one of the good 'ole boy reenactors didn't like that Vernon was black."

"Black man gets shot out in a field, surrounded by a bunch of white folks wearing Confederate uniforms and pointing guns. Don't need no rocket science degree to come to that conclusion." Geneva frowned.

"So you're comfortable with that theory?"

"Comfortable!? I thought this town had started to put all that behind us. Stirring that pot again makes me about as comfortable as a rib-eye steak in a lion cage."

"I take it you have doubts, Lindsay?" Rob said.

"I don't know. It's mostly that Kimberlee just seems so sure that Vernon got along with his fellow reenactors. And we know some of the guys who were out there. They're our friends, for heaven's sake. I'm just having a hard time seeing any of them as secret KKK Grand Wizards. Maybe that kind of thing would have happened thirty or forty years ago, but this town has come a long way."

"Mmm-hmm," Geneva said in a tone that didn't sound at all like agreement.

"I'm with Geneva. The South has come a long way, but it's still the South," Rob said. "I still get stares sometimes because I'm Asian."

"Rob, you're a tiny Chinese guy who talks with a funny accent and walks your three-legged cat through town on a leash. There are precious few places outside of Northern California where you're not going to get stares," Lindsay said.

"You know that the leash is intended to build Beyoncé's confidence! The vet says it might help with her self-esteem issues!"

"I didn't mean to make fun of Beyoncé," Lindsay said.

"Good, because you're her godmother. She needs to know that you support her therapeutic process."

Lindsay turned toward Geneva and sighed. "All I'm trying

to say is that being black hasn't stopped your kids from becoming dentists and lawyers and whatever else in this town. I know Mount Moriah isn't exactly Amsterdam, but it's more libertarian than reactionary."

"Linds, you've got to remember that you're white and straight and Christian," Rob said.

"I did the same diversity training as you two did. Having pale skin doesn't make me The Man," Lindsay answered crossly.

Geneva raised her eyebrow. It was an eyebrow raise born of years of being a black woman in the South. It was an eyebrow raise that invoked slavery, Jim Crow, and Civil Rights. Lindsay threw her hands up. "Fine. But just because this isn't a bastion of diversity doesn't mean that Mount Moriah is full of neo-Nazis who would kill Vernon in cold blood just because he was black. I just can't believe that about this town. I've known some of these people for my whole life."

Geneva shook her head. "I don't like to think that way about people either. But what we like to think and what's true are sometimes two different things." Geneva sighed heavily. "Lindsay, girl, I truly hope to Jesus that you are right. I truly do. But I just don't know."

Chapter 11

After she had finally entered the last of her notes into the computer, Lindsay left the hospital and returned to Kimberlee's house, intending to work on the memorial arrangements they'd left unfinished on the previous night. She pulled onto the Youngs' street, and was surprised to find half a dozen cars filling the Youngs' driveway and spilling out along the road. As she walked toward the house, the low murmur of voices seeped out, even though all of the windows were closed.

Lindsay had to ring the bell three times before a heavy-set man finally answered the door. He wore jeans and a Demon Deacons t-shirt—its scowling, top-hatted cleric logo confronting Lindsay. The man's thinning grey hair was cropped close to his scalp. A flush of color rose from his thick neck, flooding his cheeks with patches of red. His face was scrunched in concentration, as if he were trying to balance a spoon on the end of his nose.

"Hello. I'm Lindsay Harding. I think we met at the hospital. You're Keith, right?"

His expression softened with recognition, though a deep wrinkle still creased his brow. "Oh, yeah. Kimberlee said you're doing the service for Vernon. Come on in. We're having a family powwow right now. I'm afraid we've had another shock. You see, the police came around again…" he trailed off as they stepped inside. "I reckon I'll let the girls tell you."

Keith gestured toward the couch, where Kimberlee sat, tear-stained and red-faced. The three Bullard sisters circled tightly around her like covered wagons ready to fend off a gang of marauding bandits. All the sisters were pudgy, most of them were blonde, and all of them seemed to be talking at the same time. Lindsay could only catch snippets of their conversation. "Can they even do that? That sounds made-up to me." "That Warren Satterwhite is trickier than a magician's rabbit." "And meaner than a bag of rattlesnakes."

Lindsay called a loud greeting over the din. They turned toward her, a hydra-headed mass of freckles and highlights.

"Oh girl!" Kimberlee exclaimed, jumping up from the couch and running to embrace Lindsay. "They think I did it!"

"Did what?" Lindsay said, still not quite following the conversation.

"Killed him! The police think I killed Vernon!" She burst into a fresh torrent of tears and buried her face in her hands. Even during the long hours at Vernon's bedside, Lindsay had never seen Kimberlee break down so completely. Keith ushered Lindsay and Kimberlee over to the couch, where the sea of sisters parted to make room for them. Before any further explanation was offered, all eyes turned toward the stairs, where the heavy thud of footsteps could be heard.

Versa Bullard, the family matriarch, sailed down the stairs with the iron-clad solidity of a battleship. She wore a sleeveless denim shirt embroidered in a pattern of red and white fireworks and children waving American flags. A pair of fuchsia reading glasses dangled from a beaded chain around her neck. White hair seemed to explode from her head like a sunburst, moving as a unit when she spoke.

She addressed her children: "Well, he's settled down now. Those tranquilizers did the trick. I swear if we hadn't gotten those pills down him, we'd have had another death on our hands—either his from a heart attack or that skunk Warren Satterwhite's from a beating." With a little shooing motion, Versa directed Keith to vacate the armchair where he was seated. He popped up obediently and stepped aside while she arranged her ample bulk upon the pink leather.

"I guess you've heard by now," Kathilee, the oldest sister, said to Lindsey.

"Actually, I haven't. What in the world is going on?"

The twins, Kristalene and Kennadine, both began talking at once. During the time she spent with the Bullards at the hospital, Lindsay had never really figured out which twin was which. She now came to realize that it didn't really matter.

"They came over here this morning with a warrant to search the house. Pulled out everything from all the closets and basically ransacked the place," one twin said.

"Who came?" Lindsay asked.

"Warren Satterwhite and a bunch of police, and then some other guy I think was from the FBI or something. They brought him in special to work on Vernon's case," the other twin answered.

The first twin continued, "Then they came back a few hours later and said they just wanted Kimmie to come over to the police station and answer a few more questions. She knew something funny was going on 'cause they were acting all shifty."

The other twin elaborated, "And when they got her to the police station, that scary, serious-looking detective or agent or whatever he was pulled out this piece of paper with all these horrible things written on it and asked her if she's seen it before…"

Twin #1 lamented, "Terrible things! Like about Vernon being black, only they didn't say black, they called him a such and suching you-know-what…"

Twin #2 concurred, "And it said how he shouldn't be married to a white woman and how he shouldn't do his Confederate army man thing…"

Twin #1 explained, "And the detective was asking Kimmie if she saw this paper before…"

Twin #2 clarified, "Which, of course, she never had…"

Twin #1: "And then they said that they'd run some kind of test…

Twin #2: "Which I don't even think they can do, anyway. It just sounds made-up…"

Twin #1: "No, it's not made up. They can do that. I told you I saw that on *CSI.* Regular *CSI*, not *Miami*, which I don't even watch anymore because I don't like that one fellow who they have on there now."

Twin #2: "But anyway, they said they ran this test on some piece of paper that Warren Satterwhite took from here last night that had a poem or something on it, and they said it was printed on the exact same printer that the horrible letter about Vernon was printed on! And that that was Kimmie and Vernon's printer!"

"That slimeball!" both twins said simultaneously.

Kathilee, the non-twin sister, interjected with a brief aside. "We never liked the Satterwhites, you know. Warren's cousin Jake used to throw sticks at our dog when he walked past our house on his way to Little League practice. And Gremlin was a sweet old thing and hardly ever bit anyone."

The twins nodded in agreement. "Satterwhites are just like that. Do you remember old Zeb Satterwhite?" The twin who was speaking paused for effect. "He was a ped-o-phile."

"Well, maybe not a pedophile, exactly, but he was near on fifty and married a girl of about eighteen," the other twin explained.

"And that fancy, serious-looking detective—he didn't even have the good manners to introduce himself—was acting all high and mighty. Said he used to work in Los Angeles."

The other twin said gravely to Lindsay, "L.A." She spoke the letters as if they summed up the man's character.

"Anyway, the police were being real mean to Kimmie and saying 'Why did you do it?' and 'Why weren't you at the reenactment?' and saying they were going to bring Momma in for questioning! Something about establishing her alibi or something."

Lindsay looked helplessly around the room. "I'm not sure I understand what is going on."

Kathilee stepped in to explain. She seemed to be the family spokesperson, serving as a sort of translator who interpreted the Bullards' familial ciphers for the outside world. "You see, the police think that our Kimmie had something to do with Vernon's death. I guess they don't have enough evidence to arrest her, so they were trying to get her to confess. She told them she didn't do anything wrong and had nothing to do with it. Kennadine's husband, Marshall Pickett, is a lawyer. You might know him? He has those commercials on cable where he dresses up like a cowboy and chases after the Malpractice Kid? Anyway, Kimmie told them she was going to call him to come over and wouldn't say anything else without him there. When Marshall showed up, he asked them was she under arrest. They said no and they had to let her go."

"We all came running over when we heard," one of the twins said.

Versa smiled at her children. "Daddy about broke a land speed record getting over here. He was so riled up we had to give him something to calm him down. I crushed up a couple of them pills that the doctor gave him and put it in his sweet tea. He's upstairs now resting." She crossed her arms with a self-satisfied expression. The compression over her chest somehow, improbably, meant that the line of her cleavage shot out of her shirt like the mercury in a thermometer, reaching up to the base of her throat.

"Daddy's too pigheaded to take his medicine when he needs it," Kathilee said. "His heart ain't as strong as it once was, and he can't take all this stress with Vernon and whatnot."

At the mention of Vernon's name, Kimberlee sprang back to life. She grabbed Lindsay's hand as if she were holding on to the edge of a cliff. "When Vernon died, I thought it was the worst thing that could ever happen to me. This, though…I just can't see a way through this. I have never been so scared in my whole life. The police took all the stuff I'd printed out for the memorial service for 'evidence'." She paused. "I wish Vernon was here. I know that doesn't make sense, because if he was here, none of this would be happening in the first place. But I can't help but feel that if Vernon was here, he would know exactly what to do."

Kimberlee's words shot through Lindsay's brain like a jolt of electricity. Kimberlee might be more right than she realized. Vernon Young would know what to do—and maybe he had already done it. It was only a hunch, but it was a hunch that Lindsay intended to follow up at the earliest opportunity.

Chapter 12

When Kimberlee's siblings and parents finally left late that evening, Lindsay and Kimberlee drafted the program for Vernon's memorial service. Kimberlee's bravado had disappeared after the accusations of her involvement in Vernon's death, and she was more than happy to let Lindsay take over organizing the memorial. She was quiet and submissive and agreed to every one of Lindsay's suggestions—including allowing more time for quiet reflection and the addition of a eulogy. Lindsay offered to type everything out at home, since Kimberlee's printer and computer had been confiscated by the police. It was after midnight when Lindsay finally got back to her house, but she dutifully sat down on her bed, propped her laptop on her knees, and began arranging text on the page. She had an early shift the next morning and she had to get the program finished before she left. At some point around 2 a.m., the pillows seemed to become softer, the bed more comfortable. Lindsay turned out the light. She was nearly done anyway. Maybe she should just rest her eyes for a minute…

Lindsay woke up hours later, restless and sweaty. Her computer had put itself to sleep, too, and it lay dark and silent on the bed next to her. She realized that she'd forgotten to turn on the air conditioning when she got home. She lay there, too hot to sleep, but too tired to get out of bed and lower the thermostat. In her fevered half-sleep, she had terrible nightmare of a thin-faced man. He peered in through her window; his otherwordly green eyes glowing in the moonlight, drilling into her.

The sinister presence from her dream was still with her when the alarm sounded at 5:45. She silenced the alarm with a blunt blow from her fist. She lay in bed for a few minutes, letting her vision adjust to the gray predawn light and trying to erase the glowing green eyes from her mind. She silently cursed herself for taking an extra shift this week—a 7 a.m. Friday shift to boot. In theory, Lindsay, as one of the staff chaplains, should have had a fairly regular schedule, with mostly 8:30a.m.-5:30p.m. shifts and the occasional night or weekend on call. Chaplaincy residents, like Geneva, were supposed to be the ones paying their dues by keeping erratic hours. In reality, though, Lindsay's schedule was almost always unpredictable. Rob liked to try out new ways to schedule the chaplaincy rota—hence the invention of the 7 a.m. shift. He claimed that these little experiments were aimed at making the service more efficient. Lindsay was pretty sure that their actual goal was to rob her of sleep and a social life. As if Rob's diabolical scheduling tendencies weren't bad enough, the other chaplains always called on Lindsay if they needed someone to cover for them. As one of them had innocently reminded her, "With no kids and no husband you must have so much free time." It was hard to disagree. It took a frigid shower, two cups of coffee, and a giant cinnamon bun for her to put together something resembling consciousness and leave her house.

##

As usual, her shift gave her no respite. Almost as soon as she arrived, she was summoned up to the cardiac unit by the duty nurse. The nurse explained that the family of a patient, a seventy-five-year-old smoker with congestive heart failure, was undermining the course of treatment. They held very deep-seated religious beliefs that they didn't feel were being adequately addressed by the staff. The duty nurse called for Lindsay, hoping that she could persuade the family to cooperate.

"Can't nobody reason with them," the duty nurse said. "I was raised in Lumbee swampland down east, but these folks is about as country as biscuits and gravy. They make my people look like city slickers. They ain't never even seen an escalator before they came up in this hospital!" She smacked her lips and made a little "umm" sound. "I'm just prayin' you can get through to them before they kill that old woman in there."

Lindsay agreed to give it a try. She approached the patient's room with caution. Although the door was shut, the sound of raised voices bounced along the corridor, and as she got closer, she could make out snatches of conversation.

"Y'all need to calm down and listen to me," one voice instructed.

"I'll calm down when *you* listen to *me*," a second voice responded harshly.

By now Lindsay was just outside the room. She leaned in, placing her ear against the door. The metal felt warm against the side of her face, as if the first flames of a fire were smoldering just on the other side. The two voices once again became distinguishable. "I'll just come back when you have calmed down," said the first.

"We'll be calm when you listen to us and stop killing Mama!" shouted the second.

Without warning, the door clicked open and swung inward, sending Lindsay careening into the room. She stumbled forward until she flopped gracelessly across the hospital bed of an ample-bodied old woman whose elaborate grey braids crisscrossed her head. Lindsay quickly righted herself, doing her best to straighten her white chaplain's coat and smooth the blonde curls that fell across her eyes.

"Oh, hello. I'm Lindsay…uh…Chaplain Lindsay Harding. I'm one of the chaplains here at the hospital." She extended her hand to the person closest to her, a balding man whose starched dress shirt was buttoned all the way to his pale, scrawny neck.

"Luther Peechum," the man replied.

He accepted Lindsay's handshake, though he eyed her with suspicion. Lindsay tried her best to appear, if not professional, then at least less ridiculous than the clumsy, eavesdropping mess that had just crashed into their midst. She greeted each of the room's occupants. A pretty, pert nurse with a plastic clipboard extended her hand and introduced herself as Cynthia. She had a strawberry-blonde bob and wore bright pink clogs that were self-consciously "fun," while still practical and efficient. A pinched woman in an ankle-length skirt wordlessly shook Lindsay's hand. The look of contempt in her eyes almost froze the smile off of Lindsay's face. Finally, Lindsay extended her hand to the old woman whose bed she had so unceremoniously face-planted into. A thin plastic oxygen tube ran under the woman's nose. A thousand tiny wrinkles creased her skin.

"Welcome, Reverend," the old woman said, wheezing heavily.

"Thank you," Lindsay said.

Lindsay took in her surroundings. The room's three small windows stood open to the blue and gold morning light. The screens were lying stacked in a corner. Warm, moist air clung to everything like wet wool. Lindsay was suddenly aware of the prick of a mosquito, which had alighted on the back of her hand. She slapped it dead, splattering a droplet of her own blood.

"It's best to just leave 'em be. Killing 'em only makes the bite itch worse," the pinched women said.

Lindsay recognized the voice as the one she'd heard accusing the nurse of attempted murder. Looking at her now, Lindsay realized that she was very young, perhaps Luther's teenage daughter. Or teenage wife.

"I suppose you're right," Lindsay replied brightly. "But I never could countenance letting a mosquito sink his teeth into me."

"They ain't teeth. That's a proboscis. And it ain't a him. Only the females suck blood." The young woman's proclamation was followed by silence. They all stood staring at Lindsay, while she awkwardly scratched at the red lump that was beginning to rise on the back of her hand.

"So," Lindsay began. "I heard there was a little misunderstanding about the window screens."

"Ain't no misunderstanding," Luther Peechum said, looking pointedly at Cynthia, who hugged her clipboard to her chest. "Windows are open so the Holy Spirit can enter to heal Mama. Them doctors and nurses reckon that jabbing her with needles and stuffing her with pills is going to heal her better than Jesus can."

"They've got no faith. That's why she keeps getting worse." The young woman seemed close to tears.

"She keeps getting worse because she has a serious, chronic condition that is threatening her life," Cynthia snapped back. "A condition that you are preventing us from treating."

There was a silence. They seemed to be waiting for Lindsay to respond. She dug in her chaplain's bag of tricks for a time-worn technique from her CPE training days: active listening. Active listening challenges the listener to suspend his or her judgments and responses, instead focusing on the speaker. The listener must try to hear not just words, but underlying emotions, feelings, and preconceptions. The technique promoted a feeling of common purpose and mutual understanding in situations of conflict. Usually. "It sounds like everyone here is frustrated." Lindsay paused and waited for a response. The room's occupants just stared at her.

Lindsay continued, "I hear the Peechums saying that the nurses and doctors lack faith. The doctors and nurses seem to feel that Mrs. Peechum's condition will get worse unless they are given the freedom to treat her as they see fit."

Luther nodded. "Yeah, like you said. They are Godless heathens."

Cynthia stomped her foot. Lindsay struggled to maintain her equanimity. Okay, apparently she had just actively listened her way into accusing the hospital staff of being idol-worshipping pagans. She tried a different tactic: diplomacy.

"Now, Mr. Peechum, the doctors and nurses do have faith. Could we agree that it just might be a different kind of faith?"

"Aint' but one kind of faith that can truly heal Mama," Luther barked.

Silence again descended on the room. Cynthia exhaled loudly and pressed the clipboard more tightly to her thin chest.

"There is no sense in reasoning with them. I've tried. They refuse to be realistic about this woman's prognosis."

"Get this atheist out of here!" the young woman shouted, her body drawing in on itself, like a coiled spring.

"How dare you?" Cynthia said, the peachy glow of her cheeks igniting suddenly with a burst of furious redness. "I happen to be on the bake sale committee at the New Life Baptist Fellowship. And I led our youth group's mission trip to Dollywood two years in a row."

"When is the last time you got down on your knees and prayed to Jesus to forgive your faithlessness?" the young woman said.

Lindsay cut in abruptly, saying loudly, "That's funny."

"Funny?" Luther said. "I don't see nothing funny."

"It's funny that they sent me to the wrong room. You see, I was told that there was a very sick lady in here who was in dire need of some help. I was told that there was a room full of people who were all trying their level best to help her. But that's not this room."

Lindsay's eyes moved around the room. One by one, the gazes of those present fell to the floor. Lindsay was quite sure that shaming was not a technique endorsed by the Association of Professional Chaplains. But she was equally sure that the Holy Spirit wasn't about to climb through old Mrs. Peechum's third-story window like some kind of miracle-spewing cat burglar. Now that the warring parties were again silent, Lindsay leaned gently toward to the old woman and said, "We all want to help you. Tell me what you need me to do."

"I need prayer, Reverend." The old woman extended a hand for Lindsay to take. The others joined hands to form a loose circle around the old woman's bed. Cynthia continued to stand a little way off, sniffing loudly. Lindsay took the Peechums' hands, closed her eyes and cleared her mind.

"We pray for the Holy Spirit to enter Mama and make her whole again," Luther said. He appealed to God for health, happiness and protection from harm. Lindsay relaxed, letting herself be lulled by the familiarity of the sentiments and the repetition of the words. Here they were, she thought, all calmly praying together. She allowed herself to bask in a smug little victory. She alone had succeeded in earning the trust of this difficult family. She had diffused their anger and brought their focus back to their loved one's plight. Her attention drifted. She hardly noticed when the cadence of the prayer changed. It wasn't until the hands that held hers started to spasm and shudder that she was jarred out of her self-satisfied reflection. Lindsay ventured a peek at Luther, who stood directly across from her. His eyes were open, but his eyeballs had rolled back into his head. His body seemed to pulse and vibrate and his voice dropped to a raspy whisper. The women joined in the prayer, each chanting out their own rhythm. Their voices were unnaturally deep, and the words of the prayer were no longer English, nor indeed any language that Lindsay recognized.

The prayer went on like this for several minutes, increasing in volume and intensity. Luther suddenly regained his ability to speak English and cried out, "Lay your hands on her, Reverend, the power of the Spirit is in you."

Lindsay hesitated for a split second, like a diver poised on the three-meter platform. She took a deep breath and placed her hands on top of the old woman's head. Lindsay closed her eyes and began to chant, "Ora pro nobis peccatoribus, nunc, et in hora mortis nostrae." She repeated the words over and over, allowing herself to be caught up with the others in the rhythm of the prayer. After a few minutes, the prayer came to a crescendo. Lindsay ended it with a ringing, "Santa Maria!" and threw her hands heavenward.

##

Later that morning, Lindsay stood at the nurses' station in the cardiac unit, sipping a cup of heavily sugared coffee with the duty nurse who had summoned her to the Peechums' room. Luther Peechums and his wife/daughter had finally gone home to get some rest. The elder Mrs. Peechum lay contentedly watching a Discovery Channel special about a man who lived his whole life with his own unborn twin inside him. The window screens in her room had been replaced, and the windows were firmly closed against the rising heat of the day.

Cynthia, the pretty nurse who had been in the room during the boisterous prayer session, joined Lindsay at the nurses' station.

"I can't believe you convinced them to get with the program," the duty nurse said to Lindsay. "At least six different nurses and doctors have tried and failed."

Cynthia nodded. "I guess they just needed someone to do all that nonsense with the speaking in tongues." She blushed deeply. "I'm so sorry. I just meant that they needed someone from their own religion."

"I have no earthly idea what religion they are," Lindsay said. "Snake-handlers, for all I know."

Cynthia's mouth dropped open. "If you're not one of them, then how did you know how to do the laying on the hands and the speaking in tongues?"

"I was reciting the Hail Mary in Latin. I had to learn it in college for a class on Medieval Christianity." Lindsay said.

Cynthia gaped like a fresh-caught bass. "But you tricked them."

Lindsay shrugged. "I got caught up in the moment. Besides,

speaking in tongues and saying the Hail Mary are both ways of trying to talk to God."

"But you told them you had a vision. You said you saw an angel who spoke to you and said that if they radiated God's love and compassion to all the nurses and doctors, and listened to what they said, their Mama would be comfortable and at peace!"

Lindsay pointed to the duty nurse's name badge: Angel Bledsoe. "I was paraphrasing a bit. But Mrs. Peechum will be a lot more comfortable and peaceful now that her family has stopped tormenting everyone who's trying to help her." She drained the rest of her coffee and pitched the paper cup in the trash. "God works in mysterious ways, and so do His employees."

Chapter 13

After her encounter with the Peechums, Lindsay made her way down to the cafeteria to grab a bite to eat. It was only 10:30 in the morning, but the cafeteria was already buzzing with the early lunch crowd—nurses, doctors, and housekeeping staff who worked the seven a.m. to three p.m. shift. Lindsay inched her plastic tray along the line, declining a gelatinous blob of mac-n-cheese, declining a celery-laden, mayonnaise-drowned heap of chicken salad, declining the spinach lasagna with a shudder. Anyone who knew anything knew that the hospital cafeteria oreganoed that lasagna within an inch of its natural life. The bread rolls were good, though. She took three. By the time she reached the end of the food line, Lindsay had gathered three rolls, a banana, and half a dozen packets of butter—appealingly monochromatic, acceptably nourishing, and touching on several different hieroglyphs of the food pyramid. She packed everything into a white paper sack, intending to sneak off and eat in her office—eating alone in the cafeteria conjured up too many unpleasant school memories. As she passed through the main dining room on her way out, however, she locked eyes with Drew Checkoway, who was seated near the door. He was resplendently clean-shaven—Apollo in green surgical scrubs. He waved Lindsay over to the table he was sharing with Anna.

"Hiya, Linds," Anna said brightly, flashing her surfer girl smile. Anna gestured across the table. "I was just trying to convince Drew that he needs to stop listening to local radio immediately, before it does any further damage to his critical faculties."

Lindsay registered the twangy strains of the latest blonde diva's country pop anthem playing quietly over the cafeteria's PA system.

"No way!" Drew protested. "WZNC is doing a phone-a-thon to raise $1,000 for new band uniforms for the high school.

You call in with a pledge and you get to request a song. I've already heard this one four times today. This is great. Real salt-of-the-earth stuff."

Anna patted the seat next to her. Lindsay sat down, setting her lunch bag on the table in front of her. Without even seeing the contents of the bag, Anna intuited that Lindsay's lunch would fall short of her high nutritional standards, and pushed some of her carrot sticks toward Lindsay. Lindsay accepted a few and glanced briefly at the food in front of Drew and Anna. Drew was halfway through a salad, dressed with fat-free vinaigrette and topped with grilled chicken. Anna had minestrone soup and crudités. Lindsay became keenly aware that her own lunch was essentially a paper sack full of butter. She extracted the banana. Grown-ups ate bananas.

"The fundraiser doesn't bother me as much as how the DJs personally know everyone who calls in," Anna said.

Drew turned his attention to Lindsay. The twinkle of his green eyes nearly took her breath away. "What do you think? WZNC, for or against?"

She inhaled deeply, willing her cheeks to remain blush-free. "Well, this morning, I called the DJ, whose mother gave me piano lessons when I was a teenager, and donated $25. I requested Patsy Cline."

Anna gesticulated forcefully with a spear of cucumber. "Lindsay can't judge this! She's not impartial. She's an insider. She has lived here almost all her life and doesn't know any better, poor soul."

"I, for one, always listen to the local radio stations when I move somewhere new," Drew said, leaning conspiratorially toward Lindsay, "It helps me get a feel for a place."

"And how does my place feel?" Lindsay asked. She immediately regretted her choice of words and began to blush crimson. The banana in her hand seemed to have suddenly morphed into a giant phallic symbol.

Not taking his eyes off Lindsay, Drew said, "I haven't quite figured it out yet, but I hope to."

Lindsay tried to take a nonchalant bite of banana, but ended up nearly choking herself. Her cheeks burned furiously. The song had ended and the station began to play the typical commercials—for the local car dealership (Partee Auto World, where Lindsay had bought her used Toyota on the day of her high school graduation), for the upcoming open day at the Christian military boarding school out by the highway (The Milton Academy, where Lindsay's father had constantly threatened to send her). Then a gospel choir began to sing, as a deep-voiced announcer intoned, "This weekend, at the county fairgrounds, experience the power of Jesus' abiding love at Pastor Jonah Harding's 17th Annual Tent Revival. Gates open at 10 a.m. on Saturday and the soul-saving reverie will continue on into Sunday night. Bring your Bible but don't forget your bib, because there's going to be all-you-can-eat baby back ribs. Come on out and make sure you get your name entered in the raffle drawing for a brand-new Kawasaki jet ski. It's gonna be a weekend of miracles with Pastor Jonah Harding."

Drew smiled broadly. "Wow, Jesus and a jet ski. Now I'm sure I'm going to like it here. Don't suppose the soul-saving, finger-licking Reverend Harding is any relation to you?"

"Actually, yes. He's my father."

"You're joking."

"My jokes aren't as funny as that."

"Huh, so I guess Daddy's little girl became a minister to make her papa proud. I thought you'd have a more interesting back story," Drew said.

Lindsay studied his expression. He seemed to look at her the way one looks at a baby animal in a zoo enclosure, with equal parts fondness and condescension. It was much worse than Anna's open contempt for all things small-town.

"Sorry to disappoint," Lindsay said, her mouth in a razor-thin line. "You know what? I'd better be going." She rose from her chair. "Busy day."

Drew swiftly reached across the table and took Lindsay's hand in his. He tilted his head sheepishly. "Sorry. Really. I was just teasing. Sometimes I just don't know when to stop pushing on a sore spot."

Lindsay sat back down. She lowered her eyes. "It's okay."

"I really am interested. Why did you become a chaplain?"

"Yeah, Linds. I don't know the answer to this one either,"

Anna said. "My theory has always been that you were either raised by nuns in a leper colony or that you killed a man in cold blood and became a woman of the cloth to atone for your sins."

"Zip it, Melrose," Drew said. "Let the woman speak."

Lindsay softened. It was so easy to forgive a man with a face like that.

"Well, I used to go with my dad on hospital visits to members of his congregation. Once, when I was 11 or 12, I went with him to see a woman from the congregation who was dying of a very aggressive cancer. She wanted to marry her boyfriend, who was a Catholic, before she passed. My father wouldn't do the wedding unless the man converted. The man refused. His priest wouldn't do the ceremony either, unless the woman converted. She refused. The couple scrambled to find another minister to do the wedding, but they didn't find one in time. I don't think I made up my mind right then, but that experience kind of percolated with me for a long while. I wanted to make that story turn out different. So I suppose you were right. I did become a chaplain because of my Daddy."

"Huh," Anna said. "It's one of those Darth Vader and Luke Skywalker dynamics where you make up for the failings of your father."

"Like Hamlet going after Claudius to avenge his father's murder," Drew said, nodding his head.

Anna crossed her arms and raised her eyebrows. "Luke went after Darth so that the forces of Light could triumph over The Man. The Man in that case being the Evil Empire and the Death Star. In Lindsay's case, The Man is the inflexible dogma of institutional religion. Parallels between similar situations make a good metaphor. Your metaphor, by contrast, sucks. Hamlet kills, like, twenty guys, including at least a dozen innocent bystanders, messes with his girlfriend's head until she drowns herself, and poisons his own mother! Lindsay is Luke Skywalker. And you," she stabbed the air in front of Drew with her raised spoon, "have bad taste in radio stations and an inability to craft a decent metaphor. Hamlet? Hamlet?!" She clicked her tongue. "Please."

Chapter 14

Lindsay ended her shift just as the sun was just beginning to duck behind the loblolly pines. Her shift was technically over at 3 p.m., but, as usual, entering the day's case notes into the chaplain's office's prehistoric computer had delayed her departure considerably. She hadn't felt the outside air since early morning, when the maintenance men had finally sealed up the windows in Mrs. Peechum's room. The cloying humidity of earlier in the day had evaporated, leaving behind an uncharacteristically fresh and windy atmosphere. Food wrappers, grass clippings, and other parking lot detritus were propelled ahead of Lindsay on strong gusts of wind, out and up into the rapidly darkening sky. Lindsay found herself strangely discomfited by the coolness. She was happy to climb inside her car and let the warm, stale air wrap around her like a blanket.

Her conversation with Drew and Anna had dogged her all afternoon. She hated the feeling of vulnerability that always followed revelations about her past. Through her chaplaincy training, she had been forced to confront it all: the childhood she had spent in the moldy old house on the Outer Banks, with her father's coolly aloof great aunt…the sudden reunion with her father and subsequent forced march into his newly-discovered world of sweet Jesus and the Holy Spirit…the cigarettes, alcohol, and defiant sprees of her bitter teenage rebellion…the implosion of her long engagement to Timothy Farnsworth. She had stared it all down and tamed it. But her past crouched like a circus tiger, ready to rake its claws across her body if she dropped the whip, if she gave it even a moment's liberty.

As she drew closer to home, the sinking sun was blocked out by a line of dark thunderclouds rolling in from the West. When she finally eased her Tercel into her wide gravel driveway, the sky loomed low and black. The table lamp glowed in her living room. "Must have left it on," she thought. Her heart beat quickened, however, when she caught sight of a man's shadowy form through the sheer ivory curtains that hung in the front windows. The man moved from room to room, with his head bent low. She cut the headlights and positioned the car behind the stand of trees at the top of the drive. Through the screen of trees, she saw the intruder cross the windows again, this time carrying what appeared to be a large box. Was it her laptop computer? What would a thief want to take from her? She had nothing of value.

The shadow moved across the window again. Her heart tapped out a furious tattoo. Overheard, a deep growl of thunder broke across the sky. Lindsay grabbed a heavy flashlight from behind the passenger's seat. The solidity and heft of it in her hand gave her a surge of adrenaline, and she moved quickly toward the house. The rising rush of the wind masked the crunch of her footsteps on the gravel. She pressed her body into the wooden siding and slid along in the small space between the house and the line of low-slung landscaping bushes that surrounded it. When she reached the big window next to the front porch, she slowly rose and peered in through the lowest window pane. Suddenly, the window flew open, sending her flying backwards into the bushes.

"Lindsay!"

"Dad!"

"You scared me! I heard rustling in the bushes and thought someone was trying to break in!"

"*I* scared *you*!? I thought I was being robbed! Where the hell is your car?"

"Don't curse. I rode my motorcycle. It's parked out back."

Lindsay began to untangle herself from the spiky bush in which she was half-lying, half-sprawling. Her voluminous, curly hair clung to the branches, twisting tighter with her every move. She winced with pain as she tried to pull it free.

"Don't move. You're making it worse. I'll come out and help you. Let me go and get a pair of scissors."

Lindsay lowered her head back toward the bushes. She was in an awkward form of the yogic Camel Posture, on her knees with the top half of her body arched backward. She stared straight up as a white scar of lightening raked the blackened sky. The first drops of rain began to fall. She watched them gather along the edge of the gutter, until they fell, swollen and plump, into her upturned face. Droplets accumulated on her glasses and dripped down her cheeks and chin, pooling in the hollow at the base of her throat. She twisted her body sideways to try to shield herself from the rain. She succeeded only in allowing the prickly spines of the bushes to pierce her clothing and drag themselves painfully across her skin.

"Hurry up, Dad!" Lindsay called impatiently, wiping her face with her damp shirtsleeve.

Jonah Harding emerged from the house a moment later, wielding a pair of scissors. He bent over her, trying to determine the best place to start cutting. A wide smile crept across his face. "Huh, you look a little like I'd imagine Absalom looking, hanging by his hair from the oak tree."

The Biblical reference was apt, Lindsay decided. "Yes, but Absalom was punished for trying to kill his father. I haven't done that…yet."

"If you're going to be cantankerous, I can just leave you there to undergo Chinese water torture."

"Ha-ha."

Lindsay looked at her father's face as he leaned over and began to snip away her tangled curls. He was still youthful, despite having celebrated his fiftieth birthday earlier that year. He had a full head of wavy sandy blond hair, which he kept neatly trimmed. The hair around his temples was shot through with streaks of silver. His warm, brown eyes crinkled slightly as he concentrated on his task.

"There was a message on your answering machine from your mother," Jonah said. "She wondered if you got the card she sent."

The rain intensified and Jonah shifted his torso to try to shield Lindsay's face from the rain. Discussion of Sarabelle Harding, Lindsay's erstwhile mother and Jonah's faithless wife, always set off a powder keg of emotion and accusation between the two of them. Lindsay had yet to figure out if she resented Sarabelle more for abandoning them, or for the fact that Jonah still loved her, despite her having abandoned them.

"Why are you listening to my answering machine messages?"

"You never check them. I thought I'd write them all down for you so you'd see who called. There was also one from the dry cleaners saying that they are going to give your clothes away to charity if you don't come and pick them up. Unfortunately, that one was dated the fourth of May."

Lindsay and Jonah were quiet for a moment, letting the noise of the thunderstorm and the snipping of the scissors fill the space between them.

"I'm drowning here." Lindsay complained. "How much more is there to go?"

"Just a couple of snips. Are you coming to the tent meeting this weekend?"

"You know that I love my theology sung by a praise band with electric guitars."

"I don't appreciate your mockery, Miss. The Lord can speak through electric guitars just as loudly as he speaks through His divine miracles," Jonah said, punctuating his words with a sharp snip of the scissors.

If it is possible for an eye roll to be stifled, Lindsay stifled an eye roll. Her father's sincerity, as usual, made her feel childish and ashamed. "I'll try, Dad, but I'm really busy this weekend. I'm doing a memorial service tomorrow."

"What about on Sunday?"

"I'll try."

"I think that's the last one." Jonah made a final snip and hoisted Lindsay to her feet.

They walked inside the house, Lindsay making a beeline for the medicine cabinet, where she retrieved a small first aid kit. She tended to the long, painful scratches that covered the backs of her legs and arms. She snuck a quick glance in the mirror to survey the results of her unintended haircut. Even in the best of times, her hair looked slightly disheveled, but it had now taken on the appearance of an exploded mattress, with curls of varying lengths springing out in every direction. She closed her eyes and cursed softly under her breath.

Lindsay made her way back into the living room, where the mysterious box she had seen through the window was revealed to be filled with pastries.

"Why were you carrying that around my house?"

"Mrs. Bugbee came by the church this afternoon with a big batch of buns. I know how much you like them, so I brought some over for you."

"Thanks," she said, flopping on the couch beside him.

Mrs. Bugbee's Nutty Buns were famous, at least among those who frequented the mid-Piedmont evangelical church bake sale circuit. Mrs. Bugbee, a stout, middle-aged parishioner at Jonah's church, guarded her Nutty Buns recipe like a Knight Templar guarding the Holy Grail. The gooey cinnamon and pecan concoctions covered at least three of the seven deadly sins—pride (Mrs. Bugbee's downfall), envy (engendered in the minds of her co-bake sale ladies), and, closest to Lindsay's heart, gluttony. She stuffed a piece of bun into her mouth.

"You know, you really need to start locking your doors," Jonah said.

"Tell me about it."

"Honey, I'm serious. If you thought I was a burglar, why didn't you just drive to the neighbors or call the police on your cell? What would you have done if I really was a robber? Or a rapist? Or a drug addict coked out on angel dust?"

"'Coked out on angel dust'?" Lindsay rolled her eyes. "I had an excellent plan. I was going to peak in through the window to see what was going on. Then if I thought you needed to be taken out, I would sneak up from behind and bludgeon you with my flashlight. Well, not *you*, the robber."

Jonah pressed his index finger and thumb into the corners of his closed eyes. "I appreciate the boldness of your cunning plan. But somehow I don't think you can rely on all five feet and a hundred pounds of you to take down a villain."

He considered a moment, stroking the stubble on his chin. It was a familiar gesture, remembered from many Sundays watching him on the pulpit. The chin stroke was usually preceded by a particularly emphatic reading from the Bible and followed by a particularly rousing bit of preaching. Sure enough, Jonah turned toward her with an earnest expression.

"I wasn't going to tell you this, because I didn't want to frighten you unnecessarily. But I think you need a little bit of sense scared into you. When I pulled up to your house before, there was a white four by four parked out front. It drove off when I turned in here, but then I saw it circle back a few times, driving real slow. That's why I ran to the window when I heard something outside. Anything could happen to you out here. It's too secluded."

"The seclusion is the reason why I like it. You worry too much. That SUV was probably just somebody lost in the neighborhood. It's not easy to find your way around back here if you don't know where you're going."

"Well, that may be. I need you to promise me, though, that you'll be more careful next time."

"I promise that next time you come by my house unannounced wielding a box of pastry, I will confront you with a machine gun a'blazing and a pack of ferocious Rottweilers."

Jonah settled himself into the couch and helped himself to a Nutty Bun. "I liked you better when you were stuck in the bushes."

Chapter 15

Although Lindsay had the day off, she got up early on Saturday morning. She had to be at the country club for Vernon's memorial by noon, but she first wanted to spend a few hours following up on the idea that had struck her during her evening with the Bullards. Vernon had told his wife that his research at the county library had uncovered something big. Lindsay intended to find out for herself what that something was. If anyone had asked her why she was taking this upon herself, she probably would have answered that she wanted to help Kimberlee out of her predicament. If there was another possible motive for Vernon's murder hidden in the old diary, maybe it would exonerate Kimberlee. However, if God deigned to peek down into the grey folds of Lindsay's little human brain, he would have seen one motive looming above all else: she needed to be the one to help. She wasn't a martyr, exactly—just someone whose whole personality rested on a compulsion to ease the suffering of others.

But before Lindsay could do anything at all, for any motive whatsoever, she had some personal grooming to attend to. Leaning over a small trash can, she tried to rectify the previous nights' follicular butchery. It took twenty minutes of cursing and pruning before she was able to discipline the coils and helixes of her hair into something that might charitably be called a hairstyle. It was a sort of triangular bob, coming in at an unflattering angle just above her chin. That gruesome task done, she hopped into her car and drove to the squat brick building over in New Albany that housed the county library and archives.

It was still early, and the library's only patrons were a few old men who sat on torn vinyl chairs reading the morning newspapers. A librarian with a wide coffee-colored face and a lumpy, undulating body arranged papier-mâché animals on display shelves in the foyer. Lindsay skirted past them all and began to wander up and down aisles. She had rarely set foot in a library since college, and she drifted down row after row of books with titles like *Passion at Rosewood Ranch* and *The Companion Guide to Appalachian Birdwatching*. After a few more minutes of futile searching, she located the rotund librarian and asked for her help.

"I'm looking for an old book. A diary written by a freed slave. I can't remember his name."

The librarian's ample jaw dropped open. "Don't tell me you want Samuel Wilcox's journal!"

"Yes, that's the one."

"Well, you're gonna have to take a number. That thing is suddenly a popular item. There's already someone else in the special collections room reading that very book. I can take you over there anyway. Maybe he's not using the whole thing."

"The whole thing?"

"You'll see," the librarian replied with a mischievous glint in her eyes.

The woman steered Lindsay down a long hallway, past a dripping water fountain and fading posters that emphatically exhorted young people to READ! BOOKS!

The librarian turned to Lindsay and said, "Now we keep this door locked, so if you need to use the bathroom or something, you'll have to come and find me to let you back in." She unlocked a squeaking metal door and ushered Lindsay inside. The small windowless room was lined with lockable glass cases that were filled from top to bottom with books of every shape and size. In the center of the room, a thin, red-haired man bent over the dark wooden table. He looked up at the sound of the door.

"Well snatch me bald-headed and call me Kojak, if it isn't the Archbishop of Mount Moriah Medical Center!" Warren said cheerfully.

Lindsay strode across the room and grabbed a handful of Warren's hair. From his seated position, his eyelevel was slightly below Lindsay's. "You're lucky that I don't snatch you bald-headed, you two-faced liar. Hasn't Kimberlee been through enough? How dare you come to her house all friendly and eat her chicken and pie and then have her arrested the very next day!? And then smile at me like butter wouldn't melt in your mouth?"

The librarian let out a little squeal of astonishment.

Warren reassured the woman, placing his hands firmly over Lindsay's to keep her from tightening her grip. "It's all right, ma'am. We're old friends."

"Are you sure you don't want me to call the police? She looks dangerous."

He released one of Lindsay's hands and pulled his badge out of his shirt pocket, laying it on the table in front of him. "I am the police, as a matter of fact. A sergeant with the New Albany force. And this woman," he said, prying Lindsay's hands from his hair and forcing them to her sides, "is a Christian minister."

The librarian acknowledged the badge, but continued to eye the pair suspiciously.

"We've just had a little miscommunication, but it's okay now. Isn't it, Lindsay?"

Lindsay shook herself free from Warren's grip and crossed her arms over her thin chest. She turned on her heel and faced the librarian, giving her a sweet grin. "Yes, ma'am. Sorry for the disturbance. We just have a little difference of opinion over whether or not it's okay to harass a grieving widow and try to bully her into confessing to a crime she didn't commit."

"See there?" Warren said, echoing Lindsay's sugary smile. "We're fine. Just a little disagreement between old friends. Would you mind giving us a moment, please?"

The librarian's eyes darted to the cases of rare books that filled the room. Seeing this, Warren reassured her again. "Don't worry, ma'am. We won't hurt anything. If she acts up again, I'll just handcuff her to the table."

Clicking her tongue in disapproval, the librarian closed the large door and left them.

Warren turned to face Lindsay with a stern expression. "What's the idea of flying at me like that? You're lucky I didn't let her call the police on you and have you taken down to the station."

"Yeah, I suppose I am lucky, since that's what you seem to like to do to defenseless women."

"Well, judging by how you pounced on me like a rabid wildcat, I would hardly call you defenseless." He rubbed his scalp with his fingertips. "Now would you please dismount your high horse for a minute while I try to explain what happened with

Kimberlee?"

Not taking her eyes off him, Lindsay marched to the opposite side of the table and thumped into a chair. Clasping her hands and placing them on the table, she raised her eyebrow to indicate her consent for Warren to begin speaking. Warren rubbed his face with the tops of his closed fists. Looking at him now, Lindsay could see the fatigue in his eyes. He had a day or two's worth of peach-colored stubble spreading across his cheeks and chin. He leaned forward in his chair. "I have my own doubts about whether Kimberlee had anything to do with Vernon's murder. I'm afraid, though, that I might have set off something that's taking on a life of its own. If you're here for the reason I think you are, you might be able to help me stop it."

Chapter 16

"That night when I came to see Kimberlee at her house, I just wanted to hear her side of things for myself. I already told you that Vernon had brought in that threatening letter the week before. We told the officers who were doing crowd control at the state park for the reenactment to keep an eye on him and look out for anything suspicious. But they had enough on their hands trying to keep teenagers from smoking pot under the bandstand and reuniting lost kids with their parents. Like I said, we're not the Secret Service. It was Vernon's decision to go that day, in spite of us warning him against it.

"I don't know how much you know about these battle reenactments. I didn't know much myself before last week. It's almost like a play, where each person has a role set out for him. Before each battle, they come up with a list of guys who are supposed to take 'hits.' In theory, this would correspond to the proportion of casualties on each side in the actual battle, but in practice, no one wants to play dead in the grass for an hour and get eaten by mosquitoes and fried by the sun. So they draw straws, and come up with an order that those who are chosen have to take their hits. About half the guys were on the list; it was a bloody battle for the Rebs. Vernon was one of the ones picked to go down early, so no one thought much of it when he took his hit. A few people saw him from a distance, rolling around on the grass, but they thought he was just trying to get into a more comfortable position on the ground.

"So, Vernon had been lying down for what we reckon was about twenty minutes. One of the reenactors is designated as a 'medic' who goes around checking on all the 'casualties.' Basically the medic just makes sure nobody who's been laying there needs sun block or a snack. The medic, a wiry old timer by the name of Joe Tatum, came over and checked on Vernon. When Joe saw Vernon was in trouble, he dragged him over to a shady spot, gave him some water, and ran to one of the ambulances that were on site. They've always got a couple of ambulances at any kind of public event of this size. Anyway, I suppose Joe's moving him was a good thing to do in terms of making Vernon comfortable, but unfortunately, it made a right pig's supper of the crime scene."

"I've known the Tatum family for years," Lindsay said. "Old Joe does things his own way."

"That's putting it mildly. It has been well nigh impossible to get any coherent information about the way Vernon was positioned or the timeline of events or what all Mr. Tatum might have touched or disturbed. In his initial statement, he said that Vernon was still conscious when he found him. He has since changed his story and said he's not sure if he was or he wasn't. All this is by way of saying that we couldn't really rule anything or anybody out based on what happened out there."

"Well, then, what gave you the notion that Kimberlee was involved in Vernon's death?" Lindsay asked.

"There were a few things that didn't seem to add up. Kimberlee said that Vernon's catering business was going great. But when we talked to her father, Buford, he said that the restaurant was just scraping by. Kimberlee says that she and Vernon had a perfect marriage, but a couple of the busboys at the restaurant heard them arguing loudly a number of times during the week right before Vernon died."

"Did they say what the arguments were about?"

"No. Only that they kept saying something about Buford, and Vernon said something about him 'finding out' about something. All this might be beside the point, though, if Kimberlee's whereabouts could be accounted for on the day of the murder. But neither her mother, nor anyone else, knows where she was during the period of time when Vernon was shot. Kimberlee herself said that she can't remember exactly what she was doing. How can you not remember what you were doing less than a week ago? She says that she ran out to do some errands for about an hour at one point, but she's very vague on the timeline.

"Those things were already in my head when I went to talk to Kimberlee. Then I saw those poems and things that she had printed. I had looked at that threatening letter of Vernon's and I noticed that there was a little smear all through the ink, like from a leaky cartridge. I saw the same thing on those papers on Kimberlee's coffee table—the exact same pattern of streaking. We sent the paper off to the FBI lab in Virginia for their crime lab to look at. There was enough similarity to get a search warrant for the Young's house. The lab ran some more tests yesterday when they got their hands on the printer itself. A lot of modern color printers encode their serial number into every document they print. The threatening letter definitely came off of Kimberlee's printer."

"I can't understand that." Lindsay shook her head in dismay. For the first time, Lindsay experienced a niggling wave of doubt about Kimberlee's innocence. Lindsay dismissed the thought as quickly as it came into her head. She had seen the grief on that woman's face. She had been there in Kimberlee's darkest hour and witnessed her devotion to her husband. There simply had to be some other explanation. "Did you say you sent the paper to the FBI lab? Why is the FBI involved?"

"Well, the FBI can get involved in crimes that involve civil rights violations. Hate crimes and such. That all goes back to Jim Crow. Back then, local police forces, especially in the South, couldn't always be relied upon to devote themselves all that diligently to solving racially-motivated crimes. Times were that this sort of thing might get swept under the rug. As soon as the Feds got wind of the fact that there was a Confederacy angle to this murder, they asked us, very insistently, if we wanted them to send somebody down here to 'render assistance'—a real serious guy named Fleet. He's got more experience with this kind of thing that all the cops on the Mount Moriah and New Albany forces combined. We're lucky to have him, really. Plus, he's black."

There was triumphant tone in his voice that made Lindsay instinctively roll her eyes.

Warren glared at her. "The Mount Moriah and New Albany forces ain't exactly a Rainbow Coalition. We got two women officers and one guy who was born in Kansas City. Our Rainbow is seven shades of white. Besides, there's a lot of stuff that goes on out at that commemoration each year that doesn't tend to promote racial harmony—Sons of Confederate Veterans, the Lost Cause, all of that. You remember the hoopla about the Confederate flag flying at state capitols in the South a few years back?"

Lindsay nodded. In South Carolina, Georgia, and elsewhere, tens of thousands of activists had marched on state capitols, demanding that Confederate symbols be removed.

"Well, that gives you some indication of how raw this still is. Everyone says that Vernon Young looked at things differently than most people. It didn't matter to him that he was black and his wife was white. And as far as the reenacting, he was into the historical side of it. The guys in his regiment were like that, too, far as I can tell. But you do find some people who get into reenacting because they think that things would have been better if the South had won…" Warren trailed off, sweeping his upturned palm out in front of him and inviting Lindsay to finish his thought.

Instead, she abruptly changed the subject. She had already been through all of this with Rob and Geneva, and she stubbornly clung to her opinion that Vernon couldn't have been killed just because of his skin color. "So this Fleet guy is in charge now?"

"He isn't in charge, technically. Like I said, he's 'rendering assistance'. But we need to keep him happy. If he thinks we're stonewalling, next thing you know we're gonna have federal agents coming out of every impolite orifice in our bodies."

"And whose idea was it to bring Kimberlee in for questioning?"

"Fleet's. He wanted to see her for himself. He wanted to try to put some pressure on her about the printer and the letter. At this point, we have no solid motive, no murder weapon, and no witnesses. Not to mention that we're sitting on a powder keg if the contents of that letter get out to the general public. I think Fleet was hoping that Kimberlee'd spill her guts when they confronted her with the letter."

Even though Warren had partially exonerated himself by blaming the interrogation on Agent Fleet, Lindsay couldn't help snapping at him. "You should have known that she wouldn't just fold."

"Tell me about it. I watched the interrogation. When Fleet showed her that letter, her blood set to boiling. And when they so much as hinted that she wrote that letter or had something to do with Vernon's death, she about ripped their throats out with her teeth. For some of the guys, that was a mark against her, in terms of guilt."

"Some of the guys? So not you?" Lindsay said, raising her eyebrows.

"Look, I have no doubt that Kimberlee Young is capable of killing. Watching her in that moment, I saw her as the type of woman who might commit a crime to defend someone she loved. But I am having a hard time believing that she calculated this whole thing, and against her own husband. Whoever did this is slow and methodical."

"So you do think she's innocent!"

"Before you start doing an 'I told you so' dance, let's be clear. I'm still not remotely close to counting Kimberlee out as a suspect. All the evidence still points to her and nobody else."

"Then where does that leave us? What's this about me helping you stop something?"

"The news about that letter could get out any time now. Nobody wants to see this county ripped open, with its stuffing hanging out for all to see. Being able to put Kimberlee behind bars quickly would conveniently make the racial motive disappear; this becomes a domestic murder story. As you might imagine, the powers that be in this county are very anxious to see that. A little too anxious, if you ask me. I like to build a case on facts. That's where you come in."

Lindsay gave a little involuntary clap of her hands. The prospect of helping to solve the mystery made her indecently excited. She made sure that her voice came out calm and level when she spoke. "If this might help clear Kimberlee, count me in."

"Well, since you're here, I reckon you were also wondering if there might be something important in this journal that Vernon was so interested in. I started to have a look at it, but I'm afraid that by the time I find anything out, it could be too late." Warren paused, his face becoming stern. "Lindsay, you don't need to get involved in this. You really don't. An unsolved murder means that there is a murderer out there, running free. Someone who has killed already. I have no idea who it is, and neither do you. You could be getting mixed up in something very dangerous. For all you know, your new friend Kimberlee could be a cold-blooded murderer."

Chapter 17

Lindsay brushed off Warren's warning with a wave of her hand. She hated advice, especially advice from well-meaning men. And most especially she hated advice that got in the way of her doing what she had made up her mind to do.

"I take it that's Samuel Wilcox's journal?" Lindsay pointed to the large, leather-bound sheaf that stood open on the table in front of Warren. Lindsay leaned over. Densely-packed lines of cursive writing stretched from margin to margin across each thick, blue-gray page. The ink had faded to a dull brown with the occasional splotch where the thick-nibbed pen it had been written with had sputtered.

"Yes. That," Warren swiveled around and pointed to a shelf of identical books in one of the glass-fronted cases behind him, "and that, and that, and that."

"Whoa! How many are there?"

"Eleven. Each one covers one year of his life from 1862 to 1872. I've been reading this for almost an hour, but I'm only up to the beginning of March in the first volume. The writing is tough to decipher, so it's slow going. Now you can see why I could use some help."

Lindsay walked to the glass case and removed one of the heavy volumes. She opened it to a random page and began to read aloud. "24 February 1866. Rain. Flora sick with cough again. Stock room: ten pounds sugar, nine pounds suet, fifty pounds flour. Jeremy's fattened pig eaten by a she-wolf in the night." She looked at Warren in dismay. "Are they all like this?"

"What you just read there is about as exciting as it gets, seems to me. It ain't exactly the *Diary of Anne Frank.*"

"I guess I pictured a diary like I had when I was in junior high, with a pink pony on the front cover and a little heart-shaped lock. I wrote all my very important secrets in there."

Warren seemed to relax and return to his usual good-humored self for the first time that morning. "Now *that* sounds interesting. Right after I finish this here page-turner, the secret diary of Lindsay Harding is my next project."

Warren explained that he had arrived as soon as the library opened that morning. He had questioned the librarian, hoping to find out what Vernon had been reading right before his death. She thought she remembered him doing some genealogical research using the North Carolina census records, and she knew she'd seen him read the Wilcox diary, but she had no idea which of the volumes he had read. She gave Warren the names of the other librarians, but didn't hold out much hope of any of them knowing anything specific about Vernon's studies.

"You saw the set-up," Warren said. "The librarian lets you in, but then you're basically on your own in here. I got a little hopeful when I saw that people sign in and out using that log book over there, and mark down what all they read. But all Vernon wrote was 'S. Wilcox journal'. No volume numbers or years. So I guess we'll just have to start at the beginning. I've got 1862. Do you want to take 1863? Lindsay?"

"Hang on a minute."

As Warren was speaking, Lindsay had been flipping through the log book scrawling a series of numbers on a small corner of paper she'd torn out of it. "1867."

"What?"

"We should start in 1867. According to the log book, Vernon has spent nearly forty hours here looking at the journal. If it took you an hour to get through two months' worth of entries, then that would mean that it would take six hours to get through a whole volume. The volumes are each about the same length, so that would mean that in forty hours, you'd get through somewhere between six and seven volumes, depending on how fast you read. It seems logical that anyone reading this would start with Volume One, 1862, so we can guess that that's probably what Vernon did. If we want to read what he was reading just before he died, we should start in the sixth volume—1867."

Warren let out an appreciative whistle. "She's not just a pretty face, folks."

"Well, I hope not. With this haircut, I don't think I can

count on my looks to get along in life."

"I wasn't going to say anything, but now that you mention it, you do have a Shirley-Temple-meets-electric-socket thing going on up there. What made you decide on that particular look?"

"My father, a box of pastries, and a whole lot of thistle bushes. I'll tell you the details some other time. Let's get cracking."

Lindsay began with the 1867 volume; Warren took 1868. As Lindsay delved into the journal, she had the sensation of trying to touch a shadow—Samuel Wilcox, his family and his neighbors, the places they lived, all faint phantoms. Dry lists of possessions, mundane traces of everyday existence were all that remained of them. But it was the very palpable spirit of Vernon Young that kept Lindsay's attention rapt. She was certain that his eyes had passed over these same pages, and in them somehow triggered his own undoing. Warren and Lindsay spent most of the next several hours reading in silence, taking notes on anything they felt might be important. Finally, Lindsay looked up at the wall clock and said with a start, "I've got to get going. I'm supposed to be leading Vernon's memorial service in a little while. Have you found anything you think could be Vernon's 'big' news?"

Warren pushed his notes across the table. "Not unless there's some deep significance in Wilcox bitching about the price of cotton sacking. You?"

"There was a sad part when Flora dies. That's his wife. I don't think it's anything to do with what we're after, but he spends a fair amount of time writing about it here—how sick she is, how worried he is. Next thing you know, he's recording the price of her coffin. Poor guy."

"Well, don't you worry too much about old Samuel. By March 1868, he already has his eye on a pretty young lady by the name of Celia, who I'm guessing will be the new and improved Mrs. Samuel Wilcox before too long."

They smiled at each other for a moment. "How come you never got married? I remember hearing that you had a real serious boyfriend after college," Warren said.

"Timothy. Yeah. We were engaged."

"What happened?"

"Gay, apparently. I started dating him my senior year of college. We moved to Columbus together after we graduated. He was studying for an MBA at Ohio State. I got my Divinity and Counseling degrees at a seminary up there and started working on my PhD. About six months before our wedding, out of the blue, he announced that he needed to explore his sexual identity. He moved to DC and that was that."

"Wow."

"Yeah, I have been gifted with the ability to trigger profound psychosexual realizations. My friend Rob came out after he met me, too. You're probably going to leave here this afternoon and drive straight out to a strip club called The Manhole or The Fireman's Pole."

"Well, I was going to get some groceries and clean out my shed, but your idea certainly sounds livelier." Warren winked at her. He closed the volume he'd been reading. "Look, Linds, even if we come across whatever Vernon thought was so important, who's to say we'd even recognize it? And even if we recognize it, who's to say it would even be relevant?"

"I guess you're right. I had such a strong hunch about the diary, though. You must have, too, if you came here on your day off."

"Let's just put this on hold for the time being," Warren said.

"Just promise me that you'll keep working other angles so the blame doesn't fall on Kimberlee." Lindsay looked at her watch. She popped up from her seat and said, "I've got to beat a path to Vernon's memorial service. If I were you, I wouldn't go within ten miles of there, or anywhere else where you're likely to encounter the Bullards. They're out for your blood."

Chapter 18

Lindsay zipped along the two-lane road that led out to the country club. She had stayed far longer at the library than she had intended to, and she now found herself having to make up time by driving at speeds well in excess of the posted limits. Luckily, this northerly road through the scrubby pine forest was one that Lindsay knew well—well enough to test the limits of her ancient electric blue Toyota Tercel. She turned off the air conditioning, despite the baking heat of the day, in order to route more power to the car's tiny engine. As she began to squirm uncomfortably in the slow cooker of the car's cabin, she couldn't help but cast her mind back to another fateful trip along this road, in another kind of extreme weather, ten years before.

##

A dozen years before on a frigid Saturday in November during their junior year of college, Lindsay and Rob had loaded up Lindsay's little Tercel (a well-used car even back then) with a week's worth of laundry. They had set out to drive the forty miles from their campus to Lindsay's father's house in Mount Moriah. They were already in the car by 7:30am. These trips had become a fixed routine: spend the morning at Lindsay's dad's doing laundry and watching professional wrestling on TV; graciously allow Lindsay's dad to make lunch for them and to provision them with eatable sundries; return to campus in the mid-afternoon; nap; wake up refreshed and ready for their Saturday night social activities. For Rob, Saturday night social activities meant leading a Bible study group. For Lindsay, it meant running alone on the treadmills in the nearly-empty student recreation facility for an hour and then doing her homework. This was their Saturday ritual, and that particular Saturday had begun no differently than usual.

Rob had flicked through the glove compartment, looking

for a mix tape he accused Lindsay of having stolen. When he didn't find it (she had indeed stolen it, but it was hidden in her dorm room, in a drawer, tucked into a pair of socks), he sank back into his seat and gazed idly out the window. "I think your car needs a name," he said.

"I don't like naming inanimate objects," Lindsay said, her eyes fixed on the road.

"How dare you call Her inanimate!"

"*She* is an *it*."

"How can you see that perky little trunk jutting out with her come-hither tail lights and call Her an it? Her name is Michelle. Michelle, Michelle the Toyota Tercel."

"No."

"Darcelle?"

"Stop it."

"Chantelle?"

"Obadiah Dong Larry J. Robinson Wu!" Lindsay said, reprimanding Rob with his full name. It was one of the few tactics she knew of that were almost guaranteed to annoy him, and she hoped, distract him from his quest to find a name for her car. Lindsay was the only person besides Rob's own parents who knew that Rob had been named after his father's three heroes: the biblical prophet Obadiah, his paternal grandfather Dong Wu, and Larry J. Robinson, deputy manager of the Woolworth's discount store in Tulsa, Oklahoma, where Rob's father had briefly worked during a sojourn in America.

Rob, however, was not silenced. He quietly began to sing "Chantelle, My Belle" to the tune of the Beatles' "Michelle".

Lindsay ignored him for a few minutes, but, when he didn't stop, she said irritably, "Are you going to start naming other machines that I own? Is my hotplate going to be called Francine?"

"As a matter of fact, your hotplate is Blaze. Blaze McSizzlington."

"You are such a child."

"A car is different from other machines. Cars have personalities."

As if to emphasize his point, a deep thud arose from the engine block. The car rapidly decelerated. The sudden change of speed caused Lindsay to fishtail, but she quickly regained control. "Oh no! Chantelle is really upset with you," Rob said.

"Shut up, Rob. I think something's really wrong. Nothing happens when I press on the accelerator." Lindsay piloted the car to the shoulder of the highway. She popped the hood and the two of them climbed out of the car, the frigid air cutting through their thin clothing. Lindsay raised the hood, and after a few minutes of fiddling was able to get it propped open. Her sense of accomplishment at propping the hood was short-lived, however.

"I have no earthly idea what I am looking at," Lindsay stated glumly. There was no obvious smoke or fire, and no giant, blinking arrow emblazoned with the words Here Is the Problem! They might just as well have been looking at the blueprints for a space ship, for all they understood. She and Rob stood staring, the icy clouds of their breath filling the air.

"I once helped my uncle change a tire," Rob said. Lindsay glared at him.

They got back into the car. It was still very early, and after ten minutes, not a single car had driven past them. They hadn't dressed for the freezing temperatures and were already beginning to shiver.

"Well," Lindsay said, "we've got a weeks' worth of laundry in the trunk, so we know we won't freeze to death. I think we should try to walk to the Shoney's outside of Snow Camp. That's the closest place." By now, they had driven the route so many times that they were familiar with all the landmarks, large and small (and pancake-filled).

"That has to be five miles from here."

"Do you have another plan? Should we wait here until a one-eyed trucker with a hook for a hand offers to give us a lift?"

"Fine," Rob said. "But when we get to Shoney's, I'm having French toast and sausages. The round sausages, not links."

They bundled up, layering t-shirts over sweaters until they looked like turn-of-the-century strongmen. They trudged wordlessly along the shoulder of the road, gravel grinding and crunching under their feet. The rocks, stumps, and leaves at the edge of the forest were coated with a crisp layer of frost. In the flat, early morning light, the undergrowth looked like an attic full of dust-covered furniture.

"I am not adapted to this climate. It never gets this cold in Taiwan," Rob complained.

"You've been here for almost three years. What's Taiwanese for 'quit being a crybaby'?"

Ignoring her, Rob continued, "My feet are freezing. I should have put on extra socks."

"Do you want to run back for them? We've been walking for less than ten minutes. I don't think we've even gone a quarter mile."

"Next spring, they're going to find our frozen corpses in the ditch next to the road."

"If you don't stop whining, you might be right about them finding a corpse down there."

"Hey, is that a house?" Rob pointed hopefully to the near distance, where a column of white smoke rose like a Grecian column into the vivid blue sky. At the edge of the road ahead, a small, colorfully painted sign marked the beginning of a narrow gravel track. "Tatum's Tree Farm," Rob read aloud. "How do you farm trees?"

"Let's find out, shall we? Maybe they'll let us use their phone."

They turned down the track, passing through a hundred yards of dense forest that screened the tree farm from the road. Suddenly, there was a break in the tree line and a surreal vista opened up before them. As far as they could see, row upon row of tiny conifers dotted the undulating landscape, none of the trees more than four or five feet high. The smell of Christmas morning filled the air. The trees were a pale, silvery-green color, and they shimmered in the thin rays of early morning sun. At the crest of the next hill stood a neat two-story farmhouse. The wooden siding boards were painted in an alternating pattern of red and green. The effect was charmingly garish, as if Santa's tackiest elf had been unleashed on this unsuspecting farm. A thin plume of white smoke rose from a stone chimney. Lindsay and Rob walked up the steps and onto the porch. As Lindsay raised her hand to knock, the door flew open.

"I been watching y'all come up the road."

A small, gnome-like man with wizened reddish skin stood glowering before them. He wore red Long Johns, which revealed a surprisingly muscular frame. A crocheted white shawl was draped around his shoulders to ward off the cold.

Taken aback, Lindsay stuttered, “Oh. Uh. I mean, our car broke down on the road back there. We were wondering if we could use your phone.”

“Ain’t got one.”

“Sorry to trouble you, sir. We’ll just be on our way.” Rob was already halfway down the front steps, motioning for Lindsay to follow.

“Pop, who you talking to?” They heard a man’s low voice say from somewhere inside the house.

“Curly here and this little Chinaman say their car broke down,” the older man said. He took a step back to allow his son to see the strangers. The son was tanned and muscular, with a short-cropped beard so blond that it was almost white. Standing barely five and a half feet tall, he looked like a miniature Viking.

“Hi there. I’m John Tatum,” he said, smiling warmly and extending his hand.

Lindsay and Rob introduced themselves, still shrinking uncomfortably under the older man’s stare. “This here is my Pop, Joe Tatum. You say your car’s broken down? Where is she? Let me get my coat and I’ll take a look at her.” He disappeared inside for a moment. The old man continued his vigilant watch over them.

Rob leaned in toward Lindsay and whispered, “See, he called your car a Her.”

John reappeared a moment later, and the three of them headed back down the gravel track.

“Sorry about my Pop. You may have gathered that he ain’t playing off the same sheet music as the rest of the band.” He sighed and looked back over his shoulder toward the house. “Where’re y’all headed?”

“Mount Moriah. My dad lives there.”

“Students, then? Over at Elon?”

“How did you know that?” Rob asked, impressed by John’s intuition. John tipped his head toward the top layer of Rob’s sweater cocoon. It had the college’s name and emblem in large blue lettering across the front. "Oh."

They spent the rest of the walk learning more about John Tatum and the Tatum Tree Farm. The day John graduated from high school, he had gone to work as a carpenter in Charlotte, never intending to return. After his mother died, however, he came back to the farm to help care for his father. He recently bought an old fixer-upper in downtown Mount Moriah, and he was living in the one room he had managed to make habitable.

"Pop won't hear of moving out of the house," John explained. "Even after Momma died and he had his accident, the stubborn old codger still reckons he can take care of himself. He's right for the most part. Me and my sister take turns looking in on him, though. She comes a few times during the week, and I come on the weekends. And we both lend a hand trimming them every spring and summer and spraying the trees in the September of the year they're harvested."

"Spraying them?" Lindsay asked.

John nodded. "Do you know what photosynthesis is?"

Lindsay, ever eager with a right answer, quickly responded. "It's how trees convert sunlight into energy."

"Yep. They use photosynthesis to make chlorophyll—the stuff that turns their needles green. Did you notice how most of our trees are that shiny silver-yellow color, 'stead of green? Well, they are White Pines. They stop photosynthesis in the colder months, when they go dormant. Less chlorophyll in the needles means that the trees look bleached out and silvery. Nobody's gonna pay top dollar for a tree like that. When they grow big enough to sell, we need them to be green. We can't stop the trees from going dormant, so we spray 'em. The spray stops the color from fading."

"You spray paint the trees green?" Rob's eyes were round with horror. He looked like a child who had just been told that there was no such thing as Santa Claus.

"It's not spray paint. It's a water-based protectant. It gets washed off by rain during the fall. By the time November rolls around, the sun is low enough in the sky so as it doesn't cause fading. When we harvest 'em they are that bright Christmassy green," John said. "We have to trim 'em twice a year to get that nice triangle shape, too. Otherwise, they'd just be big, ole silvery bushes."

When they finally arrived at the car, it took John about fifteen seconds to render his diagnosis. "Your timing belt is busted. It shouldn't be too bad to fix, in this kind of car, but it ain't something I can do. You need parts that I ain't got. We gonna have to walk back to Pop's house and call somebody to come out and give her a tow into town."

"Wait, he has a phone?"

"'Course he has a phone. Whacha think this is, Little House on the Prairie?"

"Oh, it's just that your dad said you didn't have one."

"He says a lot of things," John said.

"Did I hear you say that your father had an accident?" Lindsay asked, as they began their trek back to the farmhouse.

"Yes, ma'am. He used to keep a garden out behind the house. There was this rabbit that kept getting through the fence and eating everything. Pop tried everything to keep that varmint out—fences, traps, everything—but this was some kind of daggone Houdini rabbit. It just kept on coming back. So early one morning, 'fore the sun even come up, Pop sets up a little hunting blind back there and hunkers down to wait with his .22."

"Sure enough, the daggone thing comes hopping along. The little critter hops over to the gate, leaps straight into the air, bats open the latch, and just goes in. Pop can't believe his damn eyes. He jumps out of the blind and starts firing away like Wyatt Earp at the OK Corral. Somehow, one of the bullets ricochets off a rock and hits Pop in the side of the head. Momma comes running out and finds Pop staggering around holding his bleeding head with one hand and that daggone rabbit's dead carcass in the other. He tells her to drive him to the hospital, and then get herself back home to cook him some fricassee.

"Pop was always an original thinker, but that bullet made him a bit fanciful. Hell, what I mean to say is he acts downright peculiar."

The trio arrived back at the farmhouse. They couldn't arrange for anyone to tow the car until that afternoon, so John invited Rob and Lindsay to settle in. John made hot cocoa for them and they laundered the layers of clothes that they were wearing in

Joe Tatum's washing machine. The whole morning, old Joe moved warily around the edges of the room, like a cat deciding whether to pounce or bolt.

When Lindsay and Rob finally left, they promised to stop in at the farm the following Saturday on their weekly laundry run. Even thinking back now, Lindsay could hardly make sense of all that had happened in the weeks and months that followed that first meeting. Rob and John never went on a date. The word "gay" wasn't even thought, much less said aloud. But one day that Spring, Rob wrote a letter to his parents and the American missionaries in Taiwan, explaining that he was no longer planning to become a missionary. Together, he and Lindsay packed up his dorm room, and she gave him a lift to John's house in town.

Chapter 19

Lindsay walked up the wide, circular drive that led to the entrance of Plantation Oaks Country Club. In the backseat of her car, she had wriggled into a black, long-sleeved dress, which was now serving to funnel the sun's baking heat onto her skin and create a great deal of very unladylike perspiration. As she made her way toward the building, Lindsay remembered the only other time she had been inside the country club's wrought-iron gates—her Senior Prom. The memories from that night were very murky and episodic. A steamy June evening. Clandestine cigarettes in the ladies' room. Wine coolers with PBR chasers. Here Comes the Hotstepper. Tequila from a flask. Hootie & the Blowfish. At some point, she had ended up face down in a bunker next to the ninth green. She'd had a revelation the next morning, when the icy spray of the golf course's lawn-watering sprinklers awakened her: Senior Prom would be her last bacchanal. Rebellion was exhausting. It left you shoeless, hung over, and covered in golf course sand. She decided that college was going to be about abstaining, eschewing, straightening up, and flying right. Plantation Oaks would be her Road to Damascus. And it had been. Basically.

With a rolling green golf course and a sparkling man-made lake, the grounds of Plantation Oaks seemed an impossible Eden. A $5,000 a year membership fee walled it off from the rural tableaux of dilapidated gas stations and trailer parks that surrounded it. And the name Plantation Oaks, of course, told everyone as much as they needed to know about the skin color of most of the members. For whites, plantations conjured images of mint-julep-sipping belles. For blacks, not so much. The oldest part of the clubhouse, erected in the 1950's, had been modeled after an old plantation house, and it sported the requisite clichés: bottle green shutters, stately Doric columns, and a grand porch with white wooden rocking chairs. Two massive glass-fronted, 80s-era additions clung to each side of the original building.

Lindsay passed through the wide doors of the plant-filled atrium of the west addition, noting that the Richards family seemed to mark large public spaces with the enthusiasm and frequency of dogs marking lampposts. The entrance was plaque-marked as the Ella Mae Richards Vestibule of the (plaque-marked) Lavonia Richards Reception Hall. Inside, the preparations for the day's activities were nearly complete. On one side of the room, a small dais and podium had been erected. Facing this stood rows of white fabric-covered chairs. On the opposite side of the room, dozens of round tables had been set with plateware and cutlery. A bored woman in a navy blue uniform was plunking vases of white carnations into the middle of each table.

The Bullard women were gathered near the podium, circling Kimberlee. They brandished mascara wands and powder brushes like a Nascar pit crew readying their vehicle for the next leg. In one corner, a group of Kimberlee's nieces and nephews were engrossed in a card game that involved violently walloping one another's hands every few seconds. Lindsay had the incongruous feeling that she was attending a wedding, rather than a funeral. The only indication of the real purpose of the occasion was a large display table in the center of the room adorned with photographs of Vernon Young. Picture after picture showed his broad smile and twinkling, intelligent eyes. Lindsay had begun to move toward the podium when two hushed voices caught her attention.

"I am not going to talk about this now. We are at Vernon's memorial service, for Pete's sake."

"You 'been avoiding talking about this for weeks. Something damned funny is going on, I'm telling you."

Lindsay recognized the voices of Keith and Buford Bullard coming from behind a large grouping of tropical plants near the entrance. Polite Lindsay could easily have made her presence known with a discrete little cough. Very Polite Lindsay could have walked away. Instead, she casually sidestepped her way out of sight behind a potted palm and listened. She could just make out the men's words over the gurgling of a nearby fountain and the loud hum of the air conditioners, which were struggling to keep the heat of the July sun at bay.

"If it's a mistake, I'll get to the bottom of it. If there's funny business, which I very much doubt, I'll get to the bottom of that, too. This is why you should let me handle the business side of things, Daddy."

Buford's reply came out in a low grumble, as menacing as a peal of thunder. "Just 'cuz you got an associates degree don't think that makes you some kind of titan of industry. Remember, boy, I paid for you to get that degree and I'm the one who put you in charge of the restaurant in the first place. Sometimes I think there's more common sense in the backside of a pig than there is in that thick head of yours."

"Yes, sir." The tone in Keith's voice was that of a guilty schoolboy.

"Now come on. You go see how your sister is doing. I need to change into my uniform."

Keith murmured something indistinguishable and the two men emerged from the foliage about two feet in front of Lindsay's hiding place. They spotted her immediately. "Hey, y'all," she said. She smiled nonchalantly, as if it were the most natural thing in the world for the spiritual leader of the memorial service to be lurking around among the shrubbery. Buford stalked past her with the merest grunt of a hello.

Keith was more cordial in his greeting. He waited until his father was out of earshot and then leaned in. "Don't know how much of that you heard. Dad's always getting his boxers in a bunch about something or other."

"Oh. Me? No, I just walked in. I was admiring the foliage on this bougainvillea." Lindsay indicated the flowering bush next to them. The color of her cheeks deepened to a shade of pink that she put the blossoms to shame. Keith knit his eyebrows together quizzically, but let her lie go unchallenged, and the two of them walked together toward the females of the Bullard tribe.

"Hey Sugar," Kimberlee called, giving Lindsay an unenthusiastic hug. The skin around her eyes was red and swollen, despite the makeup blitz her sisters and mother had visited upon her face. Her whole body, in fact, looked swollen, as if she were absorbing grief from the air around her. She turned robotically back toward her mother, who started applying another layer of concealer to her ruddy skin.

Kimberlee's sister Kathilee, who Lindsay thought of as the non-twin, pulled Lindsay to one side and whispered, "Kimberlee is not doing all that great. A reporter from Raleigh called today and asked her for an interview. I guess the story is getting some airplay beyond Mount Moriah. The reporter didn't seem to know that the police had taken Kimberlee in for questioning, but it's only a matter of time before this thing gets even uglier than it already is. We tried to give her one of Daddy's relaxation pills to stop her from crying, but she wouldn't take it. Try to get her to take one, if you can. She's hanging by a real thin thread."

##

Every one of the two hundred chairs at the memorial service was filled, with several dozen people forced to stand at the back. Vernon's regiment of reenactors arrived in their full military regalia. From her seat on the dais, Lindsay saw many familiar faces from Vernon's regiment: Keith Bullard, Silas Richards, John and Joe Tatum. Rob, who had come along with John, sat a few rows away from them.

Lindsay introduced each speaker and gave a brief but heartfelt homily about Vernon's life. Friends spoke of Vernon's joviality, his intelligence, and his love of food. It all went very smoothly, with the appropriate mix of solemnity and levity. After the ceremony, while the Bullards where busy greeting the mourners, John and Rob walked up to Lindsay. "That was a very nice service," Rob said sincerely. "Those poems were perfect."

"I can't take any credit. Kimberlee picked them all."

John nodded in agreement. "I can't say as I knew Vernon all that well, but I think that would have done him proud."

They all stared somberly at the display of pictures. After a moment, Rob turned to Lindsay. He gestured to her head and said, "Oh, the Jackson Five called. They want their hair back."

"Dang it, Rob, can't you stop cracking jokes for five minutes? Anyone would think you were a ninth grader on a field trip instead of the head chaplain at a hospital here to attend a memorial service," John said.

Lindsay frowned, putting her hands up to cover her unruly mane. "Do you think a headband would help it?"

Rob shook his head. "Putting a headband on that would be like putting a bowtie and cummerbund on a yak."

John glowered at Rob and opened his mouth to say something else. He was interrupted, however, by the sound of shouting and the sight of Kimberlee Bullard's plump form rushing headlong out the front doors of the building and into the midday sun.

Chapter 20

Kimberlee was followed a few moments later by a shuffling procession of the other Bullard women, whose nearly identical, stout figures gave them the unfortunate appearance of migrating penguins. The angry shouts continued from the corner of the room closest to the podium. Buford Bullard had taken hold of the collar of Joe Tatum's grey uniform and was shaking the small man violently back and forth. Keith and a few of the other reenactors tried to intervene.

John, Rob, and Lindsay rushed over just in time to see Joe duck out of Buford's clutches. Buford, red-faced and panting, lunged again, but the other men held him back. He pointed an accusatory finger, "You tell me what you said to her, you prune-faced little metal-plate-headed son of a bitch."

Joe smoothed the front of his jacket and shook his head. "You ask her yerself. Like I said, it's between her and Vernon."

John walked up to his father and said, "Pop, what's going on?"

Buford cut in, still breathing heavily. "I'll tell you what's going on. Your father there is making up stories and getting my Kimmie all upset. He tried to wreck my family once and I'll be damned if I'm gonna let him do it again. If he knows what's good for him, he'll stay away from my family."

Silas Richards, a sturdy gray-haired man with heavy, dark eyebrows stepped forward from the knot of reenactors that separated the quarreling men. He was immaculate in his Confederate regalia—an ornately engraved dress sword scabbard hung from his left side, and the brass buttons down the front of his jacket gleamed in the sunlight that streamed in through the building's glass wall. The spotless uniform, combined with his short-cropped, salt-and-pepper beard and naturally resonant voice, lent weightiness to his words. "Now then. Let us remember why we are all here. Joe, I think you need to apologize to Buford and Keith for marring the solemnity of this occasion."

Joe opened his mouth to protest, but Silas silenced him with a raised hand. “I am not implying there was anything untruthful in what you said. I doubt that anyone but Mrs. Young can judge that, because Mrs. Young was your sole interlocutor. However, I believe you need to apologize to the Bullards for further inflaming the powerful emotions they must be experiencing during this difficult time.” He turned to Buford. “And Buford, you have every right to be troubled that Joe further distressed the poor widow. However, you have known Joe Tatum for years and you know that, despite his many eccentricities, and despite your, ahem, shared history, he intends no harm.”

The two men fixed their eyes in opposite corners of the room, their eyes burning coals of anger. When it became clear that two combatants were not going to apologize, Silas turned to John. “I think it might be best for your father to take his leave now. Perhaps you would be so kind as to escort him out?”

John quickly complied, glad to escape from the embarrassing scene his father had created. He linked arms with the older man and steered him toward the door. Rob whispered a quick goodbye to Lindsay and trailed out quickly after the Tatums. The gathered men began to disperse, leaving Lindsay and Silas standing next to one another. This was the closest she had ever been to the great patron of Mount Moriah. He was a robust specimen, tall and large-boned. Next to him, Lindsay’s pale skin, myopic eyes, and slight figure seemed like the misbegotten adaptations of some soon-to-be extinct bird.

They watched as Keith Bullard guided his father to a chair in a quiet corner of the room and sat him down. “What on earth was that about?” Lindsay asked.

“It would seem that Mr. Tatum had a few words with Mrs. Young about Vernon. He told her what Vernon’s last words were.”

“I thought Vernon was unconscious when Joe found him.”

“That seems to have been what Joe reported to the police and that was certainly what he told those of us who were there on that unfortunate day. Nonetheless, he took Mrs. Young to one side a moment ago, and he appears to have conveyed to her that Vernon had given him a message for her.”

“What was the message?”

"I am afraid that I didn't hear it. A few of us were assembled here when he advised Mrs. Young that he had a message to impart to her from her late husband, but whatever the message was, only Mrs. Young knows. Mr. Tatum whispered it in her ear. The next thing I witnessed was the unfortunate woman rapidly retreating from the room."

"And then Buford Bullard tried to throttle Joe."

Silas nodded. He eyed Lindsay closely. "I don't believe I've had the pleasure of making your acquaintance?"

Lindsay extended her hand. "I'm Lindsay Harding."

"Silas Richards." For her, at least, the introduction was unnecessary. There were few people in town who didn't know Silas Richards. Silas shook her hand. "You delivered a moving eulogy. Do I take it that you are the Bullards' minister?"

"I'm a chaplain at the hospital. I stayed with them when Vernon was in the coma, and Kimberlee asked me to lead the service."

Silas stroked his beard a moment. "Harding, you said? Any relation to the Reverend Jonah Harding?"

"He's my father." The touch of pride in her own voice caught her off guard. For people like Drew Checkoway, the connection with Jonah Harding tethered Lindsay to petty small town concerns. For someone like Silas Richards, however, someone enmeshed in the web of families and churches that strung Mount Moriah together, the connection meant that Lindsay had a clear identity.

Silas's face widened into a broad grin. "Then I will no doubt see you at the fairgrounds tomorrow for the tent revival. I would have been there this afternoon, but for this unfortunate affair."

"Um, yes, I'll be there." Lindsay paused. "Can I ask what you meant when you mentioned Joe and Buford's 'shared history'?"

"Since you are a minister, I trust that what I am about to impart will be held in the strictest confidence." Silas raised one of his magnificent eyebrows and bent toward her conspiratorially. "Years ago, before either of them married, Joe Tatum courted Versa Bullard. There was even a slanderous rumor that the romantic entanglement may have continued after Versa and Buford married, and that Mr. Tatum might have fathered the eldest Bullard child, Keith. I believe that this rumor was put to bed, if you will pardon the double entendre, long ago. Still, the feelings clearly run deep...on both sides." Silas straightened up, bringing their moment of shared intimacy to an abrupt end. "Well, Reverend Harding, I must bid you adieu." He touched the air, as if tipping an imaginary cap. He glided smoothly through the crowd and passed into the main building of the clubhouse. Lindsay had no time to absorb the astonishing revelation. Instead, she turned and headed quickly in the opposite direction, outside through the big glass doors to check on Kimberlee. On the way out, she passed the Bullard women, minus Kimberlee, as they were making their way back inside.

"We can't find her," said one of the twins.

"Looked all over. But she couldn't have gone far because none of the cars are missing," added the other.

Kathilee said, "Lord knows what that old crank Joe Tatum said to her, but it really got her riled up. She just busted out crying like somebody had flipped a switch."

Versa clucked, "I guess we'll just have to get inside and keep things going. I'm sure she'll come back in once she's settled down." She was wearing a black lacy dress with a coordinating sequin bolero jacket, equal parts Spanish bullfight and French brothel. Her hot pink reading glasses rested on their chain across her ample chest.

Lindsay nodded. "Someone may want to check on Mr. Bullard. He seemed pretty irate."

Kathilee shook her head disapprovingly. "This whole mess has been terrible for Daddy's health. He hates to see any of us girls upset. First, there was Vernon getting killed. Then the police saying it was murder. Then the police saying they think that Kimmie did it. Now this thing about Vernon having some kind of secret last words. There's nothing Daddy can do about any of it, and it's all just too much for him."

The Bullards went inside, leaving Lindsay alone. She thought back to Senior Prom, and scanned the grounds of the country club. She turned and walked in the direction of the large willow tree at the edge of the fairway.

Chapter 21

Lindsay ducked through the curtain of low-hanging willow branches, letting the warm, still air under the tree envelop her. As Lindsay had expected, Kimberlee sat on a carved stone bench. She looked like a medieval saint, bathed in shimmering green and gold light. Lindsay walked over and sat down next to her. They sat silently, looking at the thin line of parched, hay-crisp grass at the edges of the lush emerald fairway.

After a few moments, Kimberlee said softly, "Me and Vernon lost a baby." She sighed deeply and continued, "He was born too early. A little boy we named Buford, after Daddy."

"I'm so sorry."

Tears streamed down Kimberlee's cheeks as she spoke. "I'm pregnant again. Vernon was the only person who knew, and since he's been gone, I haven't been able to talk about it with anyone." Her shoulders heaved with violent sobs and she covered her face with her hands. "We were going to tell everybody soon, but I wanted to wait a bit longer, to make sure everything was okay first. Now I don't know how to tell them.

"One of the last things I did was lie to Vernon about it. He didn't want to find out the gender. I did, though. I felt like it wouldn't seem real to me unless I knew. I wanted to pick out names. We argued about it constantly the last few weeks. I finally told him that I wouldn't find out, but then I decided to do it anyway, and just not tell him about it. I scheduled the ultrasound appointment for last Saturday. I was just going to sneak out for an hour while Momma and I were doing the Richards' order."

"And that's why you didn't tell the police where you went the afternoon that Vernon was shot."

"Yeah. My own mother didn't even know about me being pregnant. I wasn't going to tell a bunch of nasty policemen who had just ransacked my house and accused me of murder." She continued, "Vernon found out about the appointment. The doctor's office called the house to confirm it and he took the call. He was real mad at me. We argued about it again the last time I spoke to him. I hate that we left things that way."

"That explains about the busboy at the restaurant hearing you two argue about 'Buford' and whether or not you should tell someone something." Lindsay shook her head. "Well, honey, you can't let that argument weigh on you. I'm sure Vernon knew that you loved him."

"Well, from what Mr. Tatum said, now I can know for sure." She smiled and wiped her cheeks with the backs of her hands. "Mr. Tatum said when he found Vernon, he was just laying still and peaceful, looking up into the sky. Mr. Tatum saw some blood coming out of his mouth and knew he was hurt bad. When he started to move him, Vernon said, 'Tell my wife: Grant and Lee.' Those were the last words he spoke, so I know he forgave me."

Lindsay raised her eyebrows, looking bewildered. "Grant and Lee? The Civil War generals?"

"Oh. Well, you see, we're having twins," said Kimberlee. "Identical."

"That's fantastic! But…I still don't quite follow. Vernon saying something about Grant and Lee let you know that he forgave you?"

"Vernon and I decided that if the babies were boys, he was going to name them. I'd pick the girls' names. He kept teasing me, saying that he was going to name them after Civil War generals. Stonewall and Pickett, he said."

Finally catching on, Lindsay said, "So Grant and Lee were his choices for names?"

"Yes. I'm so glad their Daddy got to name them."

Lindsay couldn't help but admire Kimberlee's resilience and capacity for optimism. "So you're having boys? That's wonderful."

"Actually, I don't know. I didn't go through with the ultrasound. They had jellied me up with that goo and were just about to start when I decided I didn't want to know. If Vernon was going to be surprised, I decided I wanted that, too. To share that with him." After a moment, Kimberlee said, "How did you know to look for me under here?"

“I saw you here once a long time ago. Senior Prom. You were in here with Jesse McCrae.” Lindsay blushed at the memory and said hurriedly. “So I knew that you knew about this spot.”

Kimberlee nodded, the slight hint of a smile on her lips. “Yeah, me and Jesse were hot and heavy back in those days. Did you know he became a gynecologist?” She gave Lindsay a mischievous wink. “Can’t say I’m surprised.”

Chapter 22

Kimberlee and Lindsay made their way back across the steamy fairway toward the clubhouse, where the memorial luncheon was already well underway. As soon as they stepped through the door, the fleshy, pink faces of the Bullards closed in around them. They all began speaking at once.

"What did Joe say to upset you that way?" Versa asked.

"Did he tell you anything about the S.O.B who shot Vernon?" Keith asked.

"Do you think Vernon really gave him a message?" Either Kennadine or Kristalene said, while the other interjected, "Or was he just telling stories?"

"Hang on everybody. Give me some room to breathe," Kimberlee said holding her hands up. "I can't talk about it just yet. I'm sorry, y'all. I don't mean to be so mysterious. But I'm overwhelmed and I need to think about what he said for awhile and decide what to do."

Lindsay surveyed the assembled Bullards. One round pink face was missing from the tableau. "Where's Buford?"

"Silas Richards took him to a room upstairs. We all thought he'd better lay down for a spell, and for once, he agreed," Kathilee said. "Momma just sent Keith to check on him a minute ago. He said he'll be back down presently. Speaking of which, we'd better get some food into you, Reverend Harding. You're such a skinny thing that a strong wind could send you flying."

Versa and the twins clicked her tongues and nodded in agreement. Lindsay joined them at the head table and they all sat down. The round tables were laden with large platters of fried chicken, mashed potatoes, and green beans with ham—a veritable wonderland of bacon grease and butter. Lindsay dutifully loaded up her plate; she could either appear to go along willingly, or risk being force-fed by the Bullards.

After a few moments, Silas Richards entered the room and walked rapidly toward the Bullards' table. "I am very sorry to intrude upon you, but I need you to follow me upstairs immediately." Looking at each other with surprise, the Bullards, along with Lindsay, rose and followed Silas out the door. They hurried anxiously and wordlessly after Silas up the grand central staircase, turning down a series of plush carpeted hallways until they reached a large pine door. A uniformed member of the club staff stood just outside. Silas dismissed him with a patrician wave, "Thank you, Cedric, that's all now." Turning toward the Bullards, he continued. "One of the waiters came in a moment ago to see if Buford wanted anything. He knocked on the door, but there was no answer."

Silas pushed the door open. Lying unconscious on the floor next to a leather and mahogany couch was the prone body of Buford Bullard. A tall, awkward-looking teenager in a waiter's uniform stood nervously to one side as another teenage girl in a bathing suit and board shorts was performing CPR, counting chest compressions aloud.

The Bullards rushed toward Buford, but Silas stopped them. He gestured to the young woman on the floor. "Jaime is a lifeguard at the club's pool," he said. "Like all the lifeguards in the employ of this club, she has obtained her Red Cross certification in cardio-pulmonary resuscitation. If you will be kind enough to leave her some room to work, she is equipped to handle this kind of situation."

Lindsay, who had seen even doctors and nurses grow flustered in emergencies, was impressed with the young lifeguard's calm demeanor. There was an uncharacteristic quiet among the Bullards, who seemed transfixed by the young woman's rhythmic counting and breathing.

"Andre found Mr. Bullard lying on the ground." Silas said quietly, indicating the man in the staff uniform. "He immediately summoned the emergency services and then very wisely ran to the pool area to alert Jaime, who began administering CPR at once. The ambulance should be here any second." As if on cue, three black-garbed paramedics hurried through the door. One of them took over chest compressions as the other two measured vital signs and made preparations to administer some medication.

"Everybody out!" one of the paramedics barked without taking his eyes off the needle he was preparing. There was a moment of collective immobility. No one seemed able to process the command. "Out now!" he repeated. Jaime the lifeguard ushered people into the hallway like a rancher moving a herd of recalcitrant cattle.

In the hallway, the Bullards began to speak for the first time since Silas summoned them. "It was his heart. I just know it. The strain was too much for him," Versa said. "If I get my hands on Joe, I'm gonna wring his scrawny chicken neck."

"Not if I get to him first!" Kathilee said. Her hands were clenched at her sides and she stomped her foot as she spoke. The twins stood like nightclub bouncers, their arms crossed and their faces twisted into identical scowls of menace. Keith's florid face was lit up in red-hot fury.

Kimberlee raised her hand, trying to throw a little calming oil on the roiling waves of their anger. "Don't be mad at old Joe, y'all, it's not his fault. The one we should be angry at is whoever shot my Vernon."

"What have I done to deserve this?" Versa covered her face with her hands.

Silas put a consoling arm around her shoulder. "I know you must feel as if the plagues of Job have descended on your family. I implore you to remember, ma'am, that your husband is a man of strong spirit. I am sure he will recover." The words were spoken with the authority of Moses proclaiming the Ten Commandments. His tone awakened in Lindsay memories of her adolescence, when she used to sit wide-eyed in the front pew on Sunday mornings, cradled in the solemnity and assuredness of her father's words. The door to the office slammed as the paramedics barreled out, bearing Buford on the stretcher. "Y'all can follow us to the hospital," one of them shouted as they hurried past.

As the family hastily pursued the paramedics down the stairs, Kathilee turned and said to Lindsay, "Can you let all of them downstairs know what's happened?" Lindsay nodded, as the Bullards swept past on a tide of black dresses and puffy hair. Lindsay dutifully returned to the reception hall, where the luncheon was in full swing. In her job as a chaplain, she was often the bearer of bad news. Today, however, she felt more like the Angel of Death as she cut through the polite chatter with the latest revelation. As the astonished guests absorbed the news, each seemed to select some combination of thoughts from a menu of three: 1.) Joe Tatum was a no-good, rabble-rousing so-and-so with blood on his hands; 2.) the Bullards were an unlucky family, Mount Moriah's version of the Kennedy clan; and 3.) Buford Bullard's high-strung nature and lifelong diet of deep fried everything had finally come home to roost. The guests dispersed quickly, leaving half-eaten portions of banana pudding and blueberry pie. At last Lindsay was left standing alone and exhausted in the glass atrium, surrounded by vases of drooping white chrysanthemums and trays piled with glistening chicken bones.

Chapter 23

Lindsay decided not to go straight home. It was early afternoon and the sun was just beginning its slow descent toward the horizon. Lindsay's brain was as used up as a dry corn husk; somehow, a month's worth of drama had been packed into a few short hours. She drove slowly down Church Street, Mount Moriah's main thoroughfare, past the glass and steel facade of the hospital, which looked molten in the afternoon heat. Every one of the town's four stoplights caught her, leaving her to bake in the powerful sun. At last, she pulled into the little alley that led around to John and Rob's large Victorian house.

When John bought the house years before, it was practically derelict, having stood empty for the better part of a decade. He initially undertook only structural improvements, reinforcing the foundation, rewiring the electrics, and rebuilding the wide front porch that opened onto Church Street. He lived for years like a monk in one bare-walled room. After Rob moved in, however, the two of them threw themselves into the renovation. Rob, in particular, worked with such untiring vigor that he seemed to be remaking something within himself with each alteration he made to the house. After his abrupt departure from college, he worked ten hour days on the house, while at the same time finishing his undergraduate degree in social work at a nearby state school. His spiritual thirst could not be slaked, however, and eventually, he enrolled in a Masters of Divinity program at a Unitarian Universalist seminary. The well-meaning PC liberals there were only too happy to welcome a gay, Asian fundamentalist refugee into their funky, free-thinking fold. Like so many people whose sexual or spiritual orientations made them unsuited for or unhappy with mainstream churches, Rob at last found a home for his ministerial calling in working as a hospital chaplain.

Lindsay had never expected to become a chaplain herself; she had wanted get her PhD and teach religion at a Christian college. But, like Rob, she found her plans undone by love. Her engagement to Timothy Farnsworth exploded in her face, and she retreated to the safety of Mount Moriah and hospital chaplaincy. She moved in with John and Rob, and, like Rob, had rushed headlong into the work of renovating their massive house. John taught her how to hang drywall and use a band saw; the arduous physical labor had been her therapy and consolation.

The end result of those tumultuous years was a house of breathtaking beauty. A million little details worked into the building by John's skilled hands, when combined with Rob's careful planning and Lindsay's playful use of color, made the house look like an elaborate wedding cake. Lindsay still had a key to the house and one robin's egg blue bedroom was still designated as "Lindsay's room," though she hadn't slept there in a long while.

Lindsay's spirits lifted when she caught sight of the whimsical lines of the house's roof. And she was even more heartened when she saw Rob and the two Tatum men on the screened-in back porch, pitching gently forward and backward in mismatched rocking chairs. John and Rob had changed into shorts and t-shirts, but Joe still wore his full Confederate regalia. The shadows cast by a stand of sugar maples shaded the porch from the late afternoon sun. As Lindsay got out of her car and approached the house, Anna emerged from the back door carrying an ice-filled cooler of beer. "Hey Linds, the boys were just telling me about all the excitement out at the golf club," she said, placing the cooler at Joe's feet.

"I'm afraid that that's not even the half of it," Lindsay replied, opening the screen door. She took a seat next to Anna on the wicker sofa, and she quickly filled them in on the rest of the day's events—her encounter with Warren in the library, the whispered conversation of the Bullard men, the collapse of Buford Bullard, and the subsequent disintegration of the memorial lunch. She avoided any discussion of Kimberlee's revelations under the willow tree. Unloading all the information that had been bouncing around inside her head began to restore Lindsay's equanimity. The beer also helped.

"Wow, and all I did today was patch up a fractured rib and prescribe Demerol for a guy with a kidney stone." Anna took a long swig from her bottle of MGD. She leaned in closer to Lindsay. "With all that going on, how did you find the time to skin a poodle and glue its pelt to your head? I'm assuming that's what happened, anyway."

Lindsay pinched the soft skin under Anna's arm and smiled. "Have I ever told you how much I appreciate your friendship?"

"Ouch! I thought circus clowns were supposed to have a good sense of humor."

"This thing with the Bullards is getting mighty heavy, Linds," John said. "I don't know if you should be getting yourself involved any more than you already are."

"Yeah, Linds," Anna agreed. "The spunky amateur girl detective always ends up hogtied in a subterranean lair or trapped in the attic of the Old McCoy Mansion as the villain sets it on fire."

"They're right," Rob said. "For all you know, Kimberlee Young is a homicidal maniac."

"I'm even surer now than I was before—Kimberlee did not kill her husband. That's why I need to be involved. The police are so focused on railroading her, they might be letting the real killer get away." Lindsay turned to Joe. "Oh, but speaking of homicidal maniacs, you're going to want to steer clear of the Bullards for the time being. They are on the warpath." She paused. "Gosh, that is the second time today that I've had to warn someone about them. They are actually a very loving family, underneath all the threats and bluster."

"They didn't look so loving when Buford Bullard had Pop by the neck."

"Never you mind that, Son. Buford was just protecting his little girl, same as any father would," Joe said.

"I just wish you'd tell us what you said to her."

"That ain't none of your damn business. It's between Vernon and his missus, so stop asking. And you, Little Miss Busybody," Joe said, pointing a sinewy finger in Lindsay's face, "need to stop sticking your nose in where it don't belong."

"Pop, lay off. Lindsay was just…" John began.

"Boy, unless you want me to cut a switch and tan your backside, that best be the end of this conversation." Joe rose abruptly, stormed into the house, and slammed the screen door behind him. They all sat still for a moment, stunned into silence. Joe's cantankerousness was a given, but he had never spoken so crossly to Lindsay before. He had taken a shine to her early on, and, for all these years she had been exempt from his tirades. She thought now of Silas's revelations about Joe and Versa's romance and wondered how much that played into his fit of temper.

"Silas Richards said something strange at the memorial. Something about Versa and Old Joe being, uh, closely acquainted back in the day," Lindsay said.

John took a long swig of beer. "Yeah, I've heard something along those lines. Not from Pop, mind you. Just talk."

"So there's nothing in that?"

"Well now, if my Momma was still with us, she'd have a thing or two to say on the matter." He took another slow drink before continuing. "Momma said she was forever grateful to Versa for throwin' Pop over so that she could have a shot at him herself."

"Versa dumped Old Joe for Buford?"

"No. She dumped him for Silas Richards."

"What?!"

"Versa was quite the hot commodity back in the day. Or so I hear. My momma said that Versa threw herself at Silas. Wouldn't even give Pop the time of day once Silas came on the scene. One day, Versa found herself in the family way. No ring was forthcoming from Silas, but another of her beaux stepped in to fill the breach."

"Buford?"

"Yep."

"Come to think of it," Lindsay said, "I do remember hearing rumors to that effect. It was so long ago, I'd forgotten all about it."

"All is know is what Momma said. Who knows. We're talking about a woman who believed that the sun shined out of Pop's backside. The story she told suited her view of things."

Rob gave a long whistle. "So you like to think you know this town, huh Linds?"

"Fine. I didn't remember the details of a forty-year-old paternity scandal. Jerry Springer would have trouble keeping track of all that."

Just then, Lindsay's phone chimed to indicate an incoming text. "It's from Kimberlee. Buford is alive, but unconscious. He's in the ICU. I can't believe they're doing a bedside vigil again. It's so hard on a family. It was only a week ago today that Vernon was there."

"Are you gonna go over there?" John asked.

"Not now. I might stop by tomorrow, after the revival."

"The revival?! I thought you steered clear of those things," Anna said.

"Usually I try to schedule an emergency, last-minute, couldn't-possibly-get-out-of-it shift at the hospital, but I think I'm going to go this year," Lindsay said. In the dozen years since she had left Mount Moriah for college, she had only attended the revival once. She was no longer a regular attendee at her father's church, either. After a week spent ministering to patients at the hospital, she always found that by Sunday, the only communion she wanted or needed was a jog out in the countryside.

"Do you have sins to atone for?" Rob teased.

"Robinson Wu, you should know me better than that," Lindsay said. "I'm attending this revival out of a heartfelt desire to support my father in his essential work of helping people on their path to healing and wholeness. Plus, I love baby-back ribs."

They all laughed and then fell silent, sipping their beers and enjoying the deepening cool of the evening.

"Seriously, what made you change your mind about going? You hate those things," Rob said.

"Guilt, I guess. I was talking to Silas Richards at the memorial today and he just seemed to assume that I would go because I'm Jonah's daughter. There's something about Silas that actually reminds me a little bit of my dad. That got me thinking about how disappointed Dad always is when I don't go. He knows I'm just making excuses. It's the church's biggest event of the year and I always skip it."

"What happens to all the money they raise at these things anyway?" Anna asked after a moment. "I heard it was over $10,000 last year."

"They do something different with it every year. This year, it's going to an orphanage in Guatemala. Sometimes it's for building projects at the church or charities in North Carolina," Lindsay said.

"Charities, huh? No using the money on a gold-plated, air-conditioned house for your Chihuahuas like Jim and Tammy Fae Bakker? No hush money payments to male escort services?" Anna said.

"Nope. My dad is about as squeaky clean as they come. No scandals, no embezzlement, no Chihuahuas. My only pet growing up was a goldfish and it lived for 11 years in a bowl on my dresser, and I'm reasonably sure that my dad has never had a meth-fueled night of pleasure with a male prostitute."

"Then he doesn't know what he's missing," Rob said, coyly batting his eyes at John.

"If I find out that you bought a Chihuahua without telling me, I'm gonna be pissed," John said.

Chapter 24

When Lindsay arrived at the county fairgrounds on Sunday morning, the gravel parking lot was already teeming with cars. A group of white tents covered several hundred yards of ground. Next to them, a row of portable toilets stood shoulder to shoulder like regimental soldiers. A five-foot high banner decorated with a portrait of Christ hung over the entrance to the main tent. He looked like a rock star in flowing robes; his outstretched hands invited people to "Come to Jesus!" Signs directed the crowds to a Prayer Tent, a Puppet Theater, and something called the Bible Bazaar. Beyond the tents, Lindsay saw a group of men readying the grills for the afternoon's rib feast.

She sighed deeply and entered the shade of the main tent. As a kid, she had obediently attended all manner of functions, watching as Jonah grew his church from a small meeting in the high school gym into the multi-pronged ministry it was today. But as she grew older, she had begun to dread the tent revivals. There was something improper about seeing her father—usually so straight-laced and be-suited—out here on preaching in a t-shirt and jeans. It was like running into your teacher buying condoms at the pharmacy counter.

The main tent was set up as she remembered, with folding chairs facing the stage, next to which stood a portable baptism pool. She herself had received the Holy Dunk in that very pool when she was about thirteen, shortly after Sarabelle had disappeared from their lives. Back then, her main duties at the revival included passing the collection baskets and leading a special prayer and song for the children. Her cheeks burned now at the memory of herself up on the stage self-consciously singing "He's Got the Whole World in His Hands".

Inside the main tent, dozens of people were milling around, waiting for the next sermon to begin. Lindsay scanned the crowd distractedly, looking for Jonah. Her search was interrupted by someone shouting her name. Lindsay turned to see a stout, middle-aged woman heading straight for her.

"It is you! I knew it! I can't believe my eyes. It's been years. I keep asking your father what's become of you!"

Lindsay greeted the woman with a tight smile. "Hello, Mrs. Bugbee. How have you been?"

"Me? Well, I've been fine, honey. The real question is, how have *you* been?" Mrs. Bugbee replied. "We all heard, of course, about the sad breakup with that boy up in the Northern States a few years ago. Such a pity. His name was Timothy, right? Timothy Farnsworth?"

"Uh-huh."

"You were engaged, right? And you got cold feet and broke it off?" She sucked her teeth. "Well, I suppose when you were in your twenties it probably seemed like you had a lot of time in front of you. So, have you met someone else?"

"I'm not really seeing anyone at the moment." Lindsay said, thinking that Mrs. Bugbee's legs in wide khaki shorts looked like the drip sandcastles she used to build on the beach. She tried hard to sweep those thoughts from her mind and to concentrate instead on smiling.

"You're kidding! Well, as luck would have it, my son—you remember Courtland Jr.?—he just broke up with his girlfriend! She was a sweet girl, though she had been divorced, bless her heart, and she was nearly thirty-seven. Being older like that can make a woman, you know…" Mrs. Bugbee gave Lindsay a meaningful look. "Anyhow, Courtland Jr. is around here somewhere. Let's just see if we can see him." She craned her stubby little neck and scanned the crowd.

Lindsay remembered Courtland, Jr. all too well. He was a sullen man with all the charm of a plastic bag.

"Oh gosh!" Lindsay exclaimed. "I forgot…something. In my car. Catch up with you later! Tell Courtland I sincerely hope he can work things out with his girlfriend."

Outside, Lindsay saw a number of familiar faces from her father's church. A congregated circle of white-haired ladies began to whisper to each other, gesturing at Lindsay with small, discrete inclinations of their heads. She was beginning to seriously regret her decision to come. She looked around again. If she could just find her father, she could say a quick hello to him and leave—her daughterly duty done. He was nowhere in sight, though, and the group of old ladies advanced on her like lions stalking their prey. Lindsay turned on her heel and walked in a wide arc around the portable toilets, emerging on the back side of the tents. A heavy sheet of undyed canvas hung across the intersection of the large tent with one of the smaller side tents, covering the tent pegs and the supporting frame. She looked around to be sure that no one was watching her, and she deftly unbound the cable ties that held the sheet in place. She stepped behind the sheet, quickly re-securing the ties and concealing herself in the small space. She inhaled deeply and looked around.

Sharp shafts of light filtered in between the gaps in the canvas. Lindsay remembered how, as a teenager, she used to hide in the interstices of these tents, smoking cigarettes and reading V.C. Andrews novels, while her unwitting father preached a few yards away. She sat down now on the damp grass and closed her eyes. The air in her hiding spot was almost unbreathably thick. Her reverie was disturbed by the sound of voices close by. Peering out through the gap between the canvas sheet and the edge of the main tent, she saw Silas Richards and a younger man approaching her hiding spot. They stopped just on the other side of the canvas sheet and spoke in hushed, urgent voices.

"It appears that it is all settled now," Silas said, lighting a cigarette and inhaling deeply. "I conferred with my lawyer yesterday and she does not foresee any further obstacles."

"That was a real lucky break we got. I mean, I hate that a man had to die, but that mess would have caused me no end of problems," said the younger man. "We're already having to work overtime to make up the time we lost."

Lindsay now recognized the younger man as Morgan Partee, the fiancée of Silas's oldest daughter. The Partee family owned the largest car dealership in central North Carolina, the ads for which featured various members of the Partee clan waving American flags and extolling the virtues of their vehicles. Lindsay recognized Morgan as the blond-haired, blue-eyed Partee son who shouted, "Our prices can't be beat!" at the end of each commercial.

"It is tragic. Deeply tragic. You are quite right in pointing out, however, that any developments in that direction would have posed a serious setback for our project. That entire line of inquiry is one that I would prefer never to see pursued," Silas said.

"I take it that you've made sure that that 'line of inquiry', as you call it, is closed?"

"Unfortunately, he never revealed his source, and I didn't ask him. I thought it best not to seem overly interested. In any case, I assume that he must have accidentally wandered across it somehow. I am not concerned, nor should you be, my boy. If nothing else has been brought forward thus far, I feel confident that no one else is aware of its existence."

Silas flicked his cigarette to the ground, snuffing it out with the heel of his shoe.

Chapter 25

"Well, it's time we return to the festivities," Silas said. He clapped Morgan on the back and the two men walked away toward the front of the tent. Lindsay peeked out, confirmed that there was no one around, and emerged from between the tents. Her thoughts were a jumble. It was as if she had pieces from ten different puzzles all mixed up inside her head; she couldn't fit them together to make a unified picture. She could hear her father's megaphone-amplified voice in the distance, and she decided to make one last attempt to see him before she left. As she followed his voice around the corner, she was confronted by a crowd of at least a hundred people standing on the grass around a shiny, red pick-up truck. A trailer hitched to the back towed a purple metallic jet ski.

Jonah stood on the back of the truck with a bullhorn, encouraging people to enter their names in the raffle. "Less than ten minutes left now to get your name in the drawing, folks. Remember the little orphans at La Casa Esperanza, our partner orphanage in Guatemala, need your help. This is not about trying to win the brand, spankin' new Kawasaki jet ski so kindly donated by Morgan Partee of Partee AutoWorld. The Book of Proverbs tells you 'cast but a glance at riches, and they are gone, for they will surely sprout wings and fly off to the sky like an eagle.' No, folks. Buying these tickets will be your reward in itself. All your donations are going to help those little orphans. This is your chance to do some lasting good and have some fun to boot!"

Jonah jumped off the truck when he caught sight of Lindsay, greeting her like she was the prodigal daughter. "Lindsay! Surely my eyes deceive me. You said you would come, and here you are."

"Hi, Dad. I was just on my way out, but I thought I'd say 'hi' first. So, 'hi'."

His broad smile crumpled. "Aren't you going to stay for the gospel jamboree? And there will be ribs. You love ribs. They've already fired up the barbecues."

"I really can't. Sorry."

He sighed. "Well, then, at least buy some raffle tickets."

She looked at him wryly. "What ever happened to the days when you used to quote the verse from Hebrews: 'Keep your lives free from the love of money and be content with what you have?' When I was younger, you wouldn't even let me have a deck of Uno cards in the house because you said it was a gateway game that would turn me into a hardened gambler. I think your exact words were, 'It's a slippery slope between childish games of chance and a life of selling yourself on the streets of Vegas for slot machine money.'"

"I've mellowed."

Lindsay shook her head and handed over $10 to the cheerful mullet-haired woman who was selling tickets. She scrawled her name, tore off the stubs, and put them into the raffle wheel. When she turned back around, she saw Silas and Morgan approaching.

"Reverend Harding," Silas said to Jonah, showing parallel rows of big, slightly-yellowing teeth. The two men shook hands. "Of course you know my future son-in-law, Morgan Partee."

"Of course. And I'd like to introduce you to my daughter, Lindsay."

"Ah, yes, the other Reverend Harding. As a matter of fact, Lindsay and I are old friends," Silas said, smiling at his own joke. His expression quickly shifted from levity to gravity. "We became acquainted yesterday under some very unfortunate circumstances." He shook his head. "I'm sure your daughter told you all about the poignant memorial service that she conducted for Mr. Vernon Young, and the subsequent sudden illness of Mr. Buford Bullard?"

Lindsay faced her perplexed father and explained hastily. "Oh, yeah. I haven't had the chance to tell you about that, yet." Her habit of concealing things from Jonah had begun during her rebellious teenage years, when a great deal of information about her whereabouts and activities needed concealing. Somehow the habit had become a hard little knot at the center of their relationship.

"Well, I'm sure that the two of you can discuss that at a

later time. Now we are here under altogether more pleasant circumstances. Are we ready for the drawing?" Silas asked. Jonah nodded, his eyes still looking questioningly at Lindsay. Silas turned to Morgan. "Will you do the honors, son?" Jonah handed the megaphone to Morgan, who clambered onto the bed of his truck.

"Howdy, folks! Who here's ready to win themselves a jet ski?!" A collective holler rose up from the crowd. Morgan selected a pigtailed little girl and lifted her up onto the truck bed. "Well all right then! This little darlin' is gonna pick our lucky winner." The ticket-selling, mullet woman gave the wheel a spin. When it came to a stop, the little girl reached in, extracted a ticket, and handed it to Morgan. "Everybody ready? Number 684. Can't hardly read this name." He turned the ticket sideways and squinted. "Well look at that! It's Lindsay Harding! Come on up here, girl, and climb on board your brand new jet ski!" Morgan jumped across to the trailer and patted the seat of the watercraft for Lindsay. The crowd whooped and cheered; the people immediately surrounding Lindsay nudged her toward the trailer.

"Sweet baby Jesus in the manger," Lindsay said. Her heart pounded like a tin drum as she looked frantically toward her father. "I can't take it. Pick another name. I mean, how is that going to look?"

"Don't worry, sweetheart. Everyone saw the drawing. They all know that you won it fair and square. Besides, it's not about the jet ski. It's about helping the orphans."

Lindsay edged uncertainly forward, pushed along by the congratulatory crowd. She was suddenly very aware of the baking heat of the sun. Morgan hoisted her up and perched her on the seat of the jet ski. She felt as if the truck bed might drop from under her, trapdoor-like, and leave her dangling in midair. Morgan put his arm around her as she waved to the crowd, unable to muster even the faintest smile. Someone stepped forward and began snapping pictures, dazzling her with the camera's flash. As ghostly flashes glittered before her eyes, her focus was drawn to the back of the crowd, where a thin, blonde woman broke away from the assembled onlookers. The woman's eyes seemed to bore a hole right through Lindsay, even though she stood several hundred feet away. "Mom?" Lindsay whispered. Lindsay slipped from the seat of the jet ski, nearly pitching headlong into the crowd. Morgan steadied her, shouting, "This little lady is so excited she can barely stand! Let's give her another round of applause, y'all, and then let her find some shade."

The spectators dutifully applauded and those in front eased Lindsay off the trailer. Jonah jumped up on the truck and began to lead a prayer of thanks for the money that had been collected in the raffle. Lindsay continued to make her way through the spectators. They bunched tightly together, their heads bowed and hands clasped in prayer. Lindsay scanned their faces, searching for her mother's doppelganger. When she finally caught sight of the woman in the distance, she was climbing into the passenger's side of a white SUV. Lindsay pushed through the crowd, emerging near the edge of the parking lot. But before Lindsay could reach the SUV, though, it was gone.

Chapter 26

When Lindsay got home after the tent revival, she decided to go for a run. The decision was in direct violation of her own rule about daytime summer jogging, but she needed the exertion and heat to flush the toxins from her mind. She followed her usual route to the Richards Homestead, ducking under the wire fence, passing the No Trespassing signs, and entering the welcome shade of the pine forest. She leaned against a tree to wipe the stinging sweat from her eyes. In the stillness of the thick summer air, she could hear a distant buzzing. At first it sounded like locusts. After a moment, however, she realized that it was, in fact, the whine of chainsaws. She wondered if the men she saw a few days ago could have been surveying the land for logging. The growing scarcity of timber meant that even scrubby pines like these could be sold at a decent profit. She jogged away from the sound, not wanting to be harassed for trespassing on private land. Her thoughts began to drift across her mind as peacefully as the high white clouds floated across the sky. What a shame it would be to destroy this little patch of wilderness to make printer paper or cheap office furniture.

Then, without warning, the ground convulsed beneath Lindsay's feet throwing her with a hard thud into the underbrush. Red dirt and tree bark rained down over her back. She lay still, too shocked to move. After what seemed like a very long time, she climbed up slowly onto all fours. She surveyed the bumps and scratches that covered her body. She winced as her left knee came into contact with the ground. An angry, red welt was already forming on her kneecap.

"Hey!"

Lindsay turned to see a denim-clad man emerge from the other side of the trees. He covered the distance between them in long, purposeful strides. He was wearing a neon orange safety vest over the top of his shirt, and a pair of binoculars dangled from his neck.

"I thought I saw something moving over here." His voice seemed to bounce around inside the tin box of Lindsay's head. "What in tarnation are you doin' out here? I damn near blasted you to kingdom come!"

Lindsay tried to stand, but her legs refused to hold her. She settled for what she hoped was a dignified sprawl over the protruding root of a nearby tree.

"Are you blind, girlie?! There's about a million big ole signs that say 'No Trespassing' strung up all over. Do you know what that means? That means that your dim-witted, middle-of-the-day jogging behind don't belong out here."

"You almost blew me up," Lindsay said quietly, almost to herself.

"You're darn right I did. We're out here dynamiting all of these here stumps and boulders. Clearing this land." He had come nearer to Lindsay as he spoke. His tone softened when he looked over her battered, dust-covered body. "Say, do you need a doctor or something?"

"I think I'm okay." She stood up and took a few hesitant steps. She felt a strange, cool sensation across her backside and craned her neck to see what was causing it. The tattered remains of her jogging shorts tickled the backs of her upper thighs, revealing her pink bikini briefs. "Uh, I think you dynamited my shorts off."

The man colored deeply and his eyes widened.

"I don't suppose you have any extra pants or anything?"

"I'll see what we got in the trailer," the man said, hurrying back through the trees in the direction he'd come from.

Lindsay slumped back down onto the tree stump. She groaned and leaned her head against the damp moss that covered the side of an adjacent tree. Her whole body ached and the ringing in her ears was now joined by a roar like the inside of a seashell—only louder and much less pleasant.

The man emerged from the trees a few minutes later, followed by five other construction workers. He gestured toward Lindsay. "See? I told you! Nearly blew her to Timbuktu." One of the men, more smartly dressed than the others, approached her. Lindsay thought she recognized him as one of the men in white SUVs she'd seen out here the past week.

He spoke to her slowly, as you might speak to a very dim-witted toddler. “Are you all right, little lady?”

“Yes, thank you.”

“Real glad to hear it. Could I trouble you to sign this waiver?” He held out a clipboard, secured to which was a densely worded document with a highlighted signature line at the bottom. “Not that we are implying any negligence or responsibility for your little mishap. After all, you are trespassing on clearly demarcated private land. However, we do have to protect ourselves from frivolous lawsuits and such.”

Lindsay stared at him for a moment. She could scarcely believe that his first order of business after exploding her with dynamite was to ask her to sign a waiver.

“Of course,” Lindsay said. She took the clipboard and scrawled a few choice words on the signature line.

He took the clipboard, looking at what she had written. “Thank you for understanding, Miss….” he paused and cleared his throat. “Unusual name you have. Is it French?”

“You could say that,” Lindsay said, flashing her best Southern belle smile.

The man with the binoculars stepped forward and handed Lindsay a bright orange bundle. “Sorry. It’s all we could find.”

Lindsay unfolded the bundle to find that it was an oversized safety vest. She put it on over her torn clothes. It hung down almost past her knees. “Thanks.”

“Can one of the boys here offer you a ride home?” The clipboard-wielding man asked.

“No. Don’t trouble yourselves. I’ll find my own way.” She turned her back to them, and, gathering the scraps of her dignity around her, hobbled home.

Chapter 27

Nursing her wounds on the couch later that day, Lindsay had called Anna and invited her over for a girls' night in. Anna's first question, when she arrived an hour later, was, "Why is there an enormous iridescent jet ski sitting on a tow trailer on your front lawn?" Lindsay had recounted the day's events for Anna, and together they had hauled the beast into Lindsay's backyard shed. Lindsay purposely tried to hide the extent of her injuries from Anna; she didn't want to get bullied into going to the hospital. They lay now on opposite ends of the couch, flicking idly through the TV channels. "The Grave Robber" was wrestling with someone in a Neanderthal costume called "The Mastodon". The remains of a frozen pizza (for Lindsay), the remains of a Greek salad (for Anna), and a half-empty bottle of wine (for both) lay in front of them.

"I got a birthday card from Sarabelle," Lindsay said.

"When?"

"Last week."

"You'd think of all people that'd remember your birthday is in April, your own mother would. If I pushed a seven-pound human being out of my hoo-ha, you can be sure I'd remember the exact minute."

"Well, at least she tried this year, which is an improvement. And she called to see if I want to meet up." Lindsay took a drink of wine. "Actually, I thought I saw her at the revival this morning. She walked away, though, before I could tell for sure."

"Hmm..." Anna said, through pursed lips.

"What?"

"If it was your mom, why would she walk away? You always complain that your dad is too soft with Sarabelle, but you fall for the same stuff! You're getting your hopes up and serving up your tender little heart on a china dish. She'll come along and throw it in her blender of maternal neglect."

"I'm not getting my hopes up. I haven't decided whether to call her back or not yet. And I know that even if we do get together, it probably won't be that great."

"Probably won't be that great?! Like last time? When she stole $500 from you?"

"She didn't steal it. I gave it to her." Lindsay averted her eyes. "She needed a deposit for a new apartment. She'd just broken up with her boyfriend and she was having a hard time."

Anna gave Lindsay a hard stare. "I need to tell you a story. I'll start with the moral: There are some people who you've got to stay away from. They can't help themselves; they are just genetically programmed to screw you over." Anna leaned over. "You know how I've always told you that Jeremy and I split because I cheated on him? That wasn't really true. It was Jeremy who had someone else in the relationship, but it wasn't another person." She paused and exhaled sharply. "It was coke."

"Cocaine?!"

"No, Coca-Cola," Anna said. "Jeremy found it irresistibly fizzy and refreshing."

"Don't get snippy now. I'm just surprised."

"Sorry. It's a sore subject." Anna took a generous swig from her wine glass. "He'd always done it, like at parties and stuff. But I was pretty wild, too, back in those days, so I just laughed it off. It didn't really seem to be a problem. One night, though, we were on shift together. There was this freak ice storm and cars were skidding around almost like gravity was going side to side instead of up and down. The ER was packed with injuries. After hours of that, I was dragging—totally exhausted. But there was Jeremy, plugging along like the Little Engine That Could. But he was making dumb mistakes, just getting ahead of himself. Yelling at the nurses if they couldn't keep up. I looked into his eyes, and they were shining like a pair of silver dollars.

"We talked about it the next day, and he promised that it was a one-time thing. He'd had the coke on him from the weekend, and he was just taking it to stay alert. I bought that crock of crap and we went on with our lives.

"Then other things happened. We'd be out to dinner with

my parents, he'd go to the bathroom, and he'd come back lit up like a Christmas tree. We argued and I left him. He went to a couple NA meetings and I took him back. A few months later, we were at my nephew's christening and Jeremy was so coked that he could barely sit still in the pew. I took him aside after the service and confronted him. He called me a lying bitch and ripped the front of my dress. I left him again. He went to rehab for two weeks. He begged me, sent me flowers every day. I took him back.

"Every time I took him back, it was like getting a puppy for Christmas. Only the puppy came split up into ten different boxes. Ten pieces of a puppy are not each one-tenth as cute as a whole puppy, you know? And you can't build a whole puppy out of them at the end." Anna leaned back and drained her wine glass.

Lindsay sat for a moment in stunned silence. "I'm so sorry. Why didn't you tell me before?"

"I couldn't. I moved down here because I hated how all my friends and family up in New Jersey saw me as a victim. My great aunt Lydia and uncle Herb heard my husband call me a bitch in a church at a baby's christening, for God's sake. You and Rob and John are great, but you're all too…empathetic. If you'd known, you'd have felt sorry for me and been all sweet and considerate about my feelings."

"I wish you had trusted me. I know how what you're going through. How do you think I felt when I had to send out letters to all the people who had RSVPed to my wedding? Timothy didn't want me to tell anyone about him being gay because he was afraid of their reaction. I had to tell everyone that I had called it off because I got cold feet. So on top of getting my heart broken, all of our family and friends thought I was a total jerk for dumping such a sweet guy. Timothy's parents haven't spoken to me since. My dad was furious."

"You're right, Linds. I should have told you," Anna said.

Lindsay hugged her and said, "Not to mention that I've kind of thought you were a slut all this time for cheating on your poor husband."

"Guess I didn't have to worry about you being too nice to me, huh?"

Lindsay emptied the remaining wine from the bottle into

Anna's glass. "So," Anna said, lying back on the sofa, "any action on the Drew Checkoway front? He obviously likes you."

"Do you think?" Lindsay said, blushing crimson.

"Absolutely! You've got to go for him. He's a total catch. Have you noticed that he looks just like a dark-haired version of Charlton Heston?"

"Charlton Heston? Senile, gun-crazy Charlton Heston?"

"No! Young, chiseled, *Planet of the Apes* Charlton Heston. Definitely 60s-era, pre-NRA Charlton Heston," Anna said.

Lindsay pondered. "Yeah, I suppose there is a little, 'I am Spartacus!' thing going on with him."

"You'll have to see him shirtless to really test my theory, though," Anna said, playfully poking Lindsay in the ribs with her foot. Just then, Lindsay's cell phone began to chime. She got up and hobbled to the kitchen to retrieve the phone from her purse. Walking back in the room, she mouthed to Anna, "It's Kimberlee." As she stood in the doorway and listened to the voice on the other end, Lindsay's face darkened and became increasingly grave. "Okay. Hang in there. I'll see you in the morning." She hung up the phone and walked solemnly back over to the couch. "They just got the results of the tests they ran on Buford Bullard. He definitely had a heart attack."

Anna shrugged her shoulders. "Well, a burly guy like that, history of high blood pressure, terrible diet, these things happen."

"It's not just that. The doctors think the heart attack was caused by poison."

Chapter 28

Anna and Lindsay stayed up late, opening another bottle of wine, discussing their love lives (or lack thereof), and speculating about the latest happenings in the Bullard family saga. When Lindsay crept out for work just before 6:30 the next morning, she was careful not to disturb Anna, who had fallen asleep on the couch.

Lindsay spent the first hours of her shift trying to draft the sermon that she was set to deliver for the hospital's interfaith worship service the following week. Sermonizing was her least favorite chaplaincy duty by a mile. She would rather mourn with a dozen grieving families than stand up in front of worshippers who were expecting pearls of spiritual wisdom to be bestowed upon them. She always felt like such a fraud behind the little pulpit in the hospital chapel, with the seeking eyes of sick people looking up at her. Usually, she would have procrastinated with her sermon writing until the day before she was set to speak. Today, however, with her knee still tender from the dynamite fiasco, she wanted to do something that would allow her a bit of rest. For the topic of the sermon, she chose the theme of suffering. It seemed apt for so many reasons, not least because of the suffering she herself endured as she extracted each tortured word from her brain and committed it to the computer screen.

During morning visiting hours, Lindsay made her way to the ICU to check on Buford Bullard and check in with his family. Buford was still comatose. Versa sat in an armchair next to his bed, dozing. Her bright pink reading glasses stood perched on the end of her nose, and a celebrity gossip magazine lay open in her lap. Lindsay was about to depart when Versa's eyes fluttered open. "Hey. I hope I didn't wake you," Lindsay said softly.

Versa sat up. From the way she looked at Lindsay, it was immediately clear that she had woken up on the wrong side of the green vinyl armchair. Or maybe there was no right side to wake up on when you've been sleeping in a green vinyl armchair. Without preamble, Versa started in on a tirade. "Did you know that they only let us in here one at a time? The kids have to stay out in the waiting room. I know that the living dead here," she gestured to the patient next to Buford, whose wizened face was a covered in a tangle of tubes and wires, "like their sleep, but having a few of the kids and grandkids in here would liven things up a bit." She paged irritably through her magazine. "I sent Keith and the twins to reopen the restaurant this morning. We planned to do it anyway, after Vernon's memorial service. The kids think I should have waited, but there's no way I'm letting this ruin the business that Buford and I have been sweating for all these years. Buford would hate the thought." Lindsay pulled up a chair and sat down next to Versa.

"Do you know what one of my so-called friends said last night?" Versa continued. "She said that I should trust in God's plan because He has a reason for doing this. I wanted to punch her. I restrained myself in consideration of the fact that she just had her 'deviated septum' fixed." She closed her magazine with a snap and removed her glasses. "*This* is the plan!?" Her gesture encompassed the whole room. "Tidal waves washing away whole countries? Children starving to death all over the world? My son-in-law taken away in his prime? My husband getting himself poisoned and clinging to life in a hospital bed? If that's the game plan, I want a new coach."

Lindsay waited to see if Versa would continue speaking. The rhythmic sounds of the life-support machines filled the silence between them. When Lindsay finally spoke, her voice was soft and neutral. "When people don't know how to comfort you, sometimes they say what gives them comfort."

"And what gives you comfort, Miss Reverend Lindsay Harding?" Versa sunk her teeth into Lindsay's words with the ferocity of a pit-bull. "You always seem to be hovering around my family, with your feathery, little voice and your little elf face, just hugging everybody and smiling like you know a secret. Is it because you think that all the good girls and boys go up to heaven and dance around with their golden harps?"

Lindsay was caught off guard by Versa's vitriol. Even during the darkest hours of the previous week, Versa usually managed to cheer up her children or muster a smile for the grandkids. Now, though, with her children and grandchildren momentarily absent, her façade of strength was revealed to be as thin as an eggshell. Lindsay took a deep breath and recovered her equanimity. In her years of hospital chaplaincy, she'd learned that grief ran the gamut of human emotions. Tears, regrets, rejoicing, dead-eyed shock: she had seen it all. And she understood that sometimes people just needed somebody to yell at, someone to blame for their misfortune. They couldn't yell at God, at least not to his face, so Lindsay was the next best thing.

"As a matter of fact," Lindsay said, "I do know a secret. Here it is: It doesn't matter what comforts *me*. I really don't know if there is a plan, but I do know that there is a game. And unfortunately, this is it." She gestured to Buford and the other patients on the ward. "There is no other game in town, so we all play this one."

"Are you trying to say that you just pretend that life has a meaning and God is in control to make people feel better? Because I don't need that kind of comfort."

Lindsay sighed. "This job that I have is the kind that makes some people even more certain of their beliefs. I know that it has certainly deepened my faith. But it has also broadened it." She paused and shook her head slightly. "All I'm saying, I guess, is that if you are looking for *the* answers, I don't have them. *My* answer is to find meaning in just being present with someone I care about. That comfort is real. That compassion is bigger than me."

They passed the next few minutes in silence. Versa stared straight ahead, her arms crossed over her ample bosom. At last it became clear that there was nothing else for either of them to say. Lindsay rose to leave. "Take care of yourself now. And try to get some rest."

Lindsay stopped in at the ICU waiting room, where Kimberlee and Kathilee were chatting together as they crocheted some kind of hideous poncho out of fuzzy, multicolored yarn. Lindsay silently pitied the garment's intended recipient. The two women stilled their needles when Lindsay walked in. "Did you see

Momma?" Kimberlee asked.

"Yes, I saw her. This must be very rough for all of you."

"It is." Kimberlee nodded. "Speaking of rough, what happened to you? You're limping like a pirate with a peg leg full of termites."

"Oh, just a little jogging injury." A vivid arrangement of sunflowers and balloons on the table next to Kimberlee caught Lindsay's eye. "Who sent those?"

"Silas Richards," Kimberlee answered. "I can't believe how thoughtful that man is. As much as he has going on with all his charities and business dealings and political responsibilities, and he still found time to bring those over here personally. That man is a bona fide saint."

##

After lunch, Lindsay headed toward the chaplain's office to do some paperwork. As she walked toward the door, Drew emerged from inside. "Just the person I was looking for. Geneva tells me you like the Burlington Royals," he said.

"Royals?"

"Yeah. I ran into her this morning and mentioned that I had bought season tickets. Geneva said that you're their number one fan. So I thought I'd see if I could 'take you out to the ballgame' tomorrow night. Get it?"

"Ballgame?" Lindsay asked.

"You know, *Take Me out to the Ballgame*? Harry Caray?"

"Is he a player?"

"Very funny. So, can I pick you up here at six?"

"Yes. Sure. Definitely. Great. Fantastic." His was a question that needed to be answered with five kinds of Yes.

"Okay, then. See you at six. Nice haircut, by the way. It's very…bouncy."

Lindsay watched him walk down the hall and then covered her burning cheeks with her hands. She had her first date in more than a year (if she didn't count Doyle Hargreaves, which she didn't). She had to find something to wear. She had to do something about her hair. But most importantly, she had less than

24 hours to build up an exhaustive knowledge of the Burlington Royals. She decided that her first order of business would be to find out what sport they played.

Chapter 29

A quick Internet search informed Lindsay that the Burlington Royals were the local minor league baseball team. Unfortunately, her knowledge of baseball was confined to the snippets of baseball practices that she'd glimpsed during high school, while she and Julee Rae Janson (now better known on the I-85 gentlemen's club circuit as Valeria the Goth Maiden) smoked Virginia Slims under the bleachers. Right now, the only detail she could recall was how they had always snickered when someone said "base on balls." She didn't have time to pursue her quest for knowledge further during her shift. She realized with a sigh that she would have to spend the evening at home in front of the computer—she had been reduced to studying for her dates.

As Lindsay turned her car into her neighborhood late that afternoon after work, a black Ford Crown Victoria approached her, heading the opposite direction. The driver honked the horn in a staccato rhythm. She could see Warren Satterwhite through the windshield, grinning and waving at her. She pulled her car up alongside of his and rolled down her window.

"Hey, Linds. What are you doing?"

"Being stalked by you, apparently. Then I was going to go home to learn everything there is to know about baseball. Why?"

"Well, I've been over at the county archives most of the day, and I am seeing double. I was just going to see if you wanted to come over and join me. They're open until seven tonight."

"I thought we'd given up on the Samuel Wilcox angle."

"I found something today that made me change my mind. Come on and I'll explain."

"Okay, I'll come. But I need a favor from you. After I help you do whatever you're doing, I need you to tell me everything you know about baseball, with specific emphasis on the history and lore of Alamance County's own Burlington Royals."

Lindsay and Warren dropped her car off at her house, and

less than an hour later, they were again sitting at the big oak table in the special collections room at the county archives. The heavy, leather-bound volumes of Samuel Wilcox's journal surrounded them. On the drive over, Warren had explained to Lindsay what had made him renew his focus on the diary. While reviewing the physical evidence in the case, Warren had come across an entry in Vernon Young's day planner. Two days before the murder, Vernon had written "Vegetarian option and Wilcox".

"If I didn't know what I was looking for, I would have assumed Wilcox was a client of the catering business," Warren explained. "But the mention of that name, right before the murder, is an unusual coincidence."

"Especially considering what Vernon told Kimberlee," Lindsay agreed, nodding. "Have you found anything yet?"

"'Fraid not. I'm only up to 1870. I've been reading some more stuff about his second marriage. Samuel really hit the jackpot, it looks like, with his second wife, Celia. She worked as a housekeeper for an old bachelor in Mount Moriah. He didn't have any kids or any family. She nursed the geezer when he was bedridden with rheumatism. The old guy kicked the bucket just before the end of the war and his will split his house and land between two of his slaves—Celia and his manservant. Then the manservant died a few months later, meaning that Celia got the whole shebang.

"Samuel and Celia have just moved into the house and she's pregnant with their first child." Warren paused, flipping back to the previous page. "Hey, do you have any idea what a 'naval stores' farmer is? It says here that the old guy was a naval stores farmer, but Samuel thinks that that kind of farming is no longer viable," he trailed his finger along the phrase as he read. "'The war has changed the calculus. The future is Tobacco'." Warren slid the book across the table to Lindsay, and pointed to the phrase.

"Don't you remember from our North Carolina history class?" Lindsay had a near-photographic memory when it came to subjects of interest to her. She sometimes took it for granted that other people would find tidbits of knowledge about, say, the Boer War or the quadratic equation as enthralling as she did. "They used to farm the pine trees around here for their sap. It was processed it into materials to waterproof and caulk ships—naval stores. Turpentine and pitch were the plastic of their days—very versatile materials. They also burned it in lamps. After the war, though, the bottom dropped out of the market. People started using kerosene instead of turpentine to light their lamps, and the trees had all been pretty well tapped out anyway in the run up to the war."

"Well, if you aren't just a walking encyclopedia of helpful information," Warren said.

Lindsay smiled coyly and rose from her seat. "If you don't need me, I can just mosey on home..."

"Okay, okay. You are a naval stores savant and I bow to your superior wisdom."

"That's more like it." Lindsay sat back down. The contact of the hard, wooden chair with the raw skin on her upper thighs caused her to wince audibly.

"Are you all right?"

"Yeah. Some construction worker disguised as Yosemite Sam dynamited me on Sunday and I'm still feeling a little delicate."

"Dynamited you?! Is that some kind of euphemism?"

"I'm afraid not. I was running back in the woods near my house and I didn't realize I was going through a blasting zone."

Warren raised his eyebrows questioningly, but Lindsay just waved her hands and shook her head. "Un-uh. I have you believing that I am some kind of genius. I don't want to spoil your high opinion of me by revealing that I'm illiterate when it comes to 'No Trespassing' signs." Lindsay cast her eyes idly over the book in front of her. Her gaze fixed on the paragraph she'd just read regarding the farmer's will. "Huh. This says that the farmer left property to Celia and the other servant in February of 1865, right before the end of the war."

"Yeah, so?"

"Slaves were considered to be property themselves, so they weren't legally allowed to own property. But the old man didn't free Celia in his will. It says right here that everyone was surprised that he didn't free his slaves, since he had no heirs."

Warren shook his head. "But the war was almost over by then, right? Lincoln had already freed the slaves in the

Emancipation Proclamation a few years earlier. The old farmer probably saw which way the wind was blowing and knew that Celia and the other slave would be free as soon as the war was over. Or he was a Northern sympathizer and believed that the Proclamation made them free already."

"Maybe." Lindsay's realization about Celia led to a troubling possibility. There was a loophole in the story. Surely, she couldn't have been the only one to notice it. Lindsay walked over to the glass case and pulled down the last volume of the journal, 1872. She scanned the pages feverishly, reading them in reverse order. She was so intent on her search that she didn't even move the book over to the table to read it. Instead, she perched in front of the glass case, supporting the weight of the heavy book on one of the lower shelves. "He doesn't die," she said quietly.

"Who doesn't die?" Warren asked. He rose and walked over to where Lindsay stood. Lindsay silenced him with an emphatic *Shh!* He peered over her shoulder as she continued to read. It looked like more of the same—Samuel Wilcox reckoning the household bills, worrying about this and that. After another moment Lindsay murmured, "He must have seen the same thing that I did and skipped to the end, too."

"Who must have seen what?" Warren asked. Again she ignored him. He shrugged his shoulders and sat back down to continue to paging through the earlier volumes. Lindsay sat back down at the table, never taking her eyes off what she was reading. She kept on muttering intermittently as she flipped the pages. She jumped up a few times to consult other volumes of the journal. Once or twice, she popped out to one of the library computers to check references and historical facts. Several times, Warren tried unsuccessfully to read over her shoulder or ask her what she found. His probing was met with silence. After an hour passed, Lindsay leaned back in her chair and removed her glasses.

Warren looked at her expectantly. He closed the issue of *Sports Illustrated* that he had been paging through since he had given up the pretense of reading the journal. "Well?"

"I think I might know who killed Vernon. And you're not going to like it one bit."

Chapter 30

"Let me start at the beginning," Lindsay said. "Well, actually, let me start at the end. He doesn't die in 1872."

"What? Who?"

"Sorry, my mind is running in circles. Samuel doesn't die in 1872. I always assumed that the journals ended in 1872 because he died. Why else would someone keep a meticulous journal every year, and then just stop? But that's not why he stops. A few months before the last entry, in March of 1872, this mysterious relation of the old farmer, you know, the one who left Celia all the land?, shows up from Cincinnati. Second cousin twice removed or something. He comes to the Wilcoxes house one night and tells them to get out—the land and the house are his. Samuel chases him off with a shotgun. Everything goes quiet for a few weeks until the county sheriff serves Samuel with some papers saying that the cousin has filed a lawsuit to contest Celia's inheritance of the property on the grounds that the will was invalid."

"How did you know the will would be important? Why did that make you skip ahead?"

"That detail just didn't sit right with me. White people didn't make life very easy for blacks, whether they had been slaves before the war or not. But Samuel and Celia's lives seemed to be going so well. Too well. I knew that something wasn't right about the will. It was so rare for black people to own land back then. I'm sure Vernon, being such a history buff, must have had the same thought. Even though Samuel was an exceptional person in so many ways, I didn't see how it could end happily ever after for the Wilcoxes."

"Vernon studied this stuff all the time, so you might well be right about that. But how do you happen to know so much about Reconstruction?"

"American History was one of my majors in college."

"One of your majors?"

With a matter-of-fact expression, Lindsay enumerated on the fingers of one hand. "History, Religion, and Math, with a minor in Spanish. Then, in graduate school, I did a Master's in Divinity and a degree in Counseling. I had just started on my PhD in Religion when I quit. Don't look so astonished. Having no social life is a great way to accrue degrees. So where was I? Oh yeah, Samuel isn't the type to give up without a fight, so he mounts a countersuit. He basically gives himself a crash course in the law and drafts a pretty good case supporting Celia's right to the property. Remember, Samuel is no illiterate slave. He was free even before the war and worked in a printing press. He joined the Civil War on the side of the Confederacy. He was well-known and respected in the community, among both blacks and whites. It sounds like the cousin thought that Samuel was just some country bumpkin who fell off the back of a turnip truck, so he's caught off guard by the strength of the legal challenge."

"So did Samuel scare off this carpetbagging cousin?"

"This was not a pretty period in North Carolina history. The Klan was formed by former Confederate soldiers right after the war, and they had gotten really out of hand by 1870. They were so powerful that they were challenging the authority of the local governments. They lynched the black town commissioner over in Graham. The governor at the time decided to call out the militia against them that summer. He imposed martial law in two counties, one of which was Alamance. The man he appointed to carry out the action against the Klan was a former Union general."

Warren grimaced.

"Exactly. That governor became the first governor in US history to be impeached and removed from office. That was at the end of 1870. So, this contested will was happening at a very precarious time for race relations. The Klan was on the wane elsewhere in the South, but in this part of North Carolina, they had won a major battle against the state government. The Cincinnati cousin used it to his advantage." Wrapped up in the telling of the story, Lindsay unconsciously switched to the present tense. "He does a bit of rabble-rousing. First, it's behind the scenes, like stealing livestock from the Wilcox farm. But pretty soon, the house gets firebombed. Samuel and Celia only just managed to put it out before it set the whole place ablaze. By this time, Celia and Samuel have two sons, both under the age of two. Samuel decides that they have to hightail it.

"They move down to Durham. Celia has some family who can hook Samuel up with a job in tobacco processing. There is a list here of all the things he sold to raise money quickly—all their animals, lots of the furniture, all the food they have stockpiled. Samuel writes that he hopes they'll be able to return in two or three years when things quiet down in the county. But I guess they never came back, because that was the last entry—June 13, 1872."

"So what happened with the will? Who inherited the land?"

"It doesn't say here, but I think I know. There wasn't much call for naval stores right after the war, like I said. But that soil was perfect for tobacco growing. Samuel had already started clearing the land. Based on the description of the farm…"

"Silas Richards!" Warren exclaimed, cutting her off in mid-sentence.

Lindsay pouted. "Hey! I was building up to the dramatic climax! Didn't you notice that I purposely haven't mentioned the cousin's name up to now? That was so that I could dramatically reveal that his name was none other than Silas Richards! I was even going to pause and point to the book and say 'The cousin from Cincinnati was none other than Silas Richards, the First!' and your jaw was going to drop in amazement at my powers of deduction."

"Sorry. I didn't mean to steal your thunder. But when you mentioned tobacco, I realized that the meeting in Vernon's datebook must be with Silas. That's why Vernon wanted to discuss the vegetarian option—for the engagement party catering order—*and* Wilcox's journal. He must have unearthed the connection between Richards and Wilcox."

"Fine. But I bet you don't know the motive." Lindsay crossed her arms and raised her eyebrows, daring him to guess.

Warren's brow creased in concentration. "Maybe Silas didn't want a stain on the honor of his family. They've always cast themselves as more Southern than grits and gravy and the kind and generous benefactors of the county. If people found out that the original Silas Richards was a carpetbagging Klan sympathizer from

Ohio, it could have been very embarrassing. This would cost him the black vote. It would be enough to torpedo his political career."

"I think it might be all that and more. Before my triumphant 'I know the murderer' speech was so rudely interrupted, I was telling you about the naval stores farm. Based on Wilcox's description of the place, I think that it was the Richards Homestead—the land where the Richards family started building their tobacco empire. I didn't mention this before, because I didn't know it was relevant to Vernon's murder, but I overheard a conversation at the tent revival the other day. Silas and his future son-in-law, Morgan Partee, were discussing some business deal that they have. Morgan said that a man had to die because he was presenting obstacles. Silas said that everything was taken care of now, and the deal was going to happen. I bet whatever it was had something to do with the ownership of that land. It's the same land that I was jogging through when I got blown up. There's some kind of major construction project going on out there. I think that Vernon might have jeopardized that deal by finding out about Celia and the will. If the Richards family doesn't legally own that land, than whatever they are doing to it might not be legal, either. Celia's descendants might even be able to claim some kind of compensation. Now that I know about the stuff in the journal, it all fits together."

"How did you happen to hear the conversation between Morgan and Silas?"

"I was hiding from some old ladies between the tents."

Warren let this revelation pass without remark. "Based on what Silas and Morgan said, do you think Morgan could be in on the murder? Did he definitely say that a man had to die?"

"I'm almost sure those were his exact words."

Warren let out a long, slow whistle. "This is not going to be pretty. The police were hoping to wrap this case up swiftly to protect this county from a race riot. Now we've got a scenario where two of the richest and most powerful families in this part of the state could have conspired to murder a man. You add in the Civil War and the Klan, and you've got yourself a recipe for Stink Pie. Well, at least Kimberlee will be happy not to have the suspicion on her anymore."

“Relieved, yes. But not happy. She likes Silas. Just today she called him a ‘bona fide saint’. Matter of fact, I am having trouble believing this myself. If the proof wasn’t staring me straight in the face, I’d say that there was no way Silas could be involved in anything like this.” Lindsay sighed. “What happens now?”

“First off, we’ve got to prove that Vernon talked to Silas about the diary. We still don’t have a murder weapon or much in the way of physical evidence, either. And we have no explanation for how the threatening letter came to be printed off of Kimberlee and Vernon’s computer. We also don’t know if Morgan was involved in the murder, or if he just knew about it after the fact. Silas may not have been the triggerman. He’s got money; he might have hired someone. Then, we’ve got to find out what is going on with the Richards Homestead.”

“And don’t forget about Buford Bullard. If he was poisoned deliberately, maybe it was because he knew something about the murder.”

“To tell you the truth, that troubles me a whole lot. Murderers don’t usually change tactics like that. Someone who shoots a man in broad daylight in front of a crowd is arrogant. Or real, real desperate. Someone who puts poison in somebody’s food or drink is sly and careful. I’m struggling to fit those pieces together in my mind.” Warren began to stack the volumes of the journal in two piles on the center of the table. “For the moment, all’s I’m going to do is call for somebody to come over and take the journal in as evidence. Then we’ll go from there.”

Chapter 31

Lindsay waited anxiously for the police officers to arrive and collect the journal. She had a deeply uneasy feeling, as if villains could burst in at any moment and snatch the evidence of Kimberlee's innocence from out of her hands. Another part of her conflicted mind wished that someone would steal the journal. That they would destroy it and the terrible things it contained. At last, two uniformed officers knocked on the large metal door. Without even introducing them to Lindsay, Warren began issuing instructions on how they should secure the evidence. In the presence of his fellow officers, Warren was all crispness and efficiency—not a hint of the gangly, jokey Warren that Lindsay had seen in the past few days. Lindsay began to drum her fingers impatiently on the table while Warren droned on. He turned to her, looking slightly annoyed at her continued presence, "You can go home now, if you want to. We'll take it from here."

"You're my ride, remember?"

"Oh."

Just then, there was a rapid staccato of approaching footsteps in the hall outside. The door clicked open and a librarian entered, followed by a stocky black man with an almost cartoonishly square jaw and a close-cropped, no-nonsense haircut. Even the librarian seemed to have a sense of his authority, giving him a slight, almost involuntary bow as she wordlessly left the room.

"Special Agent Fleet! I didn't know you were coming," Warren said.

Fleet just sniffed and approached the large volumes that the officers were in the midst of collecting. "This it?"

"Yes."

"Nice work, Satterwhite."

"You'll want to secure that log book, too," Fleet said, gesturing to the record that detailed Vernon's visits to the reading room. "And get statements from all the librarians who've had contact with the victim."

"Already on it," Warren replied.

Fleet snapped his head abruptly toward Lindsay and then back to Warren. "And this is?"

Lindsay opened her mouth to speak, but Warren jumped in. "She is my, er, girlfriend, Lindsay Harding. She had just dropped in to bring me some supper when I came across the evidence in the diary."

Lindsay's face contorted into a number of simultaneous expressions—shock, confusion, anger, and incredulity. With great effort, she arranged her features into a sphinx-like half smile. She nodded. "Uh-huh."

Fleet bent over the journal. He turned the pages slowly. He pinched the edges of each page with the tips of his thumb and index finger, like an old woman grasping a cup of hot tea. Without interrupting his rhythmic page-turning, he said, "Sergeant Satterwhite, please ask Miss Harding to wait outside. Her presence is not required." His tone was one of scientific certainty—neutral, clinical, indisputable.

Lindsay rose and, giving Warren an acid smile, said, "Sure thing, Snookie Wookums. Don't want to interrupt y'all while you're doing your important police things." She gave Warren a firm and obvious pat on the left butt cheek and walked out into the hallway.

A few minutes later, one of the uniformed officers waddled out carrying the journal in a large zip-top bag. He was middle-aged and balding, with a pot belly and skin so pale he looked like he'd spent most of his life underground. He paused in front of Lindsay, his lively blue eyes twinkling. "I can't believe Warren hasn't mentioned that he had a girlfriend. 'Specially one as pretty as a prize peach, if you don't mind my saying so. No reason to hide you. I tell you what, my Rosaleigh's got buckteeth and a face like a brickbat, but I still put her picture right on my desk."

Like many long-single women, Lindsay had eagle eyes when it came to spotting wedding rings. She had seen Warren's thin gold band immediately the night he visited Kimberlee's house. "Maybe the secrecy has something to do with him being married," she said, amazed at the officer's nonchalant attitude toward Warren's (pretense of) infidelity.

"You mean Cynthia?" The officer laughed. "I'm surprised he told you about her. I guess he probably had to. I don't think my Rosaleigh would be as accommodating as you seem to be." The officer extended his hand and introduced himself. "Freeland Vickers."

"Pleased to meet you," Lindsay replied. "I'm Lindsay Harding." She was still stewing over Warren's treatment of her and a bit flabbergasted at Officer Vickers's casual acceptance of her (alleged) extramarital relationship with Warren. Still, she couldn't help being won over by Freeland's old-fashioned corniness. When she was growing up, Southern men issued compliments to women as a matter of course. *Why you surely are looking lovely tonight, Miss Smith. Is that a new dress you're wearing, Mrs. Jones? Your husband better not let you out of his sight looking as purty as you do, Mrs. Wilson!* There was a playful flirtation in these interactions that was dying out, suffering a death of a thousand cuts: women's lib, political correctness, or the plain old loss of neighborliness. It was a shame, Lindsay thought with an inward sigh, that, in order to progress, women had had to sacrifice being told that they looked nice.

Vickers tipped his cap to Lindsay. "Well, I best be on my way." A few moments later, Warren and Fleet emerged from the reading room. Lindsay joined them, walking along beside them in stony silence. Directly in their path, with books and papers strewn across the table in front of him, was the last person in the world Lindsay wanted to see right then…Doyle Hargreaves.

He looked up at them and made eye contact. There was no way that she could blank him—she was just too polite, too Southern. "Hi," she said, giving a nervous little wave as they approached.

"Well, hey, Lindsay," Doyle said, rising to greet her. He stood between them and the door, blocking their path. There was no way to pass him without knocking him down and stepping over his body. Which Lindsay half considered doing. "I'm glad I ran into you. I've been feeling kinda sorry about dumping you like that. I'm dating someone else now. I thought that you might take it hard if you found out. I wanted you to hear it from me."

"It's all right, Doyle. I swear to god, it really is," Lindsay said. Doyle was looking even younger than he'd looked on the day of the reenactment. He wore a Mount Moriah Falcons Baseball t-shirt and long shorts. A mild acne outbreak spread across his forehead. She tried to push past him as politely as she could, but he would not yield any ground. Out of the corner of her eye, she saw Fleet and Warren exchange curious glances.

"Good. I'm just here finishing off my homework. Remember I told you I had one more class to pass before I graduated?"

"Hi, I'm Warren Satterwhite," Warren cut in, smiling broadly. He pointed to Doyle's t-shirt. "I used to play for the Falcons. I've still got my old t-shirts and uniforms, too. So, you're graduating? What college do you go to?"

"Oh, I don't go to college. I'm finishing up Señora Smolinski's Spanish class. Did you have her? She's a real witch."

Warren's smile broadened. "So you're in high school. That's great. That's real, real nice."

"Honeybear? Shouldn't we be going now?" Lindsay put her hand in Warren's back pocket and pushed him forward.

"Yeah, I should probably get going to," Doyle said. "Carla—that's my new girlfriend—is gonna be done babysitting soon. I've gotta pick her up on account of how she's only got her permit."

When they finally got clear of Doyle, Lindsay practically ran to Warren's car. She couldn't even look at Fleet as he bid them goodnight.

"Well, I'm not sure whether to take you home or take you down to the station and book you for contributing to the delinquency of a minor," Warren said, opening the car door for her.

Lindsay stepped past him and slammed her body into the seat. She yanked the door closed. Warren got in the other side and started the engine. "Look, Linds. I'm sorry about what happened back there with Fleet." Lindsay remained silent, so he continued. "How was I going to tell him that I brought along a friend to help me work a murder investigation? How would that have looked?" Lindsay continued to stare silently out the passenger's side window her cheeks aflame with anger and embarrassment. "You're going to have to come in the station tomorrow and make a statement about the conversation you overheard between Silas and Morgan. We'll need your evidence. Is that okay?" Warren said.

"Are you sure you don't want to take credit for that, too? Maybe you were the one who heard them while I was busy ironing your shirts?"

As they pulled into Lindsay's driveway, Warren turned toward her and spoke earnestly. "Look, Lindsay. This is the biggest case of my career. Fleet already acts like we're a bunch of no-account Barney Fifes down here. For you this is just a puzzle to solve. For me, it's real."

"Real?! You think that this is just another trigonometry problem for me?"

"That's not what I meant."

Lindsay got out of the car, slamming the door, and walked toward her front porch. It had rained while they were inside the library and the night air hung around her like a thick, wet blanket. Breathing was like inhaling lungfuls of tropical Jell-O. All around, a fog of dense, steamy mist rose from the trees and the warm ground. Warren stayed parked in the driveway, waiting to see that she got into the house all right. It was the kind of overprotective thing that her dad would do, she thought, rolling her eyes. When she stepped onto the porch, she noted with surprise that, although the screen door was shut, the front door stood ajar. She paused a moment before grabbing the screen door handle and pulling it slowly open. As her eyes adjusted to the dim light given off by Warren's headlights, she looked down the long central hallway and saw that the back door, too, was also standing open. She took a step forward and called out, "Hello?"

"Is everything okay?" Warren called, emerging from his car and walking toward the house.

"Yes." Lindsay snapped back to him over her shoulder. "Fine." Her voice sounded shrill and shaky, even to herself. "My friend slept over last night. She was still sleeping this morning when I went to work. She probably just…left both doors open when she left." The explanation sounded no more plausible when said aloud than it had in her churning mind. Lindsay took a step into the house. A faint glow filtered into the hallway from one of the back rooms, revealing papers strewn around the living room and furniture in disarray. Out of the corner of her eye, Lindsay saw a shadow pass through the hallway. The back door slammed shut with a sharp crack. Warren took the porch stairs in one leap and tore past her into the house. He was down the hallway in a flash. He opened the back door and sprinted into the yard. In the distance, Lindsay heard the squeal of tires and the crunch of gravel under fast-moving wheels. Lindsay stood there blinking for a moment. There had been something disquietingly familiar about the shadowy form of the intruder.

She rendezvoused with Warren a few moments later as he emerged from the trees at the back of her yard. He was clutching his side and panting heavily. "Whoever it was, got away. I didn't get a look at them or at the car."

They walked back into the house and Lindsay began to turn on the lights. Each room had been ransacked—the intruder had rifled through drawers and overturned furniture.

"Is anything missing?"

"I doubt it. I don't really have anything valuable—not valuable to anyone but me, anyway. No jewelry or cash or anything. And my car is still parked out front."

"Maybe we got here before he had a chance to get anything. I'll call it in," he said, reaching for his phone. "They might be able to lift some prints."

"No," Lindsay said in a low voice.

"What?" Warren replied, incredulous.

She avoided his gaze. "Nothing was taken. It was probably just some kids messing around."

"Kids?! Lindsay, it looks like a tornado came through here."

"I said I'm not reporting it."

Warren stared at her a long moment before lifting his hands in surrender. "Do what you want." He turned on his heel and began to stomp down the long central hallway toward the front door.

"I will." She squatted down and righted a chair that had been overturned. As she stood, a jolt shot through her injured knee and she cried out in pain.

She felt a gentle hand under her arm, steadying her. "At least let me help you clean up," Warren said. "To make up for tonight."

Lindsay surveyed his face. He seemed sincere. She nodded and together they began sifting through the mess. A large potted plant lay on its side near the kitchen door. Lindsay swept the dirt into a dustpan and then walked outside to empty it over the back porch railing. As the dirt dropped to the ground, Lindsay let out a groan. The doors to the shed stood open, revealing the empty, cavernous interior. The motion-sensitive floodlight mounted to the shed illuminated two thin wheel ruts running through the damp grass in her yard. Lindsay could just make out the continuation of the track as it ran along the soft bed of pine needles at the back corner of her property, where the trees thinned out. She walked back into the house, shaking her head. "They took my jet ski. They must have dragged it on the trailer all the way to the main road."

"Jet ski? I wouldn't have guessed that you were a big water-sports person."

"Yeah, well, sometimes I even surprise myself."

Lindsay and Warren moved from room to room, gathering the discombobulated things into discombobulated piles.

"Whoever did this seems to have been looking for something on paper. Maybe they're identity thieves. Or maybe they were looking for some kind of paper that could be valuable in itself. Do you have any stock certificates or anything like that?"

"Stock? Hardly. I'm still paying off my student loans. I do all my banking and stuff online. I don't think I even own a checkbook anymore." In the living room, Lindsay picked up a clock that had been knocked off the side table. A deep crack snaked down the center of the glass clock face, but the hands still ticked purposefully around the dial. "It's nearly eleven. Shouldn't you call your wife and tell her where you are?" she asked.

Warren looked at her quizzically. "I'm not married."

"I just thought…your ring…"

Warren touched his left ring finger. "Oh, that. I never seem to find the time to have it cut off." He blushed and began busily shuffling and reshuffling a stack of papers as he spoke. "I was in Vegas a few months back for my cousin's wedding. It was a wild night. There was this girl there, one of the bridesmaids. We, um, we got married."

"Wow! That is unbelievably…"

"Stupid?"

"I was going to say thrilling and romantic." Lindsay burst out laughing. "But stupid, too. Definitely stupid."

"Anyway, we're having it annulled. We just need to clear up some red tape between Nevada and North Carolina and it'll be over. This ring, though, is five carat gold or something and about two sizes too small for my finger. We bought them from the wedding chapel for twenty five dollars apiece." He tugged at the ring to demonstrate. "Won't budge."

Lindsay left the room and came back a moment later with an ice pack, three large rubber bands, and a tub of Crisco. Warren let out a long whistle. "You're a kinky lady, Lindsay Harding."

"You wish. I wondered why Freeland Vickers didn't seem to think it was strange that you had a girlfriend. I thought maybe you boys in blue all just keep girls on the side or something."

"They always seem to on TV. But the reality doesn't really match up. Maybe you need to live in a big city."

Lindsay took Warren's hand in hers and folded the ice pack around his fingers. She secured it with the rubber bands as she explained, "I had the same problem with my engagement ring. I was ready to gnaw off my finger rather than wear it another day, but luckily I hit on this solution instead. Put your hand on ice for five minutes and then we'll move on to stage two."

While Lindsay continued the clean-up, Warren walked around the perimeter of the house to try to determine how the burglar got in. He came back in a few minutes later, shaking his head. "Only two of your windows are locked. Most of the locks don't even work. The deadbolt on your front door is so rusted that it won't turn. Even if your friend locked up when she left, all that the thief had to do was reach through your living room window, which was open by the way, punch out the screen and unlock the door from the inside. I know you're out in the country here, but you need to use a little common sense."

Lindsay crossed her arms and snapped, "Says the man who got drunker than a coalminer on payday and married a total stranger in Las Vegas."

"Lindsay, I'm serious. What might have happened to you if I wasn't here? What if that was a rapist? Or some kind of a psychopath?"

"Or a drug addict, coked out on angel dust?" Lindsay erupted into hysterical peals of laughter. Warren glowered at her. She wiped tears from her eyes and covered her cheeks with her hands. "Sorry. You just reminded me of something funny."

"Look, if you want to let thieves come into your home and rob you blind, that's your business. But don't expect the people who care about you to help you gratify your death wish."

"I'm sorry," she said, not meeting Warren's stern gaze. Lindsay gently took his hand. She began to unwind the rubber bands that held the ice pack on his hand. "I'm sorry," she said again. "You're right. You were right before, too. What you said in the car. What you said about this being a puzzle for me to solve." Warren tried to interrupt her, but she carried on, keeping her eyes lowered and concentrating intensely on her task. "A good man has died and his poor wife was within a hair's breadth of going to jail for it. And now we're talking locking up a respected philanthropist and politician. I didn't want to admit it, even to myself, but my first instinct *was* to be insulted that I didn't get any respect for helping to crack the case." She dipped her fingertips into the shortening and slathered the viscous white goo up and down his ring finger. She began to work the ring off his finger, twisting it as she applied a gentle upward pressure. A few seconds later, she was holding the ring in the palm of her hand. "There, now. You're free," she said, softly.

Chapter 32

Warren had spent the night on her couch; he absolutely refused to let her stay in the house alone. After putting up a mild protest, she gratefully accepted his offer, but only after he promised never to mention the encounter with Doyle Hargreaves again. When she woke up early the next morning, she tiptoed around the house for about 10 minutes before realizing that he had already gotten up and left. He left a note promising to swing by later and check that she was okay. With Warren's help the night before, she had finished most of the major clearing up—furniture uprighted, broken glass swept up—but the house was still in disarray. The rest of the cleaning would have to wait. She was going to the Royals game with Drew straight after work and she still hadn't had time to figure out how she was going to pass herself off as a baseball aficionado. She scarfed down a banana and some animal crackers, and rushed out the door.

As requested, she stopped by the police station on her way to work and gave her statement about the conversation between Morgan and Silas. She omitted any mention of her role in the library investigation. Although she was anxious to fill Kimberlee in on the latest developments, the officers she spoke to cautioned her not to discuss the details of the case with anyone, as it might compromise her testimony and endanger their investigation of Silas Richards.

The stop at the police station took far longer than she had planned, and Lindsay arrived at the hospital over an hour late for her shift. As she made her usual rounds, she was surprised at how calm and normal everything seemed. She'd half expected the chaos in her own mind to be reflected in the outside world. The patients and families that she visited were all doing well. No emergencies, no drama. She decided to go and see Kimberlee. Even if Lindsay couldn't tell her everything, the police had given her permission to reassure her that the investigation was moving away from

Kimberlee. As Lindsay turned a corner toward Buford Bullard's ward, she saw the back of Geneva's tiny salt-and-pepper head. Geneva was elevated on her toes, chatting with the duty nurse over the tall counter of the nurses' station. Lindsay stayed to the far side of the hallway, hoping to sneak past unseen. Unfortunately for Lindsay, the duty nurse was Angel Bledsoe, the "angel" she'd used to communicate her message of peace and love to the tongue-speaking Peechums.

"Hey Lindsay," Angel called cheerfully. "Where you off to in such a hurry? Gonna work some more miracles in my name?"

Lindsay returned the greeting, but hurried quickly along in the hope that she could outrun Geneva. Her injured leg, however, slowed her escape.

When Geneva caught up with her, she poked a skinny finger into Lindsay's sternum. "Well?" she said expectantly.

"What?"

"Girl." Geneva could infuse that one word with an almost inexhaustible variety of meanings. In this case—spoken in a clipped tone with a deeply creased brow—it served as both a chastisement and a demand.

Lindsay's thin charade of ignorance collapsed. "Why did you tell him I love baseball?" she whined.

"Remember when Moses was trying to free the Israelites? If the midwives hadn't lied to Pharaoh and hid the newborn Israelite babies, there'd have been a whole mess of dead Israelite babies all over that pyramid. Lesson? God helps those who help themselves. And He especially helps those that help others who can't seem to help themselves find a nice husband."

"I'm not sure that tricking Drew into taking me on a date is quite as justifiable as Moses freeing the Israelites."

Geneva batted away the criticism with a flick of her small hands. She paused. "Why're you limping? You ain't even had your first date yet. Better not be any limping until after the wedding night."

"I'm afraid that's got nothing to do with this. I was jogging out at the Richards Homestead and got caught up in the middle of a blasting zone."

"Richards!" Geneva said, slapping her forehead. "Girl, that

reminds me. Strange goings-on with that Silas Richards. I got this letter from my husband's lawyer yesterday. Seems that Mr. Vernon Young wrote to him the day before he got himself killed." She mumbled to herself as she began to search through the large white faux-leather handbag that was slung over her shoulder. As Geneva sorted through the bag, Lindsay was astonished to see that it contained, among countless other items, a full-sized pair of sewing scissors, a packet of radish seeds, and a toddler's shoe. After a few moments, Geneva triumphantly removed an envelope and handed it to Lindsay. "Our lawyer dropped this off at the house the other day. I kept meaning to mention it to you, with you being so close to the widow and all, but I've been otherwise occupied with trying to get you happily married to a handsome brain surgeon."

Lindsay scanned the letter, her eyes growing wide with astonishment. "This says that Vernon has traced the family records of Samuel and Celia Wilcox, and that your husband may be an heir to their property. Property that includes the land known as the Richards Homestead."

"I can read." Geneva deftly plucked the letter from Lindsay with a lightening-quick snatch of her bony little fingers.

"Geneva, we've got to take this to the police. This might be evidence of...." Lindsay caught herself just before she blurted out anything about the investigation. The police did not want to tip Silas off that they were on to him. Warren had shared confidential information about the case on the condition that she should be discreet. Blabbing details to one of the town's biggest busybodies seemed ill-advised.

Geneva's head recoiled into the soft wrinkles of her neck. "Evidence of what?"

"You know. Crimes and things," Lindsay said with a vague wave of her hand.

"If it's so important, the police would've come to see me about it," Geneva said.

"Why did you show it to me if you're not going to tell the police about it?" Lindsay asked.

"I know that you are friendly with Vernon Young's widow. I was thinking about giving this to her, since it was one of the last things her husband wrote."

Geneva had momentarily softened when she spoke of Vernon's death. Lindsay used it as an opportunity to grab the letter. She held it in her left hand and pointed forcefully toward it with the index finger of her right. "If it can help with the investigation, you have got to give it to the police," she said.

Geneva seized the letter from Lindsay's hand and began to fold it. "The last thing I need is the police to get me and my family involved in this whole mess," she said decisively.

Lindsay thought carefully. What she had to do now was to convince Geneva to hand over the letter—without explaining why. She changed tack. "What about the land? Don't you want to find out if you and your children are the rightful owners?"

"What do I want with some piece of dirt that some dead people may or may not have left to my husband's great, great granddaddy?" Geneva huffed. "We worked hard to get where we are. We don't need handouts from Silas Richards or anybody else."

Lindsay would never be able to outflank Geneva in a straight argument—her only hope was to play dirty. "You know, you're absolutely right. That letter should be cherished. We, as good Christians, as good citizens, have to do whatever we can do to make sure that what may very well be Vernon Young's final written words reach out from beyond the grave. If I were his widow, that's what I would want." Geneva stood there hesitantly, the letter dangling from her pinched fingers. She opened her mouth to speak, but, for once, Lindsay was too quick for her. "I'll just see that this makes it into the right hands. You don't need to worry yourself about it anymore." Lindsay hobbled away, as fast as her injured leg could carry her.

Chapter 33

Buford Bullard remained comatose but was now breathing without the assistance of a ventilator. He had been moved out of intensive care and into a private room overnight. When Lindsay stopped by to check on him, only Kimberlee was there, the rest of the family having gone home to sleep and shower. Kimberlee sat in an armchair near the window with her stocking feet perched on the windowsill. She absent-mindedly ran her hands over her slightly-rounded belly. The TV was tuned in to some schmaltzy soap opera, but Kimberlee faced away from it, staring out the window over the double-decked parking lot to the low, green hills beyond.

When Kimberlee noticed Lindsay, she chirped a cheerful hello and said, "The organ function tests on Daddy came back better, and, as you can see, he's not hooked up to as many tubes as he was." Lindsay was glad to see that some inkling of Kimberlee's usual vigor seemed to have returned.

"I've got good news for you, too," Lindsay said. "As of last night, you are off the most wanted list."

Kimberlee's face broke into a wide grin. "That's the cherry on top of my banana split today!" She paused and considered a moment. "Does this mean the police are closer to catching whoever killed Vernon? Why haven't they called me?" She crossed her arms and shook her head in disgust. "They couldn't seem to get enough of talking to me when they thought I did it. And now that they have some news that I actually want to hear, they're making themselves scarce. When are they gonna arrest somebody?"

"It's not that easy, I'm afraid."

The sound of voices reverberated down the hall and a moment later the rest of the Bullards piled into the room.

"Hey, y'all," Kimberlee said. "Lindsay was just saying that the police don't think I did it anymore. Weren't you, Lindsay?"

Lindsay nodded. A barrage of questions came from Versa and her children, who circled around Lindsay like sharks in a feeding frenzy. "Who did it then?" "Have they arrested anyone?" "How did those dimwits finally figure out that it wasn't Kimberlee?" "What about the thing with Kimberlee's printer?" "Do they know if Daddy getting poisoned has anything to do with it?"

Lindsay held her hands up to ward them off. "I know that you want to know all the details, but I can't really say anything right now. I wish I could. But I am literally sworn to secrecy. I will tell you, though, that they have a witness who may know something about the killer, and some evidence that may link up to the murder. They just need a few more pieces to fall into place and they can make their move." A collective squeal of delight rose from the Bullards. "If you want any more details, you'll have to ask the police themselves. But don't tell them that you heard anything from me! They may not be able to say much, either. I get the impression that they are going to keep this pretty close to the vest until the right time comes."

The Bullards continued to buffet her with questions, trying to get her to divulge what she knew. She refused to be drawn out, though, and was very grateful when Kimberlee drew everyone's attention away by standing up on a chair and clearing her throat. "I think we need to have a little moment of celebration. They haven't yet nailed the guy who shot my Vernon, but it sounds like the noose is tightening around the bastard's neck! And best of all, they know it wasn't me!" She threw her arms open and the Bullard women rushed forward to embrace her, cackling like a coven of jubilant witches. Lindsay found herself pushed to one side of the room, standing next to Keith and the comatose Buford. Keith stood there silently. Lindsay thought he looked unsteady on his feet, so she eased him down in a chair next to Buford's bed. He glanced at her briefly, shaking his head in amazement. As Lindsay turned to make a quiet exit, she saw Keith gently caressing his father's hand. Tears overflowed from the deep wells of his eyes.

Chapter 34

Lindsay returned to the chaplains' office, where she planned to use her break to call Warren about the letter. It wasn't the smoking gun, but it was proof that they were on the right track. She also needed, if she had time, to look up some information about the Burlington Royals in advance of tonight's date. As soon as she sat down, however, she was summoned to the ER by her buzzing pager. She sighed and dutifully trekked down to the emergency room, where she found Anna waiting for her. "Glad you're here," Anna said. "I've got this woman, the wife of a patient, who is a total basket case. They were headed down to High Point to see the husband's parents. Stopped at the rest area off of I-85, where the husband got stung on the tongue by a bee." Lindsay raised her eyebrows quizzically. Anna just shrugged. "It was in his soda can. He had an anaphylactic reaction. The wife just ran around the parking lot, screaming like a ninny—not helpful. Luckily, someone with some common sense was there. The Good Samaritan just happened to have some children's Benadryl and managed to pour some down the guy's throat. Called the ambulance.

"We've given Mr. Beetongue some epinephrine, and he'll be fine. Mrs. Beetongue, however, is annoying the crap out of everyone. I tried to give her a sedative, but she's pregnant so she won't take anything. I told her what I was giving her was perfectly safe for her and the baby, but she said that her homoeopathic doula told her that she should only use chamomile and valerian root if she needs to relax. Then she lectured me for ten minutes on the tyranny of the medical-industrial complex, paying no attention to the fact that modern medicine had just saved her husband's life and totally ignoring the fact that herbal medicines can be just as dangerous as pharmaceuticals. Now I'm ready to give myself a sedative."

Anna paused and gave Lindsay a quick once-over. Lindsay usually dressed a bit like a retired schoolteacher—cardigans, sensible shoes, and hair swept into a ponytail. Today, however, she wore a flattering turquoise linen dress. Her curls had been tamed into a wavy blonde halo. “Hey, you’ve got your date tonight, right?”

“Yep. Right after work.”

Anna nodded her head approvingly. She then spun Lindsay around and pointed out a woman near the end of the corridor. The woman was griping at one of the nurses—the shrill tones of her voice echoed down the hall. Anna pushed her forward. “Go get ‘em, tiger.”

Lindsay cautiously drew nearer to the woman. The nurse she was speaking to (or, rather, speaking at) had his back to Lindsay. She couldn’t hear all of their conversation, but the nurse repeatedly shook his head and began taking small, but deliberate, steps backward. It was the kind of cautious retreat you might make if you found yourself stuck in a cow pen with a red-eyed bull. The woman was a good bit taller than Lindsay. Her honey-colored hair was shaped into a sleek bob that skimmed the tops of her shoulders. Her round, taut belly and full breasts were set off attractively by her well-tailored clothes.

“Hello, ma’am,” Lindsay said, extending her hand. “I’m sorry to interrupt. I am a chaplain here and I’ve been told that you’ve just suffered a terrible shock. Is there anything I can to do help you?” The nurse, sensing his chance, retreated down the hallway.

The woman looked over the top of Lindsay’s head in the direction of the fleeing nurse. She ignored the proffered handshake. She scanned the corridor, mumbling to herself, “I told that doctor that we have dinner reservations for 7pm tonight. Not that the Red Lobster in High Point really counts as a restaurant.” When she finally addressed Lindsay, her tone was patronizing. “I’m sorry, dear, did you say you were a chaplain? I’m not superstitious, you see. Now where did that doctor go? My husband needs to be discharged.”

Many times, Lindsay had been dismissed by people who were “not religious.” “Not superstitious”, however, took condescension to a whole new level. This woman was a piece of…work. “I could tell as soon as I saw you that you were a confident and cosmopolitan person. It must be very frustrating for you to be surrounded by people who just aren't operating at your level."

The woman looked hard at Lindsay, trying to detect any hints of sarcasm. Lindsay's expression, however, remained inscrutable. Lindsay extended her hand again, smiling broadly. "I'm Lindsay."

"Nikki Ruskin-Farnsworth."

"When is the baby due?"

Nikki's frigid expression melted—by one degree. "He's due at the end of August."

"So you know it's a boy already?"

"Oh yes. We had all the prenatal screening done. All that nonsense about wanting to be surprised when the baby comes out is really only an excuse for not being well-prepared. We have established a tax-free college fund for baby Timothy and selected a day-care facility that caters to the particular developmental requirements of boys. Most nurseries and schools are very gynocentric, you know. Totally unsuitable for boys," she said, giving her stomach a self-assured pat.

"Timothy?"

"Yes. His name is Timothy. After his father."

"Nikki Ruskin-*Farnsworth*," Lindsay could barely whisper the name. "I remember you now." The air left her lungs as an agonizing reality dawned on her. Quivering from head to toe, she walked over and threw back the filmy green curtain that screened the patients from the corridor. There, lying in bed with raised, red splotches covering every inch of his exposed skin, was her former fiancée, Timothy Farnsworth. Although he was still groggy from the medication he'd been given, when he saw Lindsay his eyes instantly widened in recognition and astonishment.

"Gay!?" Lindsay shrieked. "Gay?!" Her voice was so high-pitched it was a wonder that her cries didn't summon a pack of stray dogs.

Timothy's speech was thick and garbled by his still-swollen tongue. "Windsay! Wah aw you doing heaw? Wet me expwain."

"No, you let me explain," she said fiercely. Everything was so clear to her now. Nikki Ruskin had been one of Timothy's fellow students in his MBA program, a year ahead of him. Lindsay had only met her once or twice, but suddenly the memory of that woman's supercilious little face filled the entire frame of Lindsay's mind. Lindsay walked over and leaned in, her face an inch from Timothy's. "You knew that I would understand if you said you were gay, because of what happened with Rob. You knew that I would let you off the hook."

"I was young and scawed. I wassunt weady to be mawwied."

A vase of flowers stood on the table of a neighboring patient. Without thinking, Lindsay grabbed ahold of the bouquet, wielding it like a battle axe. She began to pummel Timothy with the flowers, punctuating each phrase with the thwack of flying floral force. "You humiliated me! You broke my heart! You made me lie to all of our family and friends! You miserable, lying, sniveling little coward!"

Lindsay finally stopped her assault when only the bare stems of the flowers remained. She threw them at Timothy with a muted scream and turned her back to him in disgust. Flower petals continued to rain down around her like confetti. Nikki stood gaping at Lindsay, mute with shock and rage. Her round belly and glossy hair gave her the appearance of an over-inflated balloon, ready to pop. Lindsay narrowed her eyes as she regarded the other woman. "I'll pray for you," she said, and marched briskly away.

Chapter 35

That evening, Lindsay was mostly silent during the drive to the Royals' stadium, her mind still occupied by her encounter with Timothy and his wife. Despite her sour mood, she couldn't help but observe that the date seemed to be going rather well. She noted that Drew had opened the car door for her when he picked her up. Some guys were scared to be seen as chauvinists if they undertook such gestures of politeness. She also noted that he drove a sensible blue Volkswagen Passat. Too many surgeons cruised around town in ridiculous cars with vanity license plates that advertised their specialty. The anesthesiologist whose plate read, ISED8EM, for example, was someone that Anna aptly referred to as "a total asshat." Lindsay's opinion of Drew Checkoway thus far was that he was a gentleman who was not a total asshat.

When they arrived and took their seats behind home plate, the small, 3,000-seat stadium was only about half full. Children crowded around near the dugouts, hoping to get the autographs of their favorite players. Although it was nearing sundown, the day's oppressive heat lingered. Drew removed his baseball cap and mopped beads of sweat from his brow. "I miss Chicago weather. I can't believe I'm saying that, but it's true. I feel like I am in Satan's armpit. Chicago can get hot, but this is constant, searing, jungle heat. I'm going to miss having four seasons."

"What do you mean? North Carolina has four glorious seasons." Lindsay enumerated them on her fingers. "Pollen, Sauna, Drought, and Slightly Nippy." As a lifelong Southerner, she didn't take well to complaints about the weather, especially from outsiders. It was one thing to render an opinion: "It's gonna be a hot one," or "Hailstones out there are the size of pig's balls." But actually complaining about the weather was an undignified pastime of Northerners and the British.

A vendor came past and Drew asked for two light beers. As he handed her the cup, he said, "I hope you don't mind me ordering for you. I should have asked."

"Not at all." She said, minding quite a bit, actually.

Drew opened his program and withdrew a piece of paper. It was covered in boxes and diamonds and boxes containing diamonds. In the boxes along the left-hand side, he jotted down a series of numbers. Across the top, he wrote the names of the teams, the time of the game and the weather conditions. Noticing her curious stare, Drew said, "Do you keep a scorecard when you come to games?"

"Um, no. I'd rather just sit back and enjoy the, you know, artistry of the game."

Their conversation so far had stayed safely away from Lindsay's alleged love of baseball. She was entirely engrossed in her musings about Timothy's deception. Now Lindsay thought of the verse in the Book of Matthew about hypocrisy, "Why do you see the speck in your brother's eye but fail to notice the beam in your own eye?" She blinked involuntarily. Stupid beam.

She looked out over the field, where the game was now underway. A cool breeze had picked up and low clouds gathered on the horizon. Some of Lindsay's previous baseball knowledge came from movies like *A League of Their Own* and *The Natural*, and she was dismayed at the languid pace of the real game. She clapped dutifully along with the other fans, but by the third inning, the monotony of the throwing, swinging, and catching was making her yawn. "Hey, I'm going to go and get some nacho cheese. Do you want anything?"

"God, no." Drew visibly recoiled at the suggestion that he partake in Lindsay's unholy feast. "That stuff is as bad as cigarettes. It's nothing but trans-fat and hydrogenated oil. I don't think cheese even appears on the list of ingredients."

She knew it wasn't real cheese. It probably wasn't real anything. Still, the gelatinous, bright orange goo was her favorite food. When she and Rob made their annual pilgrimage to the North Carolina State Fair, she would watch, untempted, as Rob gorged himself on giant turkey legs, fried Oreos, and various foodstuffs 'on a stick'. But when they passed the nacho stand, she would ask the quizzical vendor for a paper cup full of gooey cheese—hold the nachos—and a spoon.

"That must be what makes it so tasty," Lindsay replied, undeterred. As she stood up, a bolt of pain radiated from her knee. She sat back down heavily, wincing.

"Are you okay?"

Lindsay hiked up the hem of her dress to reveal the angry, red swelling on her knee. "I had a little accident the other day. I think it's getting worse."

"That looks really nasty. May I?" He gestured toward her leg. She nodded and he began a tender examination of her leg, bending and unbending her knee and checking various points for sensitivity. As he bent over her, she caught the soapy, lemony scent of his hair—masculine, and very, very clean. If her knee hadn't already been troubling her, it was certainly beginning to feel a bit weak now. "You should stay off that leg until you've had it looked at by an orthopedic surgeon. You need to make sure there's no damage to the ligaments."

"I'm fine. It's just a little tender." She began to rise again.

Drew stopped her. "You stay there. I'll get some food for you." He handed her his scorecard and pencil. "Would you mind keeping up with that until I get back?"

She looked uncertainly at the card as he made his way down the aisle. Drew had inscribed a series of mystifying symbols in the little boxes. She realized that the diamond shapes must represent the bases. "H" was probably hits, "R" was probably runs, and the numbers along the left probably corresponded to players. Beyond that, however, she was rapidly out of her depth. The series of "Ks" Drew had written was a complete mystery, and "LOB" was certainly something from tennis, wasn't it? She looked around to see if she could find someone to copy from, but the rows in front and behind were empty. She could see Drew returning now, so she rapidly colored in some squares on the diamond and scribbled some numbers into boxes.

Drew sat down and handed her a hot dog. "It's turkey," he said. "On a whole wheat bun. That's the best I could do." As she returned the scorecard to him, a streak of lightning forked across the sky, followed immediately be a peal of thunder. Within seconds, gentle drops began to fall.

She frowned. "I asked for nacho cheese and a spoon."

"I know. I tried to buy it, but the vendor said that he wasn't going to stand idly by while I enabled your dangerous addiction." His smile was so disarming that Lindsay could almost forgive him. Drew looked down at his scorecard. "Whoa! I missed a crazy inning. Six errors and four bases on balls! Wait, how were there nine guys left on base?"

As Lindsay opened her mouth to answer, a torrent of rain swept over them. Another bolt of lightning ripped through the sky just over their heads. The players ran for the dugouts, and the grounds crew hurried out with a tarp to cover the field. Lindsay rose from her seat, but the pain in her knee again forced her back down. Drew wordlessly lifted her into his arms and carried her under the cover of the awning, where he gently set her down. They stood there a moment, watching the sheets of water blow across the sky. Lindsay wiped the drops off her face. Her linen dress clung to her like a second skin. With deepening horror she realized that the rain had rendered the light, blue-green fabric completely transparent. She was wearing a pink polka-dot bra and leopard-print panties. And now everyone knew it.

Drew, whether through delicacy or embarrassment, made no reference to Lindsay's unintentional peep show and kept his gaze above neck level. "I'll pull the car around to the entrance," he said, surveying the worsening storm. "I'm pretty sure the game is over for the night."

Chapter 36

Drew drove Lindsay straight home after their rained-out game. Not wanting the night to end so abruptly, she invited him to come inside for a drink. Her heart gave a little flutter at his instant agreement. She immediately realized her folly, however, when she opened the front door to reveal the still-disordered contents of her house. "Oh no! I forgot about the house!" She slammed the door shut and blocked it with her body.

"It can't be that messy. I'm sure mine's just as bad. I've still got boxes sitting around my apartment that I haven't unpacked yet," he said, gently wresting the doorknob from her grip. He paused at the threshold. "Okay, you were right. It's pretty bad."

"It's not usually this way. I'm actually very tidy."

"It's okay. Honestly."

Lindsay went into the kitchen to open a bottle of wine, while Drew went to use the bathroom and to try to dry himself off. She caught sight of her reflection in the glass of the pantry cabinet. She was greatly relieved to see that her dress was now sufficiently dry to have returned to its opaque state. Lindsay emerged from the kitchen a moment later carrying two wine glasses. She was startled to see Drew fling the bathroom door open with tremendous force. He backed quickly into the hallway, keeping his wide eyes fixed on some unknown menace inside the bathroom. He continued this hasty backward egress and collided hard with Lindsay, sending a crimson shower of wine arcing through the air. He let out a small scream, spun around and grabbed her forcefully by the shoulders. The glasses slipped from her hands and exploded into a hundred jagged diamonds on the wood floor. "Oh Jesus! Sorry." He loosened his grip, his shoulders relaxing slightly. Suddenly, his eyes again widened in horror, and he glanced down at his crotch. He spun away from her again. Lindsay could see him shifting and maneuvering, and she heard the sound of his fly being zipped.

"Is everything okay?"

"No, it's not," he said, his voice tremulous and uncertain. Lindsay's hands became clammy with fear.

"What is it?"

He gestured for her to be silent. He lifted bare-footed Lindsay across the broken glass to the opposite side of the hallway, and set her down next to the door to the bathroom, which gaped open like the mouth of a slavering beast. He inched along, his back pressed tightly to the hallway wall. A muffled scratching came from within the bathroom. Together, they peered around the corner of the door.

"A squirrel!" Lindsay laughed with relief at the sight of the small, grey form perched on the tank of the toilet.

"They're vermin. Those things can carry diseases! And it was this close to my, you know, exposed manhood," Drew said, holding his thumb and index finger up to demonstrate. Seeing the look on her face, he added hurriedly, "That indicates proximity of the squirrel to my manhood, not the size of my manhood."

"He must have come in through the screen. A tree branch came down against the house during a thunderstorm a few weeks ago. It busted the screen and messed up the window in there. I haven't gotten around to fixing it yet. Let's see if we can lure that little guy out of there, shall we?"

"Is there some kind of very hands-off, distant supporting role I can play?"

"No, sorry. I need your help. I don't think it can get out the way it came in. That's not a very big opening, and it's going to be kind of panicked now. You probably scared it. I'll try to catch it in a bag, but I need you to stand over there and move it in my direction."

Lindsay retrieved a heavy canvas grocery sack from the kitchen and took up a position near the door. "Okay," she said, motioning for Drew to move toward the squirrel. "Wave your arms or something."

Drew waved his arms noncommittally and made a low grunting sound through his gritted teeth. The effect was something akin to a talentless actor portraying a very unconvincing Frankenstein's Monster. He took a step toward the squirrel. Instead of fleeing away, the squirrel made some kind of irrational calculus in its terrified brain; it dashed straight toward Drew. Drew hurtled himself backward to evade it. His knees buckled as he hit the edge of Lindsay's large, claw-footed bathtub, and he tumbled head over heels back into it. The squirrel, in a surge of adrenaline-fuelled frenzy, leapt upwards. With the grace of a kung-fu master, it kicked off a wall, using its momentum to propel itself sideways out of the small opening in the window screen. No wires, no special effects. Just 15 ounces of raw squirrel power and the will to get the hell out of that bathroom.

Lindsay ran over to the tub, where Drew lay wide-eyed and gasping like a freshly-caught trout. "Are you okay?" she asked.

"Is it gone?"

"Yes. Can you move?"

"I think so." He rolled over and awkwardly extracted himself from the tub, using one hand to rub the back of his head.

She put her arm around his waist and guided him carefully out of the bathroom. They stepped into the hallway, where splattered wine was still dripping off the ceiling and down the walls.

"I'm sorry about the wine. Jeez. It looks like there was an axe murder in here. Oh, watch your feet!" He indicated the shards of the broken wine glasses.

"It's okay. I'll clean that up later. Why don't we get you to the couch? I'll get you some ice for your head."

She guided him to the couch, painfully supporting his weight on her injured knee. "Well, you sure do know how to show a lady a good time."

"Just imagine our second date. Don't know how I could top this one."

Lindsay paused to consider. "Maybe we could get caught in a blizzard at a football game. Then you could throw split pea soup over all my furniture and break your femur while evading a rampaging butterfly."

"I'll see if I can arrange that," he laughed. "Well, I think I'd better get going now before I find some other way to humiliate and degrade myself."

"Are you sure you don't have a concussion?"

"I'm fine. Luckily I have a very hard head. It's one of my

many excellent qualities."

She got up and walked him to the door. They stood awkwardly for a moment, not quite knowing how to end the night. He bent down and gave her a quick peck on the lips. "I'll see you soon."

She gave a little wave. "Thanks for an exciting night." She closed the door behind him and walked straight to the kitchen. She retrieved a mop, bucket, broom and dustpan—preparing to clean up after yet another messy night.

Chapter 37

Lindsay was working the night shift the next day, so she spent a busy morning cleaning. The sun was shining brightly, and the previous night's storm had ushered in cooler weather. The sandals and purse she'd brought with her to the baseball game were both still damp, so she set them in a sunny spot on the back porch to dry. As she emptied the contents of her purse onto her wooden patio table, she saw a number of missed calls and texts registered on the phone—three calls from her father, one from Warren, and several text messages from Rob and Anna. Lindsay first read Rob's text: *All ok with Tim & bitch/wife. Smoothed it over. U owe me. p.s. don't do this again or ur fired xx.*

Lindsay next scrolled through Anna's texts. The first one was from yesterday afternoon: *Nice flower beating of evil ex. All nurses cheered. How r u?* The next one said: *How goes date? Naked yet?* A few hours later, the message read: *Why no updates on date? That good?* Then, from earlier that morning: *Update me, punk. Thought we were BFFs.* Then: *Am trapped in a well. Help!* And finally: *Not actually trapped, but still call me.* Lindsay was notoriously negligent with her cell phone—the battery was nearly dead and the ringer had been turned off for at least two days.

Lindsay retrieved the cordless phone from the kitchen and plugged her cell phone into the charger. She sat on the top step of the back porch and dialed Anna's number. "How was it? Tell me that he swept you off your feet and you had a night of wild passion."

"Well, he did carry me for a little while when we got caught in the rain."

"Sounds romantic."

"It was. Kind of. Until the part where a stadium full of people saw my underwear and Drew ended up almost unconscious in my bathtub."

"Flashing your underwear and getting a man in your

bathtub sounds like a stellar date, if you ask me."

"He's afraid of squirrels."

"So? You're terrified of those bald cats."

"Lots of people are scared of those. Hairless cats are genuinely scary!"

"Yeah, but you freaked out that time that Beyoncé singed her back fur on the wood stove. You wouldn't go near her until it grew back."

"Well, he also bought me a turkey dog and a light beer that I didn't ask for," Lindsay continued.

"What's wrong with that? Turkey dogs are better for you."

"Yeah, but I asked for nacho cheese. He should have respected my choice."

"When you are over the age of thirty, you need to give up your feminist ideals. You should be grateful that attractive men are still willing to buy you drinks."

"Thanks, Gloria Steinem."

"This is not about turkey dogs or feminism. You, Reverend Harding, are a psychotherapist's dream—a classic case of fear of rejection leading to commitment phobia. An attractive, eligible man shows interest in you, and you don't even give him a fair chance. You've been on one date, and you are already thinking of reasons not to be with him. Remember, Linds, *I* am the bitterly-disappointed, barb-tongued spinster. Got it? Not you. Me."

"Sorry. I didn't mean to steal your thunder."

"Good, just to make sure, let's go down to the animal shelter this weekend and pick me out some cats. I'm going to need at least a dozen to cement my status as spinster-in-chief," Anna said, signing off. Lindsay closed her eyes, enjoying the cool breeze that washed through the yard and thinking about Anna's comments. If Drew liked her enough to care about the long-term accrual of cholesterol in her bloodstream, surely that was a good sign. And being afraid of the disease-carrying potential of squirrels was a little neurotic, maybe, but also kind of adorable. Actually, very adorable, she thought, remembering the scent of Drew's hair and his tall, athletic frame laid out on her couch. The squirrel attack was the kind of story that she and Drew could tell at their wedding reception. Her reverie was interrupted by the sound of tires crunching on gravel. She walked through the house to the front drive, where Warren was emerging from his police cruiser. He greeted Lindsay with a serious expression. “They’ve brought Silas in.”

“How did that come about so suddenly? I thought you still needed more evidence,” Lindsay asked.

“Richards’ secretary. She said that Vernon came to Silas’s office a couple of days before the murder to talk about the catering for the engagement party. She didn’t hear the conversation, but she remembers that Silas was very agitated. We checked his phone records. After Vernon left, he immediately placed two calls: one to his lawyer, and one to Morgan Partee.”

“Is Partee in on it?”

“He definitely knows more than he is telling. Lawyered up as soon as they brought Silas in, and won’t talk to us. Silas’s lawyer, of course, can’t say what she and Silas discussed. But we were able to run down the lead on the land out by the interstate. The Partee family, in partnership with Richards, is planning to put a huge dealership and retail park out there. Partee RV and Camping World. I had a look at the contractor’s records. The afternoon that Vernon came to see Silas, they got a stop work order, issued by Silas’s lawyer. The day after Vernon died, the work started up again. Silas also had plenty of opportunity to do the shooting. None of the other reenactors saw him for about twenty minutes during the window of time that Vernon got shot.”

Lindsay let out a long exhalation. “So I guess he did it after all,” she said, shaking her head.

Warren threw his hands up in exasperation. “Don’t tell me you are having second thoughts now. We’ve got evidence piling up by the bucketful. We’ve arrested him, for heaven’s sake, based on your testimony and the things you discovered in the diary.”

Now that the case against Silas seemed more certain than ever, Lindsay found herself voicing all the doubts that she had harbored since the moment she saw Silas’s name in the Wilcox diary. “I know. I know. It’s just that Silas owns plenty of other land and has plenty of money, enough to pay lawyers who probably would have fought off any rival claim on that land anyway. The potential of a few months’ delay in this project was worth a man’s life? It all seems so out of keeping with his character. But then," she added, remembering her encounter with Timothy, "I may be the world's worst judge of character." She suddenly remembered that she was still in possession of Geneva's letter. Oops. She had been so caught up in the drama with Timothy and the excitement of her date that she had completely forgotten to give it to Warren. "Wait here a second," she said. She went into the house and retrieved the letter. "Here's another nail for the coffin."

"This is perfect," Warren said, scanning the letter with thinly disguised glee. "It backs up the 'family honor' motive. Silas probably wanted to keep Richards family skeletons in the closet." Warren scanned the address lines in the heading of the letter. "How did you come to have this? Who is Reverend Maurice Williams?"

"He is the deceased husband of my fearsome colleague, the Reverend Geneva Williams—a colleague who, by the way, would skin me alive if she finds out that I gave this to a policeman."

"I'll try to keep the lid on it."

"Well, it's my own fault if Geneva skins me, since I led her to believe that I was going to give the letter to Vernon's poor, grieving widow and then mugged her when her guard was down. Oh, speaking of the Bullards, what about Buford Bullard? Does that tie in with Silas?"

"Silas was one of the last people to come into contact with him before he got sick. But the lab still can't confirm what kind of poison was used. And we've got no motive to tie it together with Vernon." Warren paused and looked hard at Lindsay. "Linds, this arrest is great news, especially for Kimberlee. Looking at you, though, you'd think that somebody took away the punchbowl in the middle of your party."

"The threatening letter. The printer. If Vernon came in to the police station with the letter a week before he was killed, then that means someone was already out to get him. Before Silas knew anything about the Wilcox diary. Probably before Vernon himself knew," she said.

"The letter could be completely unrelated. Lots of people had access to that printer. Kimberlee's whole family has keys to the house. Her older nieces and nephews came over all the time after school with their friends. They didn't always lock up behind themselves. Hell, for all I know, Vernon could have printed the letter himself for some reason." Warren leaned against the porch railing. "You're right to wonder, though. I don't like loose ends—especially when we are trying to build a case against one of the most powerful men in central North Carolina. We really need to get our hands on the gun. We got the firearms identification back. The gun that was used to kill Vernon was probably a very high-quality custom-made rifle-musket—almost identical to what they would have used during the Civil War in appearance, but able to shoot regular, small-caliber ammo. We're running down manufacturers and dealers."

"You're in luck, then," Lindsay said, interrupting him. "That should be fairly easy to trace. Only the more hardcore guys at the reenactment would have had guns like that. Custom-made guns cost a small fortune. Most of them probably use either cheap Italian-made reproductions that are just there to look pretty. And if the weapon that shot Vernon had been a genuine antique or a black-powder, muzzle-loader from India, you'd never trace them at all. Antiques and muzzle-loaders are mostly exempt from gun laws."

Warren let out a long whistle. "Okay Annie Oakley, how come you know so much about guns?"

"My great aunt was a bit of a gun nut, believe it or not. When I was little, she had a collection of about fifty weapons, and lots of them were antiques. She used to take me duck hunting sometimes, though of course she never let me touch the more expensive guns."

"Well, you're right about this gun being less common than the typical reenactor's gun, but it's not going to be any easier to trace. The killer could easily have bought it out of state, which would complicate things. It's not like you see on TV, where we just type something into a computer and a picture of the gun's owner pops up. And, like you said, some types of guns are exempt from registration altogether."

"Why didn't you guys wait to arrest Silas? His lawyers could tear your case to shreds. You don't have any concrete evidence linking Silas to the murder. No gun, no DNA, no witnesses to the shooting. This is Silas Richards, for goodness sake, not some sixteen-year-old who stole a car."

"We've got enough, Linds. This wouldn't be the first time we caught someone with only circumstantial evidence. You're right about his lawyer. Like as not she'll have Richards out on bail by tomorrow or the next day. But we've struck the first blow, and that's important. Besides," Warren continued, "you know the kind of pressure we were under to get this thing done quick. National papers have been calling to interview the chief of police. They've gotten wind of the racial elements and the threatening letter. We heard that the *News and Observer* was getting ready to run a feature on Sunday calling the murder a modern-day lynching. The arrest will put a stop to that."

The initial buzz Lindsay felt when she unraveled the Wilcox story in the library was gone. All she saw now was ruined lives and the prospect of more to come. "Have you told Kimberlee yet?" she asked.

"Yes. I'm just on my way back from the hospital now. She was dumbfounded, of course, and real upset. Buford is improving, though, so let's keep our fingers crossed that he wakes up and sheds some more light on what happened to him. Anyway, I just wanted to stop by and tell you. You've done great work on this case, Nancy Drew." He patted her on the back and coaxed a smile from her. "The bad guy is in jail."

"Nancy Drew? I thought we were Fred and Daphne from Scooby Doo," Lindsay said.

"If we're talking Scooby Doo, you're Velma. No question," Warren replied.

"Velma! Just because I'm short and I wear glasses?" Lindsay pouted, crossing her arms in front of her chest. "Fine then, you're Shaggy."

"I was paying you a compliment. Velma was the smart one. She was cute."

"You thought Velma was cute? With the orange sweater and the knee socks?"

"I guess I like the smart ones," Warren said. He blushed slightly and looked very much like his teenage self.

They stood awkwardly for a moment, until the sound of an approaching car caused them to turn. Lindsay was surprised to see

John's truck pull into her driveway. John hopped out of the driver's side, and walked over to them. "I heard through the grapevine that you got robbed the other night."

Lindsay nodded. "The grapevine got it right, unfortunately." She gestured to Warren. "I don't believe you two have met. John Tatum, this is Warren Satterwhite, one of New Albany's finest. He also happens to be an old friend of mine who just stopped in for a visit," she said. She felt guilty for hiding the reason for the visit from John, but she knew he would only chastise her for the extent of her involvement in the investigation. John and Warren were exchanging greetings when Joe emerged from the passenger's side of the truck, clutching a rifle. He marched right past them and took a seat on the steps of the front porch, where he immersed himself in a meticulous inspection of his gun.

Lindsay raised her eyebrows. "First the police and now an armed guard?" She gestured toward Joe.

"Oh that," John replied. "We were in town—at the police station, as a matter of fact—to pick up our reenactment guns. They had been holding them since the shooting, but they said we could have them back now. I guess there must have been some breakthrough in the case?" He looked expectantly as Warren.

Warren, however, ignored the question and took the opportunity to say goodbye. "I've got to be getting back. Pleasure to meet you, John."

John watched Warren back down the driveway. Then he walked around the back of his truck and pulled out his toolbox. "I'm here to put some deadbolts on your doors."

Lindsay rolled her eyes. She had used the robbery to excuse her lateness at work yesterday, not wanting to tell Rob about giving evidence at the police station. In contrast to John and Anna, who always clucked over Lindsay like anxious mother hens, Rob typically let Lindsay's misadventures and bad habits pass without comment. Yesterday, however, his brow had creased with a line of worry as she related the details of the home invasion. He hadn't said anything at the time, but it was obvious that he must have been concerned enough to task John with safeguarding Lindsay's house.

"Look, Linds. I know you're not helpless. You're a capable, modern, independent woman, blah, blah, blah. But I also know that

Rob told me to come over here and put some new locks on your doors. And I have to live with him, not you."

Lindsay threw her hands up as they walked toward the house. "Fine. If you guys want to bully me into home improvements, you can help me fix my bathroom window screen, too."

"Wouldn't need to bully you if you weren't so pig-headed to begin with," Joe mumbled as they passed his perch on the porch.

"Well, if there was ever a clearer case of the pot calling the kettle black, I haven't heard it," John replied.

"That may be, but pig-headedness don't suit a woman," Joe grunted peevishly.

Lindsay smiled at him and led John into the house. "Pop's in a mood," John said. "He thinks the police were messing with his gun. He's going to take the whole thing apart, clean it, and put it back together 'how he likes it'."

They walked to the bathroom where Lindsay pointed out the broken window sash. "Well, let's get started." She bent down to open John's toolbox. As she stood up, a bolt of pain shot through her injured knee. She grimaced and steadied herself on the lip of the bathtub.

"Oh, yeah," John said. "Anna also told me to tell you to have an orthopedic surgeon look at your knee."

The two of them set to work, removing the broken window from its frame. While Lindsay sanded down the window frame where the wood had splintered, John went back outside to repair the damaged screen. Lindsay had almost completely smoothed the rough wood when a loud bang punctuated the air outside. The sound was followed immediately by an even louder bang, very close at hand. Lindsay rose. Her ears were ringing from the noise. She felt like she was standing on a conveyor belt—drawn toward the front door, toward the source of the sound. She seemed to reach it without taking a single step. She opened the screen door and stepped out onto the porch. Lying there, with his gun still clasped in his motionless hands, was Joe Tatum. John knelt over him, shouting his name. The sound of his voice was muffled, far away. Blood spilled out of a wound at the side of Joe's head, leaking down through the gaps in the floorboards.

Chapter 38

Lindsay and Rob moved along the hospital corridor, laden with cups of watery, vending-machine coffee and a packet of chocolate doughnuts. Lindsay had been keeping the vigil with John and Rob while Joe underwent surgery. Now that the initial surge of adrenaline had worn off, she was exhausted and weak from hunger.

Her nebulous memories of the past few hours flashed through her mind. They had conveyed Joe to the hospital in John's pickup. Lindsay had cradled Joe's injured head in her lap. She had pressed a towel over the wound to slow the bleeding, and watched as the blood soaked the towel, and dripped down her legs and into her shoes. After Joe had been taken into surgery, Lindsay realized that her clothes and hair were covered in a russet crust of dried blood. She had made a beeline for the staff shower room and swapped her blood-soaked clothes for borrowed doctor's scrubs.

As Lindsay and Rob walked, Lindsay pondered aloud. "I just don't see how he could've shot himself. John said that the reenactors only ever load those guns with blanks, so that there's no confusion. He's sure that his dad would have had blanks in that gun. And even if some live ammo somehow got in there, Joe emptied it before he started cleaning it. I saw him empty the chambers with my own eyes."

"Maybe he didn't shoot himself by accident." Rob let the statement hang in the air. Joe Tatum was volatile and prone to extreme emotions. An accidental shooting wasn't the only possible explanation.

Lindsay dismissed the idea. "I can't see him trying to off himself. Can you? And why would he have shot himself on my porch? It doesn't make sense."

When they entered the waiting area, John was seated with his back to them. His shoulders rose with gasping sobs. He was facing Anna, who covered her face with her hands. Lindsay's heart jumped into her throat as they approached the pair. She and Rob exchanged worried looks. Lindsay set the coffee and doughnuts down on a small table and she and Rob came around to face John. Her mouth fell wide open when she saw his expression. His face was tear-streaked and contorted…with laughter. Catching sight of Rob and Lindsay, John exclaimed, "He's okay!" Lindsay and Rob broke into relieved smiles, but still didn't understand how the situation had changed so completely in the few minutes that they were gone.

"We can go in and see him," John said.

Anna led them along the corridor, explaining to Lindsay and Rob, "Head injuries almost always bleed heavily, and I know this one looked like the St. Valentine's Day Massacre to you guys. But Joe's wound was superficial. The bullet was travelling at an angle, and the extra protection from the metal plate in his head meant that, instead of a fatal wound, he's probably going to come away with a bad concussion and another scar to add to his collection."

"I knew he was hard-headed," John cut in, "but I never thought that it would save his life."

Anna laughed with the rest of them, but when she spoke, her tone was measured. "He's not totally out of the woods. We'll have to monitor him here for a few days and then I want him to follow up with Dr. Checkoway, the neurosurgeon who treated him, in a few weeks." Anna's eyes flicked to Lindsay's face, which revealed a telling blush at the mention of Drew's name. She continued. "And they had to remove the top of his left ear, so he's probably lost his chance at this year's Miss Teen USA title."

"But he's going to be okay, right?" John asked.

"I'm optimistic. We were afraid that there would be intercranial bleeding because of his previous injury, but the surgeon said that head CT looked good. Well, as normal as things can look when someone has a metal plate stuck in their head. And he's conscious and talking. We should know if he's had any impairment or loss of function in the next couple of days."

They found Joe in a recovery room. With a two-inch thick layer of white gauze around his head, he looked like a half-finished mummy. John took a seat in the chair next to his father's bedside and clasped his hand. "I thought you were a goner, Pop."

Joe's glassy, swollen eyes opened a crack. He mumbled, "I

shot him. I shot that varmint."

Anna, Rob and Lindsay exchanged confused glances. "He must be confused—thinking of the last time, with the rabbit," Rob whispered.

"Scared him good," Joe continued. He closed his eyes again, and drifted off to sleep, muttering.

Chapter 39

Once Joe was comfortably settled into the recovery room, Lindsay tracked down a certain Dr. Belinda Jesper in the ER. The doctor was old and grouchy, didn't particularly like Lindsay, and wasn't particularly interested in Lindsay's (or anyone else's) problems. She was the perfect person to examine her knee. Other doctors might advise rest, physical therapy, or even surgery. Convalescing, however, didn't seem like a real option to Lindsay. She was due to begin her night shift in less than an hour, and she had far too much to do to lay around at home with her feet up. True to form, Dr. Jesper exhibited the bedside manner of a pit viper. "I'm on break, you know," she complained, rolling up the leg of Lindsay's scrubs. She took only the most cursory look and poked the red lump on the top of Lindsay's kneecap with her thumb. "Looks infected. Haven't you spent enough time in this hospital to know that you have to keep a wound clean?" She wrote Lindsay prescriptions for a strong painkiller and a course of antibiotics. "You should really see a doctor about this," she snapped, as she tore the prescriptions off the pad. What she meant, of course, was, "You should see a doctor who gives a damn, on your own time."

Lindsay filled the prescriptions in the hospital pharmacy and immediately downed two Percocet. Within minutes, she regretted taking the medication. Although it numbed the pain, it also intensified her feeling of distraction and unease. She wandered, murky-headed, through her shift. When she visited with patients, her words seemed like garbled, meaningless sounds coming from another person's mouth.

Lindsay wandered down to Joe's room to check his recovery. As she raised her hand to knock on the door, she nearly collided with Versa Bullard, who was leaving the room hastily. Lindsay had to step backward to keep from being knocked over.

"Wrong room. These hospital corridors all look the same," Versa said.

"You confused Joe Tatum's room with your husband's?"

"Joe is in there? I saw someone wrapped in bandages, but I couldn't tell who it was." As she spoke, she looked straight at Lindsay. She didn't so much as twitch an eyelid.

"Well now, let's see if I can find Buford's room." She turned and began to walk away. Lindsay followed.

"Aren't you at all curious about how Joe ended up in the hospital?" Lindsay said. "After all, I know you two are old friends."

"I couldn't care less what that old sack of stupid does with himself."

"Well, if you did care, I'd tell you that he's going to be okay."

Versa stopped and confronted Lindsay. "Are you deaf? I do not give a rat's behind about that man." She set off again at a brisk pace. Lindsay turned to follow her but the sudden change of direction triggered a spike of pain through her knee. She let out an involuntary yelp and clutched the wall for support.

"What's wrong with you?" Versa demanded.

"I hurt my knee. I'm taking a painkiller, but I don't think it's kicked in yet, as far as killing pain. As far as making my head feel like it's full of Karo syrup, it's working like a charm."

Versa rolled her eyes. She donned the hot-pink reading glasses that always hung by a beaded chain around her neck. She rummaged in her purse and pulled out a plastic pill case with multiple compartments, each containing a selection of brightly-colored pills. The effect was like a miniaturized version of the pick-and-mix sweets tubs at a candy shop. Versa flicked open various lids and extracted two pills—one small and green, one large and ginger-colored. "Here, take those."

"What are they?"

"That one is oregano oil. It helps with inflammation. That one is olive leaf extract. It's good for the joints. I use them for my back."

"Oregano and olive, huh? Maybe I should just eat a medicinal pizza." Lindsay indicated the other compartments. "What are all those other ones in there?"

Versa flicked open the lids and enumerated. "These are

aspirins, because I get headaches from all this stress. Those whitish ones are evening primrose. These little round ones are Buford's relaxing pills. These other ones are for his heart. The pink ones, we both take for cholesterol. These are Ginkgo biloba, for memory. These big suckers are Echinacea."

"What are those?" Lindsay pointed to a compartment filled with small blue pills.

Versa hesitated. "If you must know, those are my weight-loss pills. Don't tell the kids. I told them that I'm doing that Miami Beach diet, but I'm really taking these. They're packed full of ancient Chinese herbs that suppress the appetite and speed up metabolism. The Empress of China herself takes them." Anyway, I've lost almost four pounds since May so they're really working." Versa snapped that compartment closed. She proffered the oregano and olive oil pills once again. "You should really try these."

Lindsay shrugged and deposited the pills in the pocket of her white chaplain's coat. "Can't hurt, right?"

"Of course not. They're all natural." Versa checked her watch. "I'm going home to get in a nice cool bath."

"I thought you were checking on Buford."

"I'll be back soon. Don't you worry your pretty, little head."

Chapter 40

It wasn't until several hours into an unusually hectic night shift that Lindsay finally had a moment to herself. The overnight on-call chaplain was tasked with covering emergencies—unexpected deaths, frantic ER patients. Often, Lindsay spent most of the shift tucked up in the uncomfortable cot in the chaplain's office, trying unsuccessfully to catch a few hours of sleep. Tonight, however, emergencies seemed to be the rule rather than the exception. After seeing half a dozen patients, Lindsay returned to the chaplain's office, intending to type up her notes. She plunked her stack of paperwork down on the desk along with a can of Fanta, an orange, and a bag of Cheetos. (She was in an orange food mood.) She pressed the button to fire up the aged PC. She clicked open the pull-tab on her soda can and sipped impatiently as she watched the computer creak along even more slowly than usual. A sharp tap at the door broke Lindsay's focus on the computer's seemingly endless series of boot-up maneuvers and diagnostic checks. Lindsay's mouth dropped open when her father entered the office, looking ashen-faced and haunted. He sat down in the small, wooden chair in the corner of the office, searching the room like a convict trying to find a way out of his cell. Several times, he formed his mouth into shapes as if to speak, but no sound emerged. Finally, he said, "I've been trying to reach you for days."

"I've had a lot going on."

"You never return my calls."

"Dad, I don't have time for a lecture on family responsibility right now."

"I stopped by your house. There's blood all over your porch. Do you have any idea how worried I was?"

"Well, I'm fine, as you can see." Lindsay glanced at the computer screen, which flashed an error message and informed anyone who cared to know that it was planning to restart itself in "Safe Mode".

Jonah sighed. "Your mother came to see me. She wants a divorce."

Lindsay threw up her hands. "Well, hallelujah! Did you think I'd be opposed or something? For heaven's sake, it's about time you two made a clean break." His face remained impassive, so Lindsay tried a more conciliatory tone, "If you're worried about what people at church will think, don't. A few of the old biddies will snipe, but I know everyone will understand."

Jonah's expression remained grim. "A divorce isn't all she wants," he continued. Lindsay straightened up, her tight expression now beginning to mirror Jonah's. "If I don't give her what she wants, she said she's going to come back."

"What do you mean 'come back'?"

"Come back, as in show up at the church next Sunday, take up a position in the front pew and be the pastor's wife again."

"You guys have lived apart for more than fifteen years. She's had Lord knows how many boyfriends in the meantime. Why would she want to come back?"

"Because she wants me to give her $20,000."

"What?! Where does she expect you to get $20,000?"

"From the money I embezzled from the church."

Lindsay removed her glasses. She rubbed her temples in slow circles, as if trying to conjure a genie from a magic lamp. If she was still experiencing any residual brain fog from the painkiller, it had certainly cleared now. She leaned closer to her father. All the light and air in the room seemed to be concentrated into a single crushing point that throbbed painfully between her eyes. "You took money from your own church? Jesus, Dad, how low can you sink?" She could barely spit out the words.

Jonah jumped out of his chair and began to pace the room. "I've lived in the same two-bedroom house for almost my entire life. I drive a ten-year-old Buick, when I'm not riding a 200cc motorcycle to save on gas. My annual vacation is two weeks at Aunt Harding's house on the Outer Banks. Where exactly do you think I am hiding my vast, illicit fortune? I would never, ever take money from the church. How could anyone who knows me think that?! Dag blast it, Lindsay, if even you doubt me, no wonder someone like your mother would! And I don't want to hear you using Jesus' name in vain!" During his monologue, Jonah's face had gone from almost translucently white to an unnatural shade of claret red. Lindsay couldn't recall ever seeing him so angry. In fact, she couldn't recall the last time she had seen him angry…period. Jonah crossed his arms and stared at the ceiling.

The computer emitted a series of beeps—beeps that indicated that the boot-up had failed and the whole process needed to begin again. Lindsay glanced at the blue screen and then turned back to face her father. His eyes remained fixed on the air conditioning vent above her head. "I'm sorry," she said quietly. She turned toward Jonah and began to speak, her words piling up thick and fast like snow on a frozen field. "Timothy pretended he was gay and left me. He made me lie to everyone because he said he was scared to come out. Really, though, he just didn't love me. Now he's having a baby with a Stepford wife nutcase with beautiful hair. Mom sent me a birthday card and called me. I thought she was trying to make things right, but now it's plain as a drink of water that she wanted to try to cozy up to me to get to the money she thinks you're hiding. Also, you may have heard that Silas Richards was arrested? Well, I'm the reason. And now I'm beginning to doubt he did it. This morning, Joe Tatum shot himself in the head right on my front porch."

The angry furrows on Jonah's forehead began to reorganize themselves into an expression of concern. His voice softened as he said, "Why didn't you tell me any of this?"

"I don't know," Lindsay inhaled deeply and sighed. She reached across the desk for her soda, bringing the half-empty can toward her lips. She paused thoughtfully with the can poised in mid-air. She set it on the desk and bent down to look at the computer's CPU. She tipped the machine forward, resting the front side on the ground, so that the fan and the rear cable were exposed. She reached for her soda can, extended her arm, and poured the entire contents through the air vents in the back of the computer. For a few seconds, the inner workings sizzled, sputtered, and fried. Finally, there was silence. Lindsay set the machine back upright and resumed her seat. "I suppose they'll have to buy a new one now," she said evenly, staring at the now blank monitor.

Jonah regarded her without emotion; as if Lindsay

sabotaging the office computer with a sugary beverage was the most natural thing in the world. Finally he said, "Aren't you worried about losing everyone's work?"

"It's all backed up on the hospital's server."

"Well then."

There was a moment's pause, and then Lindsay spoke. "The jet ski," she said.

Jonah did not register surprise at her non-sequitur, instead taking up the dangling thread of the conversation. "You were right. She told me that she was there that day, at the revival. That confirmed all her suspicions. She thought that we rigged the raffle so you'd win. Her mind is so addled by her own sinfulness that she can't imagine that anyone could let so much money pass through their hands and not skim off the top."

"You've got to fight her," Lindsay said with a sudden ferocity. "Let her move in. So what? You can outlast her. She'll get bored of the game. She'll see that you don't have any money. She'll go away."

"You don't understand, honey. She is my wife. She knows that I will hold up my end of the marriage contract, even if she won't hold up hers." Jonah shook his head sadly and said, "Maybe she wouldn't have pushed on me this hard in the past, but this new friend of hers, Leander Swoopes, has her wound around his little finger. He came with her when she called in. You should have seen the way he orders her around. I can't understand what she sees in him, I have to say. Scrawny little fellow with big green bug eyes. They said that they're coming over to the house tomorrow so I can give them my decision."

"They broke into my house," Lindsay said. It was the first time she had given voice to her suspicions. She couldn't help but notice that she had unconsciously chosen to state it as fact, rather than hedging with a "might have" or an "I think." Deep down, she had known that the shadowy form in the hallway that night was her mother. "I knew it was her, but I didn't understand why until now. Her calling me and sending the card must have been the soft sell. They were trying to butter me up to get to your treasure trove. Or maybe they thought I was in on the scheme. They were staking us out. That white truck outside my house the night you were over—

that was them. The weird note and the smoking man. The green-eyed man looking in my window. Then the revival. And the break in."

"When did your house get robbed? Did you call the police?"

"How could I go to the police and say that I thought my mom had robbed my house and stolen the jet ski I won at my father's church picnic? Anyway, Sarabelle and her boyfriend went through all my papers; they must have been looking for evidence of where all your money was hidden."

Lindsay's pager buzzed. With a little groan of frustration, she dialed the ER's extension on the office phone. "Hi, this is Chaplain Harding. I just got your page." She nodded as the voice on the other end spoke. When she hung up, she turned back to Jonah, "I'm sorry, Dad, but I've got work to do. I'll come by your house in the morning, and we'll sort this out. I promise. Don't do anything until we've talked some more."

##

Her shift trudged on until the early morning hours, when Lindsay found herself alone by Joe Tatum's bedside, watching his chest rise and fall with each deep breath. Rob and John had gone home to sleep, and she had promised to look in on Joe during her shift. She drew the curtains across the window, not wanting the light from the approaching dawn to disturb him. It was strange to see Joe's usually animated face so still and peaceful. The vulnerability didn't suit him at all. As she took up her seat at his bedside, there was a soft knock on the door.

"Come in," Lindsay said, rising from her chair.

Drew strode into the room. The door swung quietly shut behind him, leaving the two facing each other awkwardly in the half-darkness, like twelve-year-olds at a grade school dance. Each waited for the other to speak. Lindsay had never before had someone trigger such a jumble of emotions in her. She wanted simultaneously to kiss him, punch him, laugh at him, and run screaming from the room, never to be seen again. Whatever array of emotions Drew was feeling, he was the first to regain his composure and speak. "The nurse told me I could find John Tatum in here."

"You just missed him."

"Oh. I just wanted to tell him something." He rocked on his heels as he spoke, seeming undecided about whether to move backward or forward.

"I can give him a message."

"It wouldn't be appropriate to discuss the patient's situation with someone outside the immediate family," he said warily. He looked at her for a long moment; she could almost see him mentally flipping through the federal guidelines on patient confidentiality. The longer he stood silent, radiating a kind of bureaucratic aloofness, the further Lindsay's emotional pendulum swung in the direction of 'punch him.'

"If you're worried about HIPAA, don't be," she said, using the acronym for the patient privacy rules. "In addition to being a trusted friend of the Tatums and a Christian minister, don't forget that I am a hospital employee who is bound by the same rules as you are," she snapped. She knew that her level of annoyance was disproportionate with the situation. After all, Drew was just doing his job. Meticulously. But she found the formality of their interaction off-putting.

"Sorry. Nothing personal. Could you let John, or Mr. Tatum, if he regains consciousness, know that the police are going to stop by in a little while to ask some questions."

"The police?"

Drew had begun their interaction a little uncertainly, but now his tone was cool and commanding; it was a tone that Lindsay imagined he used in the operating room. "We pulled a bullet out of Joe's scalp. Not a piece of debris. A bullet."

"I don't understand."

"I'm not a ballistics expert, but I took forensics classes in medical school. If Mr. Tatum's gun was loaded with blanks, as his son swears it was, it is possible that some foreign matter lodged in the chamber could have become a projectile. Even with a blank in the gun, being shot at very close range can be dangerous. But this was not a blank or a piece of debris; it was an actual bullet. Either Mr. Tatum had slipped live rounds in his gun without you or his son seeing, managed to hold his gun at an incredibly improbable angle that defies the laws of physics, and then, accidentally or not, shot himself…" He trailed off.

"Or?" Lindsay demanded.

"Or someone was trying to kill him."

Chapter 41

Lindsay sat on the cold linoleum in the hallway outside Joe's room and closed her eyes. Her thought process had come completely unmoored. She felt like Dorothy from the *Wizard of Oz*, spinning wildly through the air while little snippets of the past few days' events played in a tiny window inside her mind.

She decided she should call Jonah and let him know that she might not make it to his house after all. As she fished around in the pockets of her white coat for her cell phone, she fingered the herbal remedies that Versa had given her. She pulled them out and examined them. Her knee pain had dimmed to a dull throb. The painkiller she'd taken earlier combined with Jonah's and Drew's revelations, made her feel lightheaded and giddy.

She looked up at the sound of voices and saw Warren striding quickly down the hall, accompanied by Special Agent Fleet. She pocketed the pills again and walked up to greet the men.

Warren looked dismayed to see Lindsay. He clearly hadn't expected to have to continue the charade he had begun in the library the other night. "You remember my, uh, girlfriend, Lindsay?" Warren said to Fleet. "Lindsay is a friend of the Tatum family. She was there when Mr. Tatum was shot," Warren explained, as if to excuse her presence. He turned back to Lindsay. "Is Mr. Tatum, Sr. available for questioning?"

"Available for, yes. Coherent enough for, I'm afraid not," answered a voice from behind Lindsay. She spun around to find Drew standing just behind her with his arms crossed over his chest. Avoiding eye contact with her or Warren, he addressed Agent Fleet directly. There was no doubt that he had heard Warren refer to Lindsay as his girlfriend.

"I believe we spoke on the phone. I'm the neurosurgeon who operated on Mr. Tatum." He and Fleet exchanged introductions and handshakes.

Fleet flipped through a small notebook. “What about Mr. Tatum’s son? John? Is he available?”

Lindsay sputtered, “He’s at home. They were tired. I mean, he went to sleep. At his home.”

Fleet flashed a quick, contemptuous glance at her. “If you’ll excuse us, Miss Harding, Sergeant Satterwhite and I need to have a few words with Dr. Checkoway.”

As the three men walked away, Lindsay willed a tornado to come along and sweep her into another world. Instead, she remained fixed in the middle of the hallway staring at the point where the corridor dead-ended into a large pane of glass. The black night outside was invisible; the window reflected back a forlorn image of the empty hall and Lindsay’s small white-coated frame. Two orderlies emerged from the stairwell behind her, holding sacks full of food from a nearby, all-night burger joint. The restaurant was famous for offering milkshakes in 150 flavors. The two men walked slowly past Lindsay in the direction of the window.

“Why does my order always got to be the one they get wrong?” the first man complained, sucking his milkshake disconsolately through a straw. “Blueberry Cheesecake Milkshake and Strawberry Cheesecake Milkshake. Ain’t the same thing.” He took another sip. “I don’t like strawberry. I don’t even know why I’m eating this.”

“Then quit eating it.”

“I got more than half of it left. I can’t waste it.”

“Fine, give it to me, then,” said the second man. He took a sip and stopped, looking questioningly at the first. “I thought you said that this was strawberry cheesecake.”

“It is.”

“I can’t taste no difference between this and blueberry cheesecake.”

“I think they just change what color cheesecake they use.”

“But they taste the same.”

“I still like the blueberry one better.”

The second orderly pried the plastic lid off the top and surveyed the contents. “Yeah, I see what you saying. The other color is better. This one look like blood and guts.”

Although Lindsay had only been half-listening to their

exchange, there was something in the content of their conversation that flipped a little switch in her mind and lit up the electric grid of her brain. She hurried past the two orderlies in a frantic quest to find Versa Bullard before any more harm was done.

Chapter 42

Visiting hours had long since passed, but Lindsay hoped that Versa might be upstairs with Buford. The hospital staff had gotten to know the Bullards well during the past weeks. They clearly sympathized with the family's predicament and Lindsay had observed that they now let Versa come and go as she pleased. Lindsay opened the door to Buford's room without knocking. As she'd hoped, Versa was stationed next to Buford's bed. Her hand rested heavily on top of his as she dozed in her chair. A loud-mouthed infomercial salesman exclaimed and extolled from the wall-mounted television. Lindsay shook Versa's shoulder to awaken her. "Versa, I need to see those pills again."

Versa jumped in her seat and released her hold on Buford's hand. She put her hand over her heart and shook her rigidly coiffed head. "Jumping Jehosephat! You scared the sausage stuffing out of me!"

"Sorry. I just need to see your pills. Please."

Versa wiped the sleep out of her eyes. "Don't tell me the ones I gave you wore off already."

Lindsay kept silent and held out her hand. Versa was clearly irritated. She was not a woman who was used to being commanded and she didn't take kindly to the insistence of the elfin dictator who stood before her. She weighed Lindsay up with a long, hard-eyed stare. Lindsay met her gaze head on, unblinking. After what seemed like an eternity, Versa bent her head and rummaged through her purse for the pill case. When she finally drew it out, Lindsay all but snatched it from her hand, popped open the clear plastic lid of one of the compartments and drew out one of Versa's diet pills. She turned it over and over, holding it up to the light and examining it like a jeweler assessing the brilliance of a cut diamond. "Do you have the bottle that these came in?"

"No. I threw it away." She rolled her eyes. "Don't tell me a skinny little thing like you is worrying about your weight."

Lindsay's tone became grave. "Versa, where did you get these?"

"Off the internet," Versa said. Noting Lindsay's raised eyebrows, she become defensive. "They're packed with ancient Chinese herbs that have been proven for thousands of years. It's a very reputable company."

"I need this," Lindsay said, pocketing the pill. She popped open another compartment of the pill holder and grabbed a second pill. "I need one of these, too." Without another word, she rushed out of the room.

Lindsay used her best powers of persuasion to coax the duty nurse into giving her the cell phone number of the doctor who had been treating Buford. The doctor was at home, sound asleep at this early hour, but when Lindsay explained her theory, he agreed to come over immediately. Lindsay waited near the nurses' station for thirty restless minutes until he finally appeared. She showed him the pills. The physician was a bald bookish black man named Dr. Peedie. He held the pills in the palm of his hand, scratched his hairless, freckled head, and pursed his lips. He raised them close to his thick-lensed glasses. Understanding lit up his face and he bounced on his heels like an impatient child. Dr. Peedie held the pills before him like they were shards of the True Cross and promised to get them tested as soon as he could.

Lindsay's cell phone had been vibrating almost constantly since her encounter with Versa. She pulled it out of her pocket now and saw that it registered calls from Rob, Warren, and her father. She prioritized them in her mind. Warren might have some information on Joe's shooting or on the Young investigation. Her father might have heard from Sarabelle. Rob might be calling with news about Joe. Maybe he had taken a turn for the worse. She decided that she would quickly run downstairs check on Joe to ease her mind before she returned the other calls. It would only take a minute. Lindsay rushed off down a little-used flight of stairs behind the nurses' station, gritting her teeth as spikes of pain shot through her injured leg with each impact.

The stairwell was lit by the dim green glow of flickering fluorescent lights. The only sounds she could hear were the buzz of the lights and the muted fall of her own footsteps on the rubberized treads of the staircase. She felt like she was in a dream, the kind where you desperately need to get somewhere but your body is stuck in place. The threads of normal life were unwinding—her mother's reappearance, her love life, Vernon's murder, Joe's shooting, Buford's poisoning—and the pattern that could weave it all together was just beyond her reach.

As she rounded the final switchback of the stairwell at full speed, she smacked face-first into a something large and solid. The impact sent her spinning sideways, where she collided violently with the concrete breezeblock wall. With the force of the impact, her injured knee buckled and she hurtled forward down the stairs. With each impact, pain surged over her like tsunami waves, engulfing her and sinking the small ship of her consciousness. The last thing she was aware of before she blacked out was a familiar voice calling her name and a large, dark form bending over her crumpled body.

Chapter 43

"The angle of impact was inconsistent with a self-inflicted wound. Again, I'm no expert, but the entry wound seemed too small and round for a shot at close range."

"I can't believe I didn't catch it. When I worked in Jersey, I saw GSWs almost every day. Here, maybe two or three a month. And some of those are hunting accidents. You haven't experienced hunting season here yet. A couple of cases of Pabst Blue Ribbon mixed with half a dozen good ole' boys, add guns and stir. Honestly, you haven't lived until you've tweezed a few dozen pieces of buckshot out of a redneck's butt."

"I can hardly wait."

"Anyway, I'm sure I missed it because it was Joe. That clouded my judgment. The problem with living in this Podunk town and working in this Podunk hospital is that I know half the people who roll through the doors."

"Look. I think she's regaining consciousness."

Lindsay felt her eyelid pried open. She was blinded by the intrusion of a dazzling beam of white light. Her ears had been awake for several minutes, listening without understanding to a conversation about the butts of rednecks. The rest of her, however, seemed to be stubbornly clinging to oblivion. The light flashed in her eyes again. "Hey, Linds. It's Anna. Can you hear me?" Anna leaned over her, again shining a small flashlight into her eyes. Lindsay struggled to sit upright. Her legs felt like they were encased in concrete. After a brief struggle, she gave up, and slumped back onto the pillows.

"Mount Moriah isn't Podunk, it's charming. And get that light out of my face, you Yankee snob," Lindsay mumbled. Anna smiled and stroked Lindsay fondly on the cheek. Lindsay took in the scene around her. She was seeing the familiar confines of one of the more commodious of Mount Moriah's hospital rooms, but from the very unaccustomed perspective of a hospital bed. Turning her head, she made out an arc of pink sun cresting just above the low, black hills outside the windows.

"Why am I here?" Lindsay asked.

"You've had a minor head trauma," a familiar voice explained, "and you're lucky enough to have friends who know how to score you a sweet private room." Lindsay turned her head toward the door to see who had spoken these last words. Drew was standing a few feet from her bed, looking even more handsome than usual in jeans and a forest green button-down shirt. His shirt sleeves were rolled up to reveal the lithe muscles of his forearm. Her hands instinctively flew to cover the rising blush in her cheeks—the rapid movement ripping the tape that held an IV needle in the top of her hand. "Careful, there." Drew walked over to her bedside and bent toward her, checking the needle and re-securing it to her hand. "I'm really sorry about the KO."

"KO?"

"You don't remember? We collided in the stairwell. You fell into the wall."

"That was you?"

"Yeah. I had finished talking to the investigators and was on my way out."

"I don't remember hearing any footsteps. Were you just standing in the stairwell?"

"I was lost. I was trying to get my bearings and next thing I knew, you crashed into me like a human battering ram."

"Sorry."

"No need to be sorry. I'm just glad all you came away with was a concussion and a black eye."

"I have a black eye?" Lindsay's hands rose—more slowly this time—to touch the swollen tender skin around her right eye. Before anyone could answer her question, there was a soft knock on the door.

"Come in," Anna called.

Warren and Fleet entered the room. Or rather Fleet entered the room, and Warren trailed behind him like a solicitous butler. Fleet acknowledged Drew with a subtle inclination of his head. He turned and sized up Anna, as if deciding she was worthy of whatever question he was set to pose. He opened his small notebook with a sharp flick of his wrist and began to click and unclick a ballpoint pen.

Anna was not one to endure long, deliberative silences. "Who the hell are you?" she said flatly. She was also not one to beat around the bush.

"I am Special Agent Fleet of the Federal Bureau of Investigation. This is Sergeant Satterwhite from the New Albany Police. I take it you're a doctor of some kind? Is this woman available to give her statement about the Tatum shooting? It is imperative that we speak to her as soon as possible." Interesting, thought Lindsay. Just a few hours ago, I was gum stuck to his shoe. But now that he wants information from me, I am suddenly on the VIP list.

"Why are you asking me if she's available? She's right there." Anna said.

Fleet turned reluctantly toward Lindsay. "If you're ready to speak now, Miss Harding, I would like to take your statement. For the purposes of this enquiry, Sergeant Satterwhite has asked to be present to lend moral support, should you require it. Considering your personal relationship with him, I don't think it would be appropriate for him to participate in any official capacity."

"Personal relationship?" Anna raised her eyebrows at Lindsay.

As Lindsay opened her mouth to speak, there was another knock on the door. Cynthia, the pretty nurse Lindsay had met on the night she prayed with the Peechums, entered the room. "Well if it isn't Lindsay Harding, the famous voodoo priestess of Mount Moriah! Talk to any angels lately?" She smiled brightly. "I didn't realize you had a roomful of visitors. I was just going to check your vitals, but I can come back later." She turned to leave, but stopped when she caught sight of Warren. "Warren, honey? Is that you?"

"Cynthia? What are you doing here?"

"I work here, silly. Remember?" She let out a peal of laughter and gave him a quick peck on the cheek. "Who'd have thought that I'd run into my own darling husband!"

"Husband?" Fleet asked Cynthia, shooting a sharp-eyed glance toward Lindsay. Anna looked from Cynthia to Warren to Lindsay and back. Drew looked at Lindsay and then at the floor.

Warren just plain looked like he wanted to evaporate.

"Yep. I'm Warren's missus. Isn't that right, Warren?" Cynthia laughed.

"And you know Miss Harding as well?" Fleet asked.

"Sure. If you need an expert snake-handler or tongue-talker in this hospital, Lindsay is your gal," Cynthia said. "Well, I'll come back later to check on the patient." With that, she turned around and left.

A mile-deep cavern of silence opened in the middle of the room. Everyone seemed to be either attempting to make or avoid eye contact with everyone else. Finally, Drew raised his wrist and glanced theatrically at his watch. "Well, I'd better be going. I'm very, very late," he said. He made no further explanation; none was needed. He beat a hasty retreat.

Lindsay tried to sit up again, but she couldn't get her body to cooperate. She groaned in pain. "Oh. I forgot to tell you. I had the orthopedist put casts on your foot and ankle," Anna said.

"I broke my foot and ankle?!" Lindsay threw aside the blankets that covered the lower half of her body.

"No, but you need to stay off of your knee for a few weeks and let it heal. Drew said he told you that already. Even Dr. Jesper—yeah, you thought I wouldn't find out—thought that it was in bad shape. Clearly you are what we call a non-compliant patient. Desperate measures were called for."

"Is this even legal?"

"Read the cast." A heart was scrawled in thick black Sharpie. She traced her finger along and read: *Anna + Lindsay = BFF*. Lindsay sighed deeply and slumped back onto the pillow. "I've also hidden the scrubs you borrowed and your shoes, so don't try to leave before they discharge you. Drew says you should stay in at least one full day because of the severity of your concussion," Anna said. She rubbed her hands together and surveyed the room. "Well, I'd better be on my way, too. We should talk later, Lindsay." She stood where the door blocked her from the view of the men and pointed toward Warren. "Because I'd really love to know what you've been doing in your spare time."

Chapter 44

Lindsay's interview with Fleet was about as relaxing as a carpet bombing. As Fleet asked her again and again to recount the moments surrounding Joe's shooting, Lindsay imagined that he was writing "useless witness" in his little spiral-bound notebook, perhaps adding it to the end of a long list of damning assessments. Despite her dislike of Fleet, she genuinely tried to be helpful, and grew increasingly frustrated with her own inability to shed any light on the shooting. "You were inside the house?" Fleet asked for the third or fourth time.

"I was inside. John was outside. We were on opposite sides of the window."

"And you heard two loud bangs?"

"Yes."

"And you and John Tatum found Mr. Tatum unconscious on the porch?"

"Yes. Like I said, he was bleeding from the head. Just laying still. With the gun in his hands."

Fleet paused a moment before asking the next question. "Do you have any enemies, Miss Harding? Any reason to believe that you might have been the real target of the shooter?"

"Enemies?" Lindsay had been lulled by Fleet's repetition, but this new line of questioning snapped her back to attention.

"I understand that you were recently the victim of a home invasion?" Fleet continued.

Lindsay shot a deadly look at Warren, whose eyes were glued firmly to the ground. "That is a private, family matter."

"Oh?" Fleet raised his eyebrows. "I'm not sure I understand how a home invasion could be a private, family matter." He leaned closer, his tone shifting from patronizing to severe. "It seems to me, that if my home was broken into and my property was stolen, I would want to report it to the police. Maybe you can explain why you didn't see fit to do that?"

"I think I can guess which one you get to be when you boys play Good Cop, Bad Cop down at the station," Lindsay countered irritably.

"Is this a joke to you?" Fleet said, feigning surprise. "I am trying to solve an attempted murder, and see if it links in any way to a shooting and a poisoning. I thought, as a good citizen, a good Christian, you might want to help me out with that. And if I'm not mistaken, I thought that the victims involved were all friends of yours. I guess the humor of the situation eludes me." He hadn't made eye contact with her as he spoke, instead lowering his head and jotting something in his notebook. Lindsay imagined a new line below her name saying: Uses humor as a defense mechanism. Or worse. He had snatched the moral high ground so effortlessly that Lindsay could only marvel at him from her position down in the dust. It was an old trick of her father's that she still hadn't learned how to avoid—back her into a corner, wait for her glib response, and go in for the kill with sanctimony.

Lindsay tried to move further away from Fleet, but the tug of the IV line and the tangle of the bed sheets around her cast rooted her in place. She was now even more impressed that Kimberlee had stood up under Fleet's withering interrogation tactics. "Miss Harding, if you know something that might assist our investigation, it would be in your best interest to reveal that now." He looked up from his notebook, his gaze locking with hers. "Not doing so would be…criminal." Fleet selected the last word carefully, allowing its implied threat to hang in the air. "It would be a terrible tragedy, a crime, if your friend was shot in the head for something that you did. Or because of someone that you are involved with." Fleet's face was now so close that Lindsay could feel his hot breath on her cheek. It smelled sharply antiseptic, a mix of menthol and bleach. A flood of frightening questions deluged her mind. Did Fleet know something that she didn't? Was there some connection between Joe's shooting and her mother? That would mean that not only had her mother swindled and robbed her, but also tried to kill her. Angry tears pooled in the corners of her eyes.

"Look, I don't know anything," Lindsay said, the tears beginning to stream down her cheeks. She hadn't cried unrestrainedly in years—instead, she scheduled regular "purging" sessions. She would watch *Beaches* or *Love Story* alone on a

Saturday night and sob until she had emptied the well of emotion that built up during the week. Now, however, she felt tired and hungry, and the possibility that her mother was somehow involved in shooting Joe was almost too terrible to contemplate.

"Don't play dumb with me, Miss Harding," Fleet said, standing over her and pointing an accusing finger in her face.

"Leave me alone," Lindsay whimpered helplessly, pulling the thin blanket up to her chin. She was defeated. She was a small, dispirited child with a criminal for a mother and a broken heart. The ruins of her life smoldered white-hot in her mind. Suddenly, Fleet's body jerked backward away from her. Warren stood behind Fleet with his hand clamped down on Fleet's shoulder, like a club bouncer ready to eject a rowdy patron. "You're going to need to leave now," Warren said. His voice was both matter-of-fact and menacing.

Fleet brushed off Warren's grip with an agitated flick of his hand. He spun around, squaring off with Warren. The two men locked eyes. "Sergeant Satterwhite, I am questioning this witness. Please remember that you are not here in an official capacity."

"And you need to not be here at all in about ten seconds." Warren's nostrils flared and bright circles of color pooled in each of his cheeks.

"Is that a threat?" Fleet said incredulously.

"No. That is a statement about what needs to happen." The sight of the two men facing off was like something out of Wild Kingdom—gorillas bellowing and beating their glistening chests. Finally, after what seemed like an eternity, the standoff ended. Warren had won, and Fleet stomped moodily out of the room. Warren stood with his back to Lindsay, his shoulders heaving. After a few moments, he inhaled deeply and crumpled into the chair next to her bed. He was wearing a short-sleeved gray dress shirt. He had broken a sweat, and now the thin material clung to the long muscles of his arms and chest. "I don't even know where to start," he sighed. "I suppose I should just say that I'm sorry. For everything."

Lindsay daintily wiped her nose on a corner of the bed sheets. "Everything, huh? So what would fall into that category?" She pulled herself into a sitting position, cocked her head, and itemized his offences: "Pretending I was your girlfriend, thus ruining any chance I had with a handsome, heterosexual brain surgeon? And making it look to everyone like I am not just your girlfriend, but your mistress, since you are apparently two-timing your Vegas wife, Cynthia, with me?" She smacked her head with the heel of her hand, as if another thought just occurred to her. "Oh! Or dragging me to the library, where I proceeded to find an important piece of evidence, which you took credit for, even as you allowed Fleet to belittle me?"

"And telling Fleet about the break-in at your house, which has now led him to accuse you of being a party to attempted murder." Warren said, with a guilty nod.

"I wasn't going to mention that, but, yeah, add it to the list." Lindsay said. "You know what, Warren? I am never one to hold a grudge. But in your case, I'm going to have to make an exception. I've decided to be mad at you for a good long while. You could say you're sorry again, but I'd still be mad at you. You could punch Fleet in the face for me, and I'd still be mad at you. You could singlehandedly rescue a burning busload of orphans, but I'd still be mad at you."

"So you're saying that you're still mad at me?"

"Yeah, I really am." Lindsay sighed. "Now that we have that out of the way, tell me about Joe. Is he okay? Did he see the person who shot him?"

Warren appeared grateful for the small reprieve Lindsay had given him by changing the subject. "He's fine. They think he'll be discharged tomorrow or the next day. We talked to him just a little while ago. His statement was that he saw someone crouching in the line of trees at the side of your house, acting suspicious. Joe pretended not to notice anything, but started loading his gun—real casual, so it looked like he was just checking the thing over. All he had with him were blanks, but he thought that'd do to scare the guy off. Then he saw that the person in the bushes had a gun, too, and that they were raising it at Joe. Quick as a flash, Joe emptied both barrels at him. That must have been enough to throw off the shooter's aim. The bullet he fired at Joe ricocheted off the porch rail and hit Joe in the side of the head. By the time you and John got out to the porch, the shooter must have run off through the woods."

"Did you find anything at my house? Any trace of the shooter?" Lindsay asked.

"Afraid not. We went over the whole scene, but came up empty." Warren shook his head.

"Then why does Fleet think I'm involved? What could have given him that idea?"

"I did," Warren said. He leaned in closer to her, his face solemn. "I hate to be the one to tell you this, Lindsay, but your mother is involved with a pretty dangerous fellow."

Chapter 45

"What does Sarabelle have to do with any of this?" Lindsay couldn't stand for the woman to be referred to as her mother.

"The day after the break-in, I came back to your house, and I lifted some prints from the door of your shed. I asked a friend in the department to analyze them," Warren replied.

"I told you that I didn't want to involve the police!" Lindsay's voice was shrill with rage. When she and Warren had been friendly in high school, one of the things she most liked about him was his total lack of interest in breaching the wall she had built to guard information about her home life. They made small talk, laughed at the teachers. He had never once asked her about her parents. Now he had blown her private life open for all to see, and the betrayal amplified her rage.

Warren waited a moment for Lindsay to calm down. When he spoke, he was neither defensive nor apologetic. "I was worried about you. I could tell that the break-in shook you up, and I wanted to help," he said sincerely. "And I was curious. You were acting so mysterious. There were two sets of prints: Sarabelle Harding and a guy by the name of Leander Swoopes. I'm going to guess that it's no surprise to you that your mother has had a few encounters with the law. Nothing too serious, mind you, worthless checks, forgery, and the like. But this Swoopes guy…" Warren shook his head. "Embezzlement, wire fraud, assault, and an outstanding warrant for trying to strangle his ex-girlfriend. He put her in a coma. She has permanent brain damage."

Lindsay inhaled sharply but said nothing. Warren continued, "I knew you wanted the robbery kept quiet, but how could I ignore the fact that a wanted criminal was right under my nose? I had to try to track them down. There's an all-points bulletin out for them and their car. If they're still in the area, I intend to find them."

As Warren spoke, Lindsay's anger metamorphosized into a

new emotion…fear. Fear for her father who would be getting a visit from Sarabelle and Swoopes in a few hours, fear that she was running out of time to help him, and, though she hated to admit it, fear for her mother, who might have gotten herself in over her head. "Have you found them?" she asked.

"Not yet," Warren said. "We got a rush order on a ballistics test on the bullet from Joe's head. It came back as a perfect match for the one that killed Vernon."

"Okay, so the same gun that killed Vernon shot Joe, too," Lindsay said. The tentacles of her mind were finally beginning to grasp the information that was laid out before her. "But there is no way Sarabelle would be involved in anything like that. Like you said, she's never been mixed up in anything really serious." A flicker of doubt crept into her voice. "And anyway, I still don't see why Fleet would think I have anything to do with this."

"Well, with that new ballistics evidence, the case against Silas is about as solid as Jell-O in a washing machine. He couldn't possibly have shot Joe, since he was locked up. Morgan's off the hook, too, because he was attending Silas's bail hearing at the time Joe was shot. So where does that leave us? It was partly your evidence about what you overheard Silas and Morgan say at the revival that put Silas away and cast suspicion on Morgan. It appears that your mother is linked up with this Swoopes character, and the fingerprints show that they were both at your house just before the shooting—a fact that you failed to inform the police of. You were there when Buford was poisoned, and you were there when Joe was shot. Both Buford and Joe might have information about Vernon's murder. It looks like some person or people are trying to silence witnesses. You have to admit that, to an outside observer, you seem to be in all the wrong places at all the wrong times."

"And it was convenient that just as you are casting around for a new suspect, a violent, wanted felon waltzed into town," Lindsay said.

"Exactly. Neither Silas nor Morgan could possibly have shot Joe."

Lindsay rubbed her temples. She felt like she had been watching a horror movie with her eyes taped open, and now she was drafted in as the movie's star. "So what's going to happen now?"

"Well, Silas was released on bail. Even though the case against him is a damn mess, we still have some good evidence with the diary and the meeting. It's possible that he contracted someone else to kill Vernon, and that person shot Joe on his orders."

Lindsay looked searchingly at Warren. "Tell me the truth. Do you think Sarabelle and Swoopes could be involved in this somehow?"

Warren opened his mouth to answer but was interrupted by a perfunctory knock on the door, followed by the rapidly entering footsteps of Dr. Peedie, the physician who had been treating Buford. "Sorry to interrupt, Chaplain Harding," he said, far too excitedly to be genuinely sorry. "They told me I could find you here. I just wanted you to know that you were right. The preliminary test results just came back. As you suspected, Mrs. Bullard's diet pills were the source of the poison, and the cause of the heart attack. One of the ingredients in them, sibutramine, has a proven link to heart attacks and strokes. It can be incredibly dangerous in high doses. It has been cropping up in counterfeit pills made in China and sold through third parties on the internet. The lab didn't test for it initially, however, because it's very rare. In addition to helping identify what had caused Mr. Bullard's symptoms, you might have saved Mrs. Bullard's life. Her blood also shows very high doses of the chemical in her body. If she had continued to take those pills, she was risking serious harm.

Dr. Peedie continued. "Mrs. Bullard's diet pills are so similar in appearance to the tranquilizer that Mr. Bullard had been prescribed that it's little wonder she, with her poor eyesight, got them confused." He paused, placing his fist under his chin like Rodin's Thinker. "But then, one never knows. Could it be that Mrs. Bullard poisoned herself to throw off suspicion?" He shook his head. He was no longer really addressing Lindsay. Instead, his gaze was fixed out the window at some invisible audience. "No, too risky, I would think. Perhaps someone intended to poison them both, but hadn't given either of them a lethal dose yet? It's a puzzle, and I am only one tiny, insignificant piece of the jigsaw." He smiled at the aptness of his metaphor. "I wonder if the police will interview me?" He turned his attention back toward Lindsay and involuntarily straightened his tie.

"We will. Definitely," Warren said, removing his badge from his back pocket, and displaying it for Dr. Peedie to inspect. "I'll need to hear all about your central role in solving this. For now, though, I need to finish questioning Chaplain Harding here."

Dr. Peedie's eyes grew wide. "How incredibly prompt! I only notified the police about twenty minutes ago. I'll let you carry on with your interview then." He fumbled in his wallet and handed Warren a business card. He proffered it like a teenage fan asking for an autograph. "That has my number. Oh, wait, let me write my home number on that as well. Call me anytime. Day or night. I humbly offer any assistance that I can possibly give." With that, Dr. Peedie rushed excitedly from the room.

Lindsay turned back to Warren and said, "Well, it's nice to see that at least someone is having a good time with all of this."

"You're going to have to bring me up to speed on the diet pills," Warren said, putting his badge back into his pocket. "You always seem to be one step ahead of me."

"I'll explain everything I know to you, but only if you do something for me first," Lindsay said. She fiddled with her IV needle until she was able to draw it slowly out of her hand. She sat up and hoisted her casted leg over the side of the bed.

"Anything."

"Wrap this gown around me so that it covers my butt. You're going to help me blow this popsicle stand."

Chapter 46

Lindsay and Warren followed a path of little-used corridors and stairwells; she wanted to leave the hospital unobserved. There wasn't any legal bar to Lindsay's leaving, but she didn't have time for any unnecessary hassle. The cast on her leg made her feel like she was doing a three-legged race with a sack of concrete as a partner. She glanced again at Warren's muscular arms, half-wondering if he would try to lift her off her feet the way that Drew had. Warren made no move to do so, however, offering only a supportive arm when she seemed particularly unsteady. They eventually made it, unseen, out to the lot where Warren was parked.

She scanned the lot for his Crown Victoria, but it was nowhere to be seen. Instead, he led Lindsay toward a neon green Honda motorcycle. At first she didn't believe it was his—it was cartoonish, with paint and chrome that glistened like a display of movie theater candy. The bike seemed incongruous with the buttoned-down template of Warren Satterwhite that Lindsay had constructed in her mind over the past week. This was no Harley—that mid-life crisis bike of suburban male fantasies. Nor was it the kind of cobbled-together amateur mechanic's bike that her father rode. This motorcycle was a serious, reckless piece of machinery designed to rend the air with a slash of neon green as it sped past you on the highway. Warren inserted a key in the small rear storage compartment and began to rummage inside it. He removed a rolled up pair of Cordura riding pants and a leather jacket. "Here, put these on," he said, passing the clothes to Lindsay.

Lindsay ran her hand over the heavy fabric. "I don't think these pants are going to fit over my cast. And it's way too hot to wear a jacket this heavy," she complained. The air temperature, despite the early hour, edged toward ninety, and the black asphalt of the parking lot was already unpleasantly warm against her bare foot.

"I'm going to guess that we'd get about three blocks before that blows off." Warren gestured to the flimsy, blue cotton hospital gown she was wearing. "So, unless you want to be known as the Lady Godiva of Mount Moriah, I'd suggest you try those on." Lindsay donned the riding gear without further protest while Warren issued more instructions. "Let the pants hang over your feet a little bit so you can put your heels on the footrests without frying your toes." The clothes swamped Lindsay's tiny frame. When Warren fixed the helmet on her head, she had the appearance of an astronaut whose spacesuit had been pricked with a large pin and deflated.

Lindsay had asked Warren to take her to her father's house. Even though Warren took great pains to ride slowly carefully, the roar of the motorcycle didn't allow for conversation. It wasn't until they reached Jonah's house that Lindsay was able to uphold her end of the bargain and brief Warren on how she had identified Versa Bullard's diet pills as the source of the toxin that had incapacitated Buford. "I guess I need to stop being surprised that you are a better detective than I am, and just kneel before you in admiration and awe," Warren said, with only a touch of mockery. He helped Lindsay dismount the motorcycle, holding her under the arms as she hoisted her cast-encased leg over the seat.

Lindsay took off the leather jacket and returned it to him. "Before you set up a shrine to honor my deductive genius, could you do me two more favors?" she said. "First, will you please make sure that whichever one of your esteemed colleagues questions Versa Bullard will go easy on her? If you really think I'm such a great detective you will trust me when I say that I don't think she poisoned her husband on purpose. Mind you, that warning is not so much to protect Versa as to protect whichever unfortunate police officer tries to bully her."

"You got it. What's the other favor?"

"Will you let me keep these pants for awhile? I don't think there's any way I can get them down over my cast without exposing my delicate underparts to half the neighborhood."

He shook his head and gave her a look of mock pity. "I really need those pants back right away. I can help you get them off, if you'll just bend over."

"Isn't there some kind of law against aiding and abetting my indecent exposure?"

"If there is, I'd do the time."

She punched him playfully on the shoulder, as he donned the jacket that she had returned to him and prepared to leave. He paused for a moment, holding his helmet in the crook of his arm. His expression became suddenly serious. He looked at the front of Jonah's house, and then back at Lindsay, searching her face earnestly. The look was so penetrating that a shiver ran up her spine. She felt like her face was made of glass, leaving the inner workings of her mind on display. "What?" Lindsay demanded, trying her best to draw a curtain over the broken machinery of her jumbled thoughts. She had not told Warren about the planned rendezvous with Sarabelle and Swoopes. With her father's reputation and her mother's freedom hanging in the balance, she couldn't risk involving him. The way he looked at her now, with a deep wrinkle of concern creasing his forehead, she felt certain that he knew that she was hiding something.

"Just take care of yourself. That's all," he finally said. He kick-started the motorcycle and took off down the street.

Lindsay made her way awkwardly across the dewy grass of her father's front lawn, dragging her hobbled leg behind her like a villain in a silent film. Jonah's house, where she'd spent much of her childhood, was an orange-brick bungalow with white shutters and window boxes bursting with red geraniums. There was no front porch, just a half-dozen concrete steps that led to the front door. On either side of the steps grew rows of evergreen bushes, each hand-trimmed into a perfect little cupcake of foliage. An American flag hung listlessly from a pole fixed to the wall next to the door. Attached to the left side of the house was a carport, a steel structure with a roof made of corrugated metal. In the South, a carport could serve as a garage, workshop, laundry room, patio, place to chain your snarling dogs, or all of the above. In Jonah's case, however, the carport was as neat as a pin, housing only his old Buick, a small storage cabinet, and two green plastic lawn chairs that lay stacked against the wall. Anyone who didn't know better could be forgiven for thinking it was the house of a fastidious old lady.

Lindsay went around the carport side of the house and let

herself in through the kitchen door. She found Jonah asleep at the kitchen table, still wearing the clothes he'd had on the previous night. His Bible lay open on the table next to him. The book was Jonah's most cherished possession. It bore an inscription from the famous preacher Billy Graham, with whom Jonah had struck up a brief acquaintance at a convention almost twenty years before. The book was beautiful, with an embossed leather cover and gilt-edged pages. Lindsay trailed her fingers lightly over the tissue-thin pages as she walked past the table.

Lindsay approached Jonah's ancient coffee maker. Jonah had had the machine as long as Lindsay could remember and it had long been a bone of contention between them. Chunks of coffee grounds would somehow insinuate themselves into the brew, rendering the beverage that emerged more akin to a hearty soup than to coffee. Lindsay had gone so far as to purchase new coffee makers for Jonah for three Christmases running, but he always returned them, saying, "The old one works just fine. You just need to know how to finesse it."

Lindsay removed the coffee pot and filled it with water. She put in a filter with fresh grounds—grounds that she knew would soon be sticking in her teeth. The noise of the machine and Lindsay's movements roused Jonah, who rubbed his eyes and sat up. He observed Lindsay's appearance with surprise. Her face was bruised on one side where she'd struck the wall. Her greasy hair coiled listlessly around her ears. The hospital gown that covered her top half clung unattractively to her sweaty torso. Warren's oversized motorcycle pants drooped low around her hips.

"You've looked better," he said.

"I've felt better," she replied, taking a seat at the table. She gestured to the Bible, "Any answers in there?"

"All the answers are in there, honey, as you well know." They smiled at each other, and for a brief moment they let themselves be soothed by the smell of coffee and the early morning sunlight that streamed in through the window. "What did you do to your leg?" Jonah asked. She had hiked up the motorcycle pants, and the bottom of her cast was now visible.

"It's not broken," Lindsay replied. Jonah raised his eyebrows inquisitively, but Lindsay waved his unspoken questions away with a shrug. "Long story. But since you brought it up, can I borrow your hacksaw?"

##

Half an hour later, Lindsay and Jonah sat in matching lawn chairs, drinking chunky coffee in the shade of the carport. A steady breeze was now blowing from the southeast, replacing the wet heat with a wet cool. Lindsay's cast lay in roughly-hewn pieces at their feet, like shards of ancient pottery. Lindsay had showered and changed into some clothes that she found lurking in the dresser of her former bedroom—a stonewashed denim miniskirt topped off with a Coors Lite t-shirt that she'd cut the collar out of. In her teens, Lindsay had favored the kind of clothes that would needle almost any parent—fishnet stockings, heavy metal t-shirts, midriffs—and Jonah, in particular, used to find her wardrobe infuriating. Lindsay wondered if she had subconsciously left this outfit behind in his house as a taunt. When she'd left for college, with no one there to care or complain, she gradually shifted her wardrobe to jeans and sweatshirts. These days, when she wasn't at home wearing pajamas or running clothes, she wore boring, sensible clothes and shoes with good arch support.

Lindsay and Jonah had managed to avoid discussing the imminent visit of Sarabelle and Swoopes while they were removing the cast. Now, however, a silence had descended, and the subject loomed large between them. "Did they say when they are going to be coming?" Lindsay finally asked.

"Just said sometime today," Jonah replied laconically.

Lindsay grew serious. "You need to know who you're dealing with, Dad. The police think this Swoopes guy is really dangerous." As she spoke, a violent gust of wind roared through the carport, as if to dramatize her words.

"That'll be Amanda." Jonah looked toward the low horizon.

"What? Who's Amanda?"

"The hurricane. Hurricane Amanda is supposed to make landfall around Cape Hatteras sometime this morning. She's supposed to reach here by tonight. Category 1 or 2. It's been all over the news."

"I haven't been following the news lately," Lindsay said. "I bet Aunt Harding will stay on the island." Jonah nodded. Lindsay's willful old aunt had ridden out many hurricanes on the Outer Banks. She battened down the hatches of her little bungalow like Captain Ahab making ready to confront the white whale. It usually took at least a Category 3 and a direct order from the National Guard to get her to consider evacuating to the mainland. Jonah and Lindsay had long ago ceased to worry for her safety. Another gust of wind blew in, bowing the pine trees like obedient courtiers. Lindsay waited for the rush of the wind to die down before she brought the subject back to Swoopes. "Did you hear what I said, Dad? There's a warrant out for this guy's arrest."

Jonah shook his head solemnly from side to side. "I don't want to call the police, if that's what you're suggesting. That wouldn't be fair to your mother."

Lindsay threw her hands up. "Please don't talk about what is fair to her. And please don't refer to her as my mother."

"She is, and always will be, your mother."

"Don't you think she stopped being my mother when she left? Or when she manipulated me for years? Or how about when she robbed my house the other day?" Lindsay said fiercely.

"She needs our forgiveness."

"Jesus Christ, Dad, why don't you ever stand up for yourself? When are you just going to tell her enough is enough?

"I will not hear you using that kind of language in my house."

"I can't believe that you are going to sit there and scold me about my language without saying a word against the thieving, drug-addicted slut who you had the misfortune to conceive a child with!"

"Lindsay Sarabelle Harding! Have you forgotten the commandment to honor your father and mother?"

"What about honoring your children? Huh? What about not abandoning them? Not lying to them? Not breaking promises to them? Not stealing from them? Maybe Moses ran out of space on the tablets for those commandments, or maybe they were just so goddamn obvious that he didn't think they needed to be written down!"

Jonah and Lindsay confronted each other like raging bulls. They were perched on the edges of their lawn chairs, their angry faces just inches apart. As usual, Jonah was the first to regain his composure. He took a deep breath and sat back in his chair. He sipped his coffee with a meditative calm, like an old man in a roadside diner. "We have to show your mother that we are better than that. She needs us to be shining examples of right living."

Lindsay ignored the white flag that her father was trying to raise. She could see only a furious red. "What about what I need? Have you ever considered that I might need you to stand up to her, if not for yourself, then for me?" Lindsay stomped inside the house and pulled the keys to Jonah's old Buick off the hook next to the back door. She stormed past him and got into the car. Jonah rose from his chair but didn't try to stop her. Before she drove away, she rolled down the car window and shouted, "In every relationship I've ever had, I've let myself be used and lied to. Guess what you've really taught me! Guess what you've really been a shining example of!" There was a squeal of tires as Lindsay sped away down the road, into the low clouds of the gathering storm.

Chapter 47

Lindsay drove toward her house, still fuming after her argument with her father. She knew that she probably wasn't in the right, but for once she didn't care. In fact, she wasn't even sure if there was a right and a wrong side to this argument. The problem of how to confront wickedness had baffled philosophers and politicians throughout history, and it wasn't going to be solved in a lawn chair argument between a pair of stubborn North Carolina pastors. The wind gusts that pushed in on the vanguard of the storm buffeted the car. Greenish-black clouds had begun to stack up on the horizon; the first bands of Amanda's wind and rain would be moving in soon. Lindsay found the gathering storm soothing. It was as if the weather understood her plight and was doing its best to reflect her dark mood. She rolled down the window, took deep breaths of the cool air, and began to calm down. As her anger subsided, she felt a creeping sense of worry about leaving Jonah alone to face Sarabelle and Swoopes. Half a dozen times, she considered turning the car around. In the end, however, her bitterness triumphed and she pulled the Buick into the driveway of her house, alongside her ancient Toyota. She let herself in, trying her best to ignore the trailing strands of yellow crime scene tape and the smears of Joe's blood that were still visible on the front porch.

Inside the house, the air was as thick and claustrophobic as a greenhouse. Insects buzzed lazily around the rooms, their droning alternating in pitch as they approached or flew away. A moth fluttered past. A breath of air stirred the stillness, like a leaf dropping on the surface of a puddle. Lindsay followed the source of the disturbance to the bathroom, where the half-repaired window stood wide open, screenless. John's toolbox lay open on the bathroom floor. She closed the bathroom door with a sigh. That moment just before Joe had been shot was the last slice of normal life that she could remember. Every event since then had plunged her deeper into a whirlpool of physical and psychological pain.

Lindsay changed out of her rebellious teenager outfit and pressed the button to check the messages on her answering machine. The machine responded in its monotone 2001 Space Odyssey voice, telling her that the memory was full. She tried a number of other buttons, but succeeded only in accidentally deleting all the messages. Her cell phone—along with her purse and the keys to her car—was still in her locker in the chaplain's office. She was anxious to hear news of Joe and of Buford Bullard, and even more anxious to flee the stifling hothouse of her own bursting mind. She decided to return to the hospital. She prayed that Anna had finished her shift and gone home. If Lindsay could avoid her, she might be able to temporarily stave off the inevitable haranguing she would get for deserting the hospital and removing the cast.

##

Lindsay had retrieved her belongings from the chaplains' office. No one was around, and no messages awaited her on her cell phone. She made her way to Joe Tatum's room. Her quiet knock on the door was met with silence. She opened the door slowly. The room stood as empty and still as an open grave, with a gloomy light filtering in through the closed curtains. Lindsay's stomach knotted and she scanned the room, looking for a trace, a clue that would tell her if Joe was okay. Joe's chart dangled from a hook at the foot of the bed. As she scanned it, she exhaled deeply—from what she could understand, it seemed that all was well. He had been scheduled for a routine, follow-up CT scan, and had probably been taken to the radiology department. She checked with Angel, the duty nurse, who confirmed this and told Lindsay that John and Rob had gone home to try to get some sleep.

Lindsay's next port of call was Buford Bullard's room, where the scene was the polar opposite. Versa and all her children and grandchildren crammed into the tiny space. The room was like a circus tent—with flowers, balloons, noise, and people. There was barely enough space for the door to swing open when Lindsay entered. In the center of it all sat Buford Bullard, looking drained and anemic, but conscious, and wearing a broad grin. When Versa caught sight of Lindsay, she parted the sea of people and hurried to embrace her. Versa squeezed Lindsay to her substantial chest; the embrace was like quicksand, soft and suffocating. Lindsay winced. She still bore the bruises of her previous night's encounter with Drew and the concrete wall. Her little cry of pain was muffled in the flesh of Versa's wide bosom. When she finally released Lindsay, Versa spun her around to face the room. "Buford, honey, you owe your life to this little person here," she said. "Doctor Peedie says she's the one that figured out about them pills." With that, the quicksand hugs began afresh, as each Bullard took a turn wringing Lindsay like a wet sponge. Lindsay had no opportunity to protest or explain that her findings hadn't really done anything to alter Buford's prognosis.

When at last the hugging and thanking mercifully ceased, Kimberlee waved her hand and cleared her throat, trying to get her family's attention. "Excuse me, y'all. Ahem. Excuse me." The chattering and noise showed no signs of abating, however, so Kimberlee climbed up on a chair and shouted, "Hey! Pipe down, y'all, I'm trying to tell you something." Silence finally descended. "I've been wanting to tell you all for awhile, but with one thing and another, I just couldn't. I really wanted to wait until they locked up the son of a bitch who killed my Vernon, but now, with Silas getting released, it looks like justice might not come for a long while yet. And I know that the police still haven't definitely given Momma the all-clear about how she poisoned Daddy. But they were a lot more civilized toward her than they were toward me, and I know we all took that as a good sign. Anyway, with the soap opera it's been lately, I don't know if there ever is gonna be a perfectly right time. And with Daddy being awake, now seemed as good a time as any. So, well, there isn't any other way of saying it…I'm pregnant!"

There was a collective scream from the Bullard women, which brought to mind the rebel yell of a Civil War battlefield. The women and children surged forward, their reactions ranging from congratulatory, "You are gonna be the greatest mom!" to chastising, "I can't believe you didn't tell us before!" to commanding, "Get down off that chair this minute, before you fall down and hurt my grandbaby!" When the news spread through the Bullards that Kimberlee was carrying twins, another collective scream rose from the chattering gaggle.

In the excited rush toward Kimberlee, Lindsay and Keith were pushed to the back of the group, near the door. Lindsay caught Keith's glance. Rivers of tears streamed down his cheeks as he watched his family rejoice. Lindsay had seen lots of tears in her time, but these were particularly pitiable. "You okay?" she asked.

Keith nodded. "It's just, you know, Vernon won't be here to see them born. They won't know who their daddy was. Poor Kimberlee. I feel real bad about that. Breaks my heart." Lindsay put a comforting hand on his shoulder. His flesh, even through the tight-woven cotton of his dress shirt, was strangely hot and rigid, like a brick that had been baking in the sun. Lindsay shuddered involuntarily at the unexpected sensation. Keith held her gaze for a long moment. In his eyes, Lindsay discovered a language she couldn't read.

Chapter 48

The Bullards' celebrations were drowned out by a gust of wind that rattled the windows of Buford's hospital room. The lights flickered briefly and the women's voices fell. Versa walked to the window and gazed out into the storm. Although it wasn't yet noon, the sky was as dark and grey as a November evening. "Keith, honey, you'd better go along to the restaurant and tell Dirk and them to shut up early. Can't be much business coming through anyway."

"Why do I need to go out there, Momma? I can just call them on the phone. Dirk knows what to do," Keith replied petulantly.

"It would do some good for you to show your face out there. We need to make sure everybody knows that it is still Bullards Family Barbecue Restaurant."

"Well, then, why can't one of the girls go?"

"Are you are or aren't you the manager of the restaurant? You need to deliver the good news about Daddy in person. I'm sure the staff'll all be anxious to hear," Versa turned her back on Keith to close off further argument. Keith sighed and then shuffled out of the room like an obedient dog. Lindsay left a few moments later, too distracted by her own thoughts to fully share in the Bullards' celebrations. She walked down the hospital corridor pondering her next move. Even now, Sarabelle and Swoopes could be at her father's house. Would they hurt him? Should she try to enlist Warren's help? She was so caught up in her own mind that she didn't notice Anna and Rob until they were standing almost directly in front of her.

"Ground Control to Reverend Harding," Rob said, waving his hand in front of her face.

"Oh, hi guys." Lindsay mustered a smile. "How's Joe?"

"Unbelievably…himself." Anna shook her head in amazement. "In fact, he wants to go home tomorrow. And he is being such a pain in the hospital's collective ass that they are talking seriously about letting him go. John and Rob are going to stay with him until he is discharged to make sure he stops 'accidentally' letting his hospital gown fall open in front of the female nurses." She glanced at Lindsay's now cast-free leg. "You and Joe must be vying for the top spot at the Patient Noncompliance Awards. Next time I'll superglue the cast to your skin."

"I will rest. I promise. Soon. Right now, though, I have things to do," Lindsay said.

"Like what? Lurk around the hospital on your day off?" Rob raised an inquisitive eyebrow. "Speaking of social lives, and lack thereof, tell me about your date with Dr. Drew Checkoway. Anna said you guys took a bath together!"

"Anna has put a creative spin on the truth I'm afraid. Basically, Drew tried to force-feed me with healthy food, I flashed a stadium full of people with my see-through dress, and then he almost knocked himself unconscious escaping from a rampaging squirrel."

"Come on, Linds!" Anna interrupted. "That is not at all what happened! Drew said he had a really nice time with you. He said he thinks you're really sweet."

"Uh-oh," Rob said. The playful glimmer was suddenly extinguished from his eyes. "You didn't tell me he said 'sweet'. Sweet is not good. Kid sisters are sweet. Old ladies with little knitted coin purses are sweet. Dates should be 'hot' or, at worst, 'fun'." He paused in the midst of his semantic analysis. "Wait, you talked to Drew about their date? When?"

"I don't know. Yesterday or this morning. It just came up. Drew and I were in the break room," Anna replied, blushing slightly at the mention of his name.

Rob, ever sensitive to the subtle ebbs and flows of other people's emotions, gasped. He pointed an accusatory finger at Anna. "You have a crush on Drew!"

"No, I don't! I'd never do that! He's Lindsay's," Anna protested.

"You like him! You like him! You like him!" Rob's voice had none of its accustomed mischief. Anna was his friend, of course, but it was clear that he would disavow her in an instant for Lindsay's sake. One of the things that Lindsay loved the most about Rob was on display now—he had decided long ago that the only one allowed to torment Lindsay was him. If he ever sensed that she was in real emotional danger, he protected her with the ferocity of a mother badger defending her cubs.

"I don't!" Anna retorted, backing away.

"Hey!" Lindsay said. Her raised voice sliced through the volley of accusations. "Cool it." The argument skidded to an abrupt halt. Lindsay continued, "Drew isn't 'mine'. I admit that he's nice. I admit that he's smart. And we've previously established that he is a 60s-era, pre-NRA Charlton Heston. But one thing that he's not is 'mine'. We went on one date, which was awkward. We've had several awkward conversations. I feel like an idiot every time I talk to him. I think I've been attributing all that awkwardness to sexual tension or nerves, but when I really think about it, he and I just don't have much to say to each other." She sighed deeply. "If the horse is dead, you have to take off your saddle and quit trying to ride, you know?"

Silence descended over the group. Anna and Rob seemed taken aback by Lindsay's calm, resolute tone. "Are you sure this isn't just another case of your chronic relationship-phobia?" Rob asked.

"Positive. The horse is dead."

Anna cleared her throat and looked at her shoes. "In that case," she said, "is it okay with you if I take up Drew's reins?"

"I knew you liked him!" Rob cried triumphantly.

"Mount up, cowgirl. He's all yours," Lindsay replied.

Now that it was clear that Lindsay was in no longer in danger of betrayal or heartbreak, Rob's impish streak reemerged. "That's it?" he asked. "No catfight? Come on, Linds. Smack her. Pull her hair."

"Sorry, Rob," Lindsay said.

Rob frowned. "I need to find some more interesting friends."

"Are all the shootings and poisonings happening around here not enough to keep you occupied?" Anna said.

"Shooting! Excellent idea. You two could duel, and

whoever comes out alive wins Drew!" Rob said hopefully.

##

After leaving Anna and Rob, Lindsay realized that she would have to decide quickly whether to hunker down in the hospital or ride the storm out at her house. Outside, gigantic raindrops danced sideways in the gale-force wind gusts. Soon, any kind of travel would become very difficult. Lindsay weighed her options. Geneva was on call overnight and would be sleeping in the chaplains' room. Lindsay could usually find an empty bed somewhere in the hospital to sleep, but with the storm raging and the hospital filled with on-call staff, peace and quiet would be hard to come by. She decided to brave the storm and head home.

At the front door of the hospital, Lindsay was confronted by sheets of rain. The outer bands of the hurricane had begun their full frontal assault on central North Carolina. Lindsay had a tiny folding umbrella in her purse, but recognized that it would be futile to try to keep such weather at bay with a flimsy piece of cloth and metal. She took a deep breath and sprint-hobbled toward the parking lot where Jonah's Buick was parked. She unlocked the door and dove inside. The warm air inside the car combined with the dampness in her clothes and hair and instantly covered the car windows in a layer of thick white steam. The car smelled like her father—Old Spice and freshly cut grass. As she put the key in the ignition and pulled out of the parking lot, she wondered if she should go to Jonah's instead of going home. She drove through town slowly, weighing her options. Was there really anything that she could do to help Jonah? He seemed determined to be "fair" to Sarabelle—even if that meant alienating Lindsay, risking his reputation, and possibly endangering his own life. Did he deserve Lindsay's help? Did he even want it? Given the weather, it was entirely possible that Sarabelle and Swoopes wouldn't show up at all.

Lindsay arrived at a crossroads at the edge of town. In one direction was Jonah's subdivision. In the other, her own house. She relaxed her grip on the steering wheel. It pulled slightly to the right—the direction of her house. She decided to follow this impromptu Ouija board-style omen and head home. Her father and Sarabelle would have to sort things out between themselves, by themselves, once and for all.

Chapter 49

Lindsay drove clear of Mount Moriah: past the empty parking lot of the new Walmart, past the shuttered shoelace factory, and past the former filling station that now housed John Johnson's Antiques, Memorabilia, and Beanie Baby Emporium. John Johnson's was the only thing that appeared to remain open for business, defying both logic and the approaching hurricane. Ever-larger gaps opened between ever-smaller clusters of houses. She guided the Buick along the winding two-lane road, grateful that the familiarity of the route so far compensated for the hazardous weather conditions. Rain enveloped the car with each fresh gust of wind. Lindsay eased off the gas pedal as she approached another curve. When she resumed pressure to the accelerator, there was no response from the engine. The car rapidly lost speed. She pressed her foot down more firmly, but the car continued its deceleration. Hoping to discover the source of the car's sudden malfunction, she glanced at the instrument console. Her heart sank. The fuel gauge had dipped into the barren no man's land below E.

Lindsay glided the car to rest beneath a broad-shouldered magnolia alongside the road, hoping the tree would provide a modicum of shelter against the storm. She put the gear in Park and pulled the key out of the ignition. The muffled sounds and indistinct green and gray landscape that had flashed past as she drove now became discrete. Each rain-drenched tree, heavy cloud, and booming bellow of the storm could be sensed with stark clarity. Lindsay began to laugh, hysterically, uncontrollably, with tears running down her cheeks. She hadn't checked the fuel gauge at all since she had commandeered the car that morning. Over the years, Jonah had chastised her countless times for leaving her gas tank running on fumes. By contrast, he always refueled his as soon as the gauge dipped below half a tank. This time, though, when Lindsay was blindly relying on his unfailing dependability, he had let the fuel run low.

She wiped her wet cheeks and fished her phone out from the bottom of her purse. Plenty of charge in the battery for once. She opened her wallet and pulled out her AAA membership—a gift from Jonah a few Christmases ago. If his momentary inattention had helped her get stranded, at least his over-protectiveness could help her get un-stranded. She dialed the number, and after several minutes on hold, was connected with a customer service representative. With a harried apology, the rep informed Lindsay that because of the tremendous volume of storm accidents and breakdowns, it would be at least three hours before roadside assistance would reach her. Lindsay sighed helplessly and hung up the phone. Her options were becoming increasingly limited. She couldn't call Jonah. Even if he was willing to come, there's no way he could ride through the storm on his motorcycle. Rob and John were busy with Joe at the hospital, and Anna had been talked into staying on call in the ER. She tried Warren's cell phone—he was definitely someone who owed her a favor—but her call went straight to his voicemail. Warren's recorded voice directed her to "call the New Albany police, or, for queries relating to the Young investigation, contact FBI Special Agent Valentine Fleet at (202) 542-9..." Lindsay hung up without even listening to the rest of the message. Valentine. That explained a few things. The minutes ticked by, stacking into tens and dozens. She tried Warren again, but again his voicemail picked up. She tried AAA again, only to be told that she could now expect a four-hour wait. Oceans of rain cascaded down the windows of the car, giving Lindsay the eerie sensation of being trapped in a marooned submarine at the bottom of the sea.

At last, the blazing, white headlights of an approaching pickup truck cut through the dreary landscape. Lindsay grabbed her bright red umbrella from the backseat. She hopped out of the Buick and stood on the shoulder of the road, waving the open umbrella frantically to signal the passing driver. The truck was now within a few hundred yards of her. She was sure the driver could see her at this distance, and she was sure that they would have to slow down significantly approaching the steep curve in the road. The driver did slow down; however, there were no signs of stopping. Lindsay stepped determinedly into the road in the path of the approaching truck. This could be her only chance to hitch a ride, and she wasn't going to let it go by without a fight. The driver would either have to stop or to swerve past her.

As the distance between Lindsay and the driver narrowed, the driver's features came into clear focus. Lindsay was surprised to make out the familiar, ruddy face of Keith Bullard. Keith's expression, too, revealed surprise. He slowed to a stop in the middle of the road a few yards shy of where she stood. Lindsay ran over to the driver's side of Keith's extended cab pickup truck. Keith rolled down his window.

"Boy, am I glad to see you!" Lindsay exclaimed.

"What on earth are you doing out here on a day like this? This rain is liable to drown you where you stand!" Keith shook his head. "And what are you doing running out in front of my truck? You got a death wish or something?"

"Desperate measures were called for. I've already been out here for an hour and you're the only car I've seen. Can you give me a ride back to my house? It's not far."

"Yeah, okay. Hop in."

Lindsay returned to her car, retrieved her purse, and locked the car doors. The abandoned Buick looked forlorn, and Lindsay felt an odd pang of guilt leaving it alone on the roadside. By the time she hoisted herself into the cab of Keith's truck, she was soaked to the skin. "Sorry about bringing the storm into your car along with me." Lindsay pushed aside some stray curls that the rain had plastered to her face. She turned toward Keith and noticed that he was also drenched. Spatters of reddish clay mud clung to shirt and pants. "Guess I'm not the only one who got a good dunking out there."

"Oh yeah," Keith looked down at his muddy clothes with slight embarrassment. "Only takes a minute out there."

"I hate to take you out of your way when you're already doing me such a huge favor, but I'm afraid my house is in the other direction from where you were headed. It's out by the old Richards Homestead," Lindsay said.

"It's no problem, really." Keith turned the big truck around, executing a three-point turn in the middle of the empty road.

It occurred to Lindsay that Keith was coming from the

opposite direction of Bullard's Barbecue. "Where are you coming from, anyway?" she asked. "I thought you were given your marching orders to head out to the restaurant. Don't tell me that you have the gumption to defy Versa Bullard's direct command?" Lindsay teased playfully.

Keith's response was petulant. "The guys who work for us ain't little kids. They don't need their hands held. I called and told them to shut, and I'm sure as Shinola they'll be all right by themselves."

Lindsay was taken aback by Keith's sudden burst of temper. He sat there glowering and staring at the road ahead. Lindsay shivered as the frigid blast from the truck's air conditioner chilled her wet clothes and hair. As they turned into Lindsay's neighborhood, the wind outside blew so ferociously that the massive truck shimmied slightly to one side of the road. A crack like a gunshot blasted through the din of the storm. There was a flash of black, like an enormous bird of prey swooping down from above, and then the broken top of a pine tree speared the ground on their right. Keith braked and jerked the wheel violently to the left to avoid the falling branches. Lindsay steadied herself with both hands on the dashboard. Empty soda cans and balled-up fast food wrappers rolled out from under Lindsay's seat, engulfing her feet in the detritus that dwells in the forgotten spaces of cars.

"God bless America! That was close!" Keith exclaimed.

"I'll say," Lindsay agreed. A piece of hard metal protruded from under the seat and pressed uncomfortably against her Achilles tendon. She tried to push it back with her feet, but couldn't shift it. The truck pulled into Lindsay's driveway with the familiar sound of gravel crunching under tires. Her little white house perched comfortingly on its lot. Her electric blue Toyota Tercel stood in the driveway like an old friend. "Well, here you are," Keith said. "Home sweet home,"

"I can't thank you enough for driving me. I owe you big time." Lindsay gathered her things. Her red umbrella had fallen to the floor during their near-collision with the pine tree, and she bent over in her seat to retrieve it. She caught a glimpse of the object that had been pressing against her heel. She could only make out a small part what appeared to be a piece of pipe. It was wrapped in a wet sheet, speckled with the same mud that covered Keith's clothes. She pushed it back under the seat and straightened up again.

The chill that made her tremble earlier now took hold of her entire body. With sudden, sickening clarity, she realized that she had not given Keith directions to her house. But somehow he had known exactly where it was.

Chapter 50

Lindsay glanced over at Keith, who continued to gaze straight ahead. His hands remained tightly gripped on the steering wheel. Every synapse in her brain seemed to sizzle and fry with new realizations. Keith knew where she lived. He had clearly been to her house before. He must have been following Joe that day, trying to silence him, trying to cover his tracks. Lindsay was certain now that the object she had felt under the seat was a gun. Was it the gun that he used to shoot Joe? The same gun he used to kill Vernon? She tried to breathe, but the inside of the truck was suddenly as devoid of air as the surface of the moon. She managed to squeak out a quick, “Goodbye,” and with shaking hands, opened the door. She lowered herself out into the storm and slammed the door of the pickup truck behind her, too forcefully. Had Keith noticed her behavior? Had he caught a glimpse of her terrified face?

Lindsay walked with slow, measured steps. Or should she run? Perhaps that would seem more natural—to run through the storm toward the shelter of her house? No, walking was better. Lindsay thought she could feel Keith’s gaze searing through the pouring rain, judging her every movement, burning a hole in the back of her neck. She took a few more steps. Perhaps he hadn’t noticed anything. Perhaps this feeling of intense scrutiny was her imagination. Her thin hopes of an easy escape were soon dashed, however, as she realized that Keith’s truck was no longer running. He had cut the engine. Lindsay froze. He was going to come after her. He knew. If she ran into her house, it would provide no sanctuary. Keith could break a window and be inside in a matter of moments. Or he could use the gun to shoot her through one of the large windows that were in every single room. She wouldn’t even have time to call the police. There were no close neighbors to run to. No one would even hear the gunshot. No one would even hear her scream.

Through the low howl of the wind, Lindsay heard the creak of Keith's truck door opening. The combination of noises was like the sound reel from some dreadful B-movie—the rising lid of Dracula's coffin in a storm-ravaged, cliff-top castle. There was a crunch of boots on gravel as Keith jumped out of his truck. For Lindsay, the sound was like a starting pistol. She began to run, for the first time in days feeling no pain from her injured knee. She fished her keys out of her purse as she went, never losing speed. When she drew level with her car, she darted sideways, throwing open the unlocked door and diving inside. She thrust the key into the ignition, and praised God, Jesus, and the Toyota Motor Corporation as the engine roared instantly to life. In the rearview mirror, she could see Keith running toward her, his face a mask of fear and rage. She slammed her foot on the accelerator and threw the car into reverse. Keith could only pound on the side of the car as she gunned it past him. When she reached the road, she shifted into drive and again slammed on the accelerator. Her purse was lying on the seat next to her. Struggling to maintain control of the car as she reached inside, she located her cell phone. She pulled it out, dialed 911. She counted six rings. Then seven. Finally, a recorded voice soothingly intoned, "Do not hang up. You have reached the 911 Emergency Services line. Due to the storm, all of our operators are handling other calls at this time. If you need emergency fire, police, or medical attention, please hold and a dispatcher will answer your call. Do not hang up…"

The headlights of Keith's truck appeared in her rearview mirror. Lindsay hung up. She dialed Warren's number. When it again went to voicemail, she groaned in frustration. But then she remembered that the message contained information that might help her. She listened to the whole message, and when Warren recited Fleet's cell phone number, she committed it to memory. She hung up and dialed Fleet. He answered on the first ring.

"Agent Fleet. This is Lindsay Harding. Listen to me very carefully." Lindsay outlined the situation for him as clearly and succinctly as she could. To her surprise, he did not seem the least bit skeptical of her story. All of his usual macho posturing was absent.

Fleet asked a few questions to clarify her location and then said, "Drive into Mount Moriah. Drive straight to the police station. We'll be waiting for you there."

"No." The word hung there, heavy and defiant.

"Did you not understand me?" Fleet asked incredulously.

"I understood you. But I am not going to do that. The police station is right smack in the busiest part of town. It's right next to people's houses. It shares a parking lot with an old folks' home, for heaven's sake."

"Exactly. It is a populated area. You'll be safer there."

"I know for a fact that Keith Bullard has a gun in that truck with him, and he has demonstrated on more than one occasion that he will use it against anyone who gets in his way. If he follows me into the center of town, there's no telling who he might hurt."

"And if you don't get here as soon as possible, chances are excellent that the person he's going to hurt is you."

"Even if I wanted to, there's no way I'd make it. His truck is huge and much faster than my car. He'll run me down on the long straightaway just outside town. I have to stay on the winding roads around here." Lindsay considered a moment. Keith's truck was now within yards of her car; the glare of his headlights filled her rearview mirror. "Listen. I am going to lead him out to the Richard's Homestead. There won't be anyone there, and you'll be able to trap him. How quickly can you get a whole mess of cops out there?"

"Miss Harding. I am going to tell you again. You get yourself into town. Drive there now. I will not have you endangering your life."

Lindsay knew that she was taking a risk by leading Keith away from town. But she felt that she had no choice. She replied in a voice like steel. "You have fifteen minutes. I need you to be there. Like I said, there's only one road in and out. I am fully aware that if you don't get there in time, it won't be him who is going to be trapped. It will be me."

Chapter 51

Lindsay zipped down the deserted country roads. The rain-washed landscape blurred past as she and Keith sped along. Keith's truck indeed proved capable of much higher speeds than her little Tercel. Only the circuitousness of the road layout, and Lindsay's familiarity with it, kept her slightly ahead of him. Several times, he got close enough to nudge her rear bumper. Once, he even started to pull alongside of her as they traversed a straight section of road. Lindsay had barely been able to pull ahead before he tried to run her off the road. She buckled her seatbelt. Her thoughts fragmented into tiny, disconnected pieces. With each curve in the road, a hundred scenarios played out in her head. Would Keith try to take a shot at her as they drove? Did that happen in real life, or only in gangster movies? That particular possibility played out again and again, keeping her grip on the wheel firm and steady.

After what seemed like an eternity, Lindsay saw the faded sign denoting the entrance to the Richards Homestead. She yanked the wheel hard to the right. Her car fishtailed as it moved off the main road and onto the muddy track that formed the main path in and out of the Richards property. Some naïve part of her had been hoping that as soon as she reached this point, it would be like the finish line of a race—a battalion of heavily-armed officers would magically parachute down from the heavens. Instead, she saw only windswept pine trees, low hills, and orangey-red scars in the earth, where Silas Richards's recent excavations had taken place.

Deep, water-filled ruts in the dirt road forced Lindsay to slow her pace to a crawl. Keith, however, maneuvered his big truck with ease over the difficult terrain. The folly of her plan bore down on Lindsay even faster than Keith's approaching truck. Off the paved road, her little sedan was no match for his massive truck. This section of the Homestead was relatively open, affording her a clear view in all directions. Along one side of the dirt road was a field of tangled bushes and saplings. On the other was a six-foot deep drainage ditch that was filling rapidly with storm runoff. Lindsay scanned the horizon in every direction for signs of the police, but no help was to be found. She didn't even have time to process the realization that she was all alone before she felt a violent jolt. Keith's truck had drawn parallel to her. Even through the rain, Lindsay could make out every detail of his plump, red face, as he positioned his truck to batter her again. She tried to swerve to avoid the onslaught, but it was useless. He made contact with the back half of her car, causing her to spin wildly like a whirligig.

The centripetal force of the spin soon gave way to a feeling of disturbing lightness as the car careened off the edge of the road, hanging in the air for a moment before it splashed into the rushing waters of the drainage ditch. Thick clouds of steam rose from the engine. Water sloshed up over the windshield. For a moment, Keith Bullard was forgotten. Getting out of the car was all that mattered. Lindsay unbuckled her seatbelt and pulled frantically at the door handle. No movement. Bracing her legs sideways against the console, she threw her body against the door. Again, the force of the fast-rushing floodwaters held it tightly closed. Dread crept over her as water surged up menacingly from the floor. Within seconds, the frightful chill of the water reached her shins. She could feel the car coming unmoored from the bottom of the drainage ditch. Soon it would be swept along in the flood. Her left hand rested on a familiar piece of elongated plastic and the violent storm of terror in her mind was, for a moment, quelled. This ancient car—hallelujah!—had manual windows. She cranked the window furiously, but she had only managed to unroll it a few inches when she heard the heavy tread of boots on the top of her car. He was standing on the roof. The car listed to one side under the assailant's weight, bringing the water level in the car's cabin even higher. His steps faltered for a moment as he struggled to regain his footing. The thin metal roof of the vehicle groaned as his steps advanced, slowly, deliberately.

He was standing just above her. She could see the slight bubble-shaped depressions of his feet in the roof just over her head. Some strange instinct drew her to place the palms of her hands against one of the depressions. The intimacy of the touch made her shudder. All that separated her from this murderer was a thin skin of metal. This little depression must be his right foot. The right foot of the man who was going to kill her. She braced her feet against the floor of the car and made her body rigid. She set her mouth in a hard line. No, she thought, this was the foot of the man who was going to have tried to kill her. With a sudden surge of force, she pushed both her hands upwards with all her might. He took a few stumbling sideways steps, and the car tipped even further to the left. The jolt catapulted him head over heels onto the hood of Lindsay's car. He landed with a thud and lay there, momentarily stunned. The front of the car dipped lower and water surged over the hood. The deluge roused him and he flailed around, looking for something solid to hold on to. Lindsay screamed. The face that peered at her through the windshield was not the ruddy round visage of Keith Bullard. Instead, she found herself staring into the burning amber eyes of Valentine Fleet.

Chapter 52

When she awoke, Lindsay's first sensation was surprise. She had somehow expected to wake up in her own bed, having spent the last days in a fevered nightmare. A rough, damp wool blanket scratched her skin. Her head pounded. She opened her eyes and sat up. She was in the back of an empty police car, a metal cage separating her from the front seats. The radio crackled with faraway voices. She peered out the windows. She seemed to be at the Richards' Homestead, in the midst of a raging storm. But she saw no one around, no signs of human life. Feeling suddenly claustrophobic, she tried the door handle. It was locked from the outside. She slumped back into the seat and lost consciousness.

A short while late, Lindsay awoke to the sound of voices. She saw figures approaching through the rain. The front door of the police cruiser opened and Valentine Fleet climbed into the driver's seat. He looked calm. With no preamble, he spoke. He didn't turn to face her, but instead spoke to his own reflected image in the windshield. "There is Keith Bullard, on his way to Mount Moriah Hospital." Fleet gestured toward an ambulance that was carefully negotiating the muddy road. "I'll follow Mr. Bullard to the hospital and question him there." Fleet glanced at her in the rearview mirror. "Are you injured?"

"No, I don't think so," Lindsay replied.

"In that case, go with Vickers." Fleet barked an order into his walkie-talkie, and another patrol car appeared alongside them a moment later. Freeland Vickers, whose squat form and twinkly eyes Lindsay recognized from the county library, popped out of his car. He opened the door for Lindsay and gently escorted her to the passenger's seat of his cruiser. Fleet pulled behind the ambulance, heading back onto the main road. Vickers pulled into the convoy behind him. In the rearview mirror, Lindsay could see a line of half a dozen police cars following in a grim procession.

Lindsay said nothing. She pulled the rough blanket more

tightly around her shoulders. She felt nauseous and forlorn. She was consumed by the thought—not of her own narrow escape from death—but of the Young Family, still at Mount Moriah, celebrating Buford's improvement and the announcement of Kimberlee's pregnancy. She felt sure that none of them had any idea what Keith had done. They were a remarkably resilient family, but the coming weeks and months would test them beyond anything they had yet endured. Lindsay felt like the Grim Reaper, hovering with a sharp scythe over the sleeping form of some unsuspecting victim.

Freeland Vickers drove skillfully through the raging storm and deepening night, all the while chatting as casually and inanely as an old lady at a beauty salon. He seemed untouched by the storm, Keith's arrest, or Lindsay's shocked silence. He yammered on, blithely swerving around upended garbage cans and downed light poles. When they arrived at last inside the 70s-era, two-story yellow brick building that housed the New Albany police station, Vickers settled Lindsay unto one of the shabby sofas in the officer's break room. "Sorry, sweetheart, but Fleet wants you to stay put until he comes back from the hospital," he said, fluffing up a tattered, embroidered pillow and placing it gently behind Lindsay's head. Then he added, "Hey, where's your boyfriend? He was supposed to come back this afternoon. He had to take a suspect over to the lock-up in Mount Moriah and then he was gonna stop home before coming back here. Haven't heard from him since. This isn't the time to be going AWOL, what with all the hurricanes and murderers."

"I've been trying to reach him all day. I kind of thought he might be here." A hint of anxiety crept into Lindsay's voice.

"Well, I'm sure he's all right. Satterwhite's not gonna let a little drizzle hurt him," Vickers said cheerfully. "He probably just got roped into helping out over in Mount Moriah."

Lindsay hoped he was right. Now that the immediate danger to her own life had passed, she was consumed by worry—not just about Warren, but also about her father. She had learned from Vickers that most of the telephone and electric lines in the county were down. There was no way to reach him by phone. She could only hope that the storm had kept Sarabelle and Swoopes from paying their promised visit.

Lindsay passed the better part of two hours sipping milky coffee. She tried to distract herself by flipping through the muscle car magazines that were scattered around the break room. She was mentally exhausted, but her body kept twitching and moving, preventing her from relaxing. When this nightmare was all over Lindsay decided that she would take Anna up on her threat to put a cast on her leg. In fact, she might even request that Anna give her a whole body cast and put her in traction. She could use the rest.

The wind howled outside and pitch darkness set in, broken only by occasional jagged streaks of lightning. Lindsay watched helplessly as officers hurried in and out of the station, soaked in their neon yellow rain ponchos, responding to storm-related emergencies. News of the storm flashed repeatedly across the screen of a small TV in the corner of the room. Amanda had come ashore as a Category 2 Hurricane. It was losing strength as the eye moved toward them, and would probably be downgraded to a tropical storm by the morning. Not the worst-case scenario by any means, but it still packed enough of a wallop to rattle the windows of the sturdy brick police station and knock them onto power from a diesel-fueled back-up generator.

At long last, Vickers came in. "We just had a call through from the hospital. Keith Bullard might not pull though. Fleet shot him twice, and one of the bullets hit him in the stomach. He wants to talk. But he won't talk until you're there."

"He wants to talk to me?!"

"Well, not exactly. He wants to confess with his family present. Fleet wouldn't hear of it at first. Said it wouldn't be proper procedure. But I guess Keith's lawyer was down at the hospital. You know Marshall Pickett, who does them commercials where he's the Malpractice Kid? Turns out he's married to one of Keith's sisters. He's gonna defend Keith. He's gonna defend his one brother-in-law for killin' his other brother-in-law. And apparently it was the widow's idea. Go figure. Anyhow, Fleet reckons it'll be all right to have the family present if Keith's lawyer has okayed it. Keith says if he can't talk now, his own way, they can forget about him ever talkin'."

"Okay, but how do I fit into this?"

"Apparently, Versa Bullard won't see Keith unless you're

there. She says you've been a rock of spiritual strength for her. That's a direct quote."

"You could've fooled me. Just last night she threatened me and told me to get lost."

"Well, the Lord works in mysterious ways, I reckon."

Just then, a fresh gust of wind roared around the station. The dim lights flickered and died.

##

Lindsay and Vickers left the station while the officers were still scrambling to restore generator power. As Vickers drove Lindsay to the hospital, the storm increased in intensity. It became like a living thing—a raving maniac tossing around aluminum siding and battering the car with enormous bucketfuls of rain. When they finally arrived, another officer showed them into a room where the Bullards, minus Keith, were gathered. Buford was sitting in a wheelchair. His skin was so pale and brittle it seemed like you could see through it—all the way to the cracks in his spirit. Kimberlee, with tears streaming down her face, rushed over to Lindsay. She clung to her pathetically, her body wracked with sobs. Lindsay could find no words of solace. She could only hold Kimberlee until the crying lessened.

Versa approached them. "I'm so sorry. It's all my fault. I've made so many mistakes."

Lindsay took her by the hand. "Versa, we all make mistakes. This isn't your fault. You did your best."

"I should have gone to church. I should have made the kids go."

"Oh, honey, church can't save us from bad things. But God can be there when bad things do happen. God can be here for you right now."

They marched together down the corridor, guided by a policewoman. Fleet was waiting for them outside the room. "I want to be clear," he said, addressing Marshall, "that everything that is said in here is on the record."

Marshall looked around. The Bullards nodded gravely. "We understand."

The group entered Keith's room in the ICU. By a horrible twist of fate, it was the same room that Vernon had occupied only a week earlier. Keith lay on the bed with his eyes closed. Marshall approached him and whispered something into his ear. His eyelids fluttered briefly, but he kept his eyes closed as he began to speak.

"I'm so sorry, Kimmie. I shouldn't have done what I done to Vernon. I didn't think on how hard it would make things for you. And now for your babies. I'm real, real sorry."

Kimberlee took a step toward him, but stopped. She said in a low voice, "I just need to know why you did it, Keith. Why did you kill my Vernon?"

"The restaurant was supposed to be mine, Kimmie! You all knew that. Momma and Daddy treated him more like a son than they ever treated me. He was just so damned perfect at everything."

"He didn't want to take over the restaurant. He thought he was helping. We all understood that. I thought you understood it, too."

"Nobody ever thought to ask me about nothing. It's probably because Daddy isn't my real father."

"What on earth are you talking about?! Of course Daddy is your father," Versa said.

"Everyone knows it's Silas Richards," Keith said.

"Huh, I thought it was Joe Tatum," Marshall said.

"Shut up, Marshall," Kennadine said, slapping her husband on the side of his head.

"All of you can shut your mouths. I am your father, boy," Buford said.

"Then why did I always hear rumors? My whole life. On the playground, in the grocery store. Whenever I asked Mamma about it, she just told me to hush up."

Versa began to cry. Buford took hold of her hand. "I'm so sorry, baby. I should've shoved those people's tongues down their throats."

"But you never even denied it."

"Why should your Momma care what those fork-tongued bastards say?" Buford said. "What business is it of theirs?"

"Oh, Buford. Keith is right. I should have stopped that talk. Marshall, honey, Joe Tatum never had anything to do with any of this. That was just puppy love. We barely even went past the first base." She turned to Lindsay. "When I went to him last night, I just wanted to tell him I was sorry. I'd heard that he got shot and I didn't want him to die still holding any bitterness toward me."

"What about Silas?" Keith asked.

"I guess… I guess that part of me wanted people to think Silas could be your daddy. I wanted him to be shamed for what he did to me. For throwing me out like trash. But honey, he's not your daddy. I should've protected you from that talk, honey. I didn't know that you had those doubts."

##

Keith's confession continued. Under questioning from the police, he admitted that had been siphoning off money from the restaurant for years—the entire time he had worked as the manager, he had treated it as his personal piggy bank. When Vernon had begun to look more closely at the restaurant's finances, Keith's embezzlement was on the verge of being discovered. This, combined with his jealousy over Vernon's increasingly central place in the family, pushed him to violence. As he planned the murder, he hit upon the idea of sending Vernon the racially-incendiary letter. If he could point suspicion toward white supremacy as the motive, no one would suspect him. He had used Vernon and Kimberlee's printer to produce the letter out of simple convenience—he was afraid of being observed if he used the one at work, and he didn't have a printer at home. He didn't know the source of the letter would be traceable, and he never intended to frame his sister.

Keith also admitted to shooting Joe; he thought that Vernon's dying words to Joe might have revealed him as the killer. He also talked about his reason for having the gun in the truck with him. After he shot Vernon, he had wrapped the gun in a piece of canvas and buried it in a shallow trench at the State Park. He had anticipated the police confiscating the reenacting guns, so he made sure to have a decoy hidden out in the woods. He surrendered the decoy to the police, and went back later to retrieve the murder weapon. After shooting Joe, he buried the gun in the same spot where he intended to leave it forever. The specter of the approaching hurricane, however, made him nervous. He worried that floodwater might erode the loose clay and expose the gun's resting place. He had gone out in the storm that day after leaving the hospital, to the deserted State Park and retrieved the weapon. He was on his way to throw the gun into the storm-swollen Haw River when Lindsay flagged him down.

The statement was so complete that Lindsay couldn't help but feel that it might be a sort of deathbed confession. Keith had even asked if he could be given the death penalty as his punishment. It went on—blow by painful blow—until Keith finally lost consciousness.

As everyone dispersed, Vickers took Lindsay by the elbow, walked her into an empty room and shut the door behind them. "Fleet wanted you to stay here until he could 'debrief' you," Vickers began, "but we all think you should go home and get some rest. You've been through more than enough for one day."

"Aren't you afraid of going against Fleet?" Lindsay asked.

"Naw. He'll be going home soon now that the Young murder is winding down. Everything will be back to normal in a couple of weeks."

"What about Silas Richards? I don't suppose he's going to forget about getting wrongly arrested anytime soon," Lindsay said. A pang of guilt swept over her as she recollected her own sizeable role in that fiasco.

"I can't believe Satterwhite didn't tell you! Good old Warren fixed that one up. Silas was threatening to sue, of course, almost from the moment he stepped out of the county lock-up. But Warren had an ace in the hole. Turns out some little old biddy has some kind of family claim on the land out at the Richards' Homestead. Going back to slave times. Warren got the old gal to pay Silas a call. She promised to give up any legal rights to the land as long as he agreed not to sue anybody about him getting arrested. And, she even got Silas to agree to set aside part of the land for historic preservation and to fund a museum dedicated to her husband's great, great granddaddy!" Vickers voice dropped low and his tone became conspiratorial. "Just between you and me," he added, "Satterwhite might also have mentioned that he knew that the Richards family comes from a long line of Yankee carpetbaggers. And that, if Silas wanted to keep that proud and noble lineage under wraps, it might do him good to forget this business about that little mistake with the arrest. Tell me that ain't a fine bit of police work!" Vickers slapped his knee and laughed uproariously.

"Well," Vickers said, wiping tears from his cheeks, "I'd better get you home before this storm gets any worse. I reckon we're gonna need a boat 'stead of a car if we wait much longer."

Chapter 53

The streetlights were out all over town, and Lindsay again had to rely on Vickers's adept driving and the sturdiness of a New Albany Police Department Chevy Suburban to conduct her safely through the storm-ravaged landscape. Tornado warnings and watches were blaring from the radio. They didn't see any twisters, but they had a few near misses from airborne debris sailing past them. At last, they pulled up in front of Jonah's house, which was dark, except for a faint glow of candlelight coming from deep inside. Lindsay opened her car door to take her leave when Vickers suddenly said, "Hey, I've been to this house before. Years and years ago. Yeah, I'm sure it was this place. I'd just started on the force in fact, maybe two months before. We got a tipoff that there was a couple of kids in there growing a forest full of cannabis—a guy and a girl who couldn't have been more than twenty. They had sheets and blankets hung over all the windows and every room was full of plants. Plants in the kitchen cabinets, plants in the bathtub, everywhere. It would have been funny, almost, except that they had a little daughter in there. Matter of fact, the only place they didn't have marijuana was in the little girl's room."

Lindsay pulled her car door closed again and listened intently as Vickers continued the story. Hearing the story was like discovering a photo album that chronicled a familiar event, but from an entirely new camera angle. "Yeah, the kid was maybe four or five. She cried like the dickens when we took her mommy and daddy away in handcuffs. And the parents cried, too, especially the father. He had to be dragged away. And I mean literally dragged. The man was clawing at the earth trying not to be parted from that little girl. Kept telling her that everything would be all right, and he'd come back for her. She ended up going to live with some relative or another down east. I've sometimes wondered what became of her. Probably a druggie like her folks. I doubt she ever had much chance." Vickers sighed and said, "Anyway, I didn't mean to trouble you with a miserable story like that! I guess this is what happens to us men with they get old. I'm going all soft and sentimental. Look, I've even got you crying now."

Lindsay thanked Vickers for the ride and hurried up the driveway to the side door of the house, her tears mingling with the rain. She peered through the glass into the kitchen. Jonah was sitting alone, studying his Bible at the table. She tried the door, but found it locked. She tapped hard on the glass, so her knock could be heard above the din of the storm. Jonah looked up in alarm, but his face softened when he saw Lindsay. He opened the door and folded her into his arms. For once, she did not stiffen at his embrace. "How did you get here? Are you okay?" Jonah led Lindsay inside and settled her in one of the kitchen chairs. An odd array of candles glowed in the center of the table—everything from tea lights to a chunky, glass-potted candle with the words "No. #1 Preacher" inscribed on the side with a silver marker.

Lindsay's brain formed her familiar, deflective anthem, "It's a long story. I'll tell you later." But instead of uttering those words and moving on to another topic, she found herself spilling the events and emotions of the previous weeks. Her story took nearly an hour, and Jonah listened quietly, without interrupting. When she finally finished, she braced herself for the inevitable onslaught of chastisements, solutions, and I-told-you-so's. Instead, Jonah patted her on her hand and poured her a glass of tepid sweet tea. They were like actors, accustomed to being typecast, now suddenly thrown into fresh roles. They sipped their tea in silence, their faces reflecting the warm orangey yellow of the glowing candles.

A booming knock on the front door shattered the calm. Lindsay had almost forgotten all about Sarabelle and Swoopes. She hadn't even asked Jonah whether or not they had come. The anxious look that suddenly broke across his face told her that they had not. Lindsay and Jonah crept toward the front door. They stepped cautiously, needlessly careful of making noise; the crash of the wind drowned out their footsteps anyway. Jonah straightened his spine and opened the door, ready to face whatever the storm had washed up on his doorstep. He and Lindsay let out simultaneous gasps of surprise. Soaked to the skin, alone, stood

Sarabelle. Lindsay scanned the surrounding street, but there was no sign of anyone else—just this rain-drowned woman, her eye makeup running down her cheeks in black rivulets, her white-blonde hair as limp as seaweed clinging to the shore. Lindsay had never seen Sarabelle looking anything other than immaculate. Now, harshly illuminated by a flash of lighting, she looked inconsequential and very, very old.

"Well, can I come in, or what?" Sarabelle demanded petulantly, forcing her way between them as she spoke. "I done walked here all the way from the Motel 6 over by Stuckey's. This damn wind almost blowed me outta my shoes."

"You walked here? In this weather?" Jonah asked, aghast.

"I had to, didn't I? That friend of your daughter's had our truck impounded." Sarabelle had removed the zip-front hooded sweatshirt that she'd been wearing and was ringing it out on the carpet.

"What friend of mine?" Lindsay asked, genuinely confused.

"As if you didn't know, Little Miss Goody Two Shoes. I can't believe that you would sic that bean-pole policeman on your own mother. And a' orange-haired, bean-pole policeman at that. You know that the only thing I hate more than policemen is carrot tops." Sarabelle removed her shoes, tipping a small stream of water out of each one. "Busted into our motel room this afternoon and cuffed Leander. Told me that I had ten seconds to decide if I wanted to end up in the back of a patrol car or be on my way. Said I better get well clear of North Carolina if I knew what was good for me! Can you believe that? What kind of man sends a woman out into weather like this? That carrot-top son of a bitch didn't call me a cab or nothing." She flopped down on the sofa and crossed her arms. "He's lucky I don't march right over to that police station right this second and demand his badge."

The vitriol of Sarabelle's monologue had been entirely directed at Lindsay. She now peeled the stray strands of her hair off her face and turned to Jonah, mustering her best damsel-in-distress expression. When she spoke, her voice seemed to sidle up beside him. "Sugar, can you get me a cup of coffee? Momma Bear's a little worn out from all this excitement."

Johan walked over to the door and opened it, gesturing for

Sarabelle to exit the way she had entered. "Get your own dang coffee. And get it somewhere else." His voice was as hard as stone.

"Sugar! What has gotten into you?" Sarabelle asked.

"Sense. Now get out of my house."

Sarabelle voice suddenly turned to acid. "Do you forget who you're talking to? I have as much right to be in this house as you do. I am your lawfully-wedded wife."

"Not for long, you're not. You can expect divorce papers just as soon as I can get down to the lawyer's office," Jonah said.

Sarabelle jumped off the couch as if it were on fire. She and Jonah circled each other like boxers in a ring. "If you even try to divorce me," Sarabelle began, "I am gonna make sure everyone in this town is reminded what kind of a person you really are. I'll be in the front pew at church every Sunday tellin' 'em. You can bet your sweet…"

Lindsay stepped between them and cut Sarabelle off, just as she was beginning to gather steam. Lindsay leaned toward her mother, pointing her index finger right between Sarabelle's eyes. "If you come within a hundred miles of that church, or my father, or me, I will have you arrested. Or did you forget about my friend the policeman?" Lindsay picked up an afghan that hung on the back of a rocking chair and threw it angrily at Sarabelle. "Make yourself comfortable on the couch. You can stay here until the storm lets up. Then I want you gone."

"We want you gone." Jonah put special emphasis on the plural.

Lindsay and Jonah left Sarabelle gaping like a fresh-caught fish. They retired to their bedrooms, whispering their goodnights in the hallway as they had done throughout Lindsay's childhood. Although the wind howled and raged through the night, Lindsay slept deeply and soundly.

##

When she awoke the next morning, bright rays of sun sliced through the cracks in the window blinds. The storm had passed. Lindsay wandered out into the living room. All that remained of Sarabelle was an indentation in the couch and a rumpled afghan on the floor. She walked to the kitchen, where Jonah was brewing coffee in the ancient coffee maker. "Power came back on," he said. Lindsay sat down at the table.

"She stole $400 from that empty ice cream tub I keep in the freezer," Jonah said. "I guess I should change my hiding places every couple of decades, huh?" He handed Lindsay a cup of murky brew that had a thick film of coffee grounds floating on the surface. She took a polite sip, pausing to chew some stray grounds.

"And she stole my Billy Graham Bible."

"Oh, Dad, no! I'm so sorry."

"It's all right. Really." Jonah sipped philosophically from his cup. He paused for a moment, swishing the coffee around in his mouth. Then he calmly walked over to his coffee maker. He pried off the lid that housed the inner workings. He tipped the machine backwards and dumped the coffee, chunks and all, into the heart of the machine. It sparked, then sizzled, then died. "She didn't take anything that matters."

"Well then," Lindsay said, with a broad smile.

Chapter 54

Jonah gave Lindsay a ride on the back of his motorcycle, out to the road where she had abandoned his Buick. The car looked bright and shiny from the rain. They filled the gas tank from a canister and were able to get it started up on the first try. Lindsay bid goodbye to Jonah, and drove his car to her house. It wasn't even nine AM, but the slow boil of the Carolina summer day had begun. Sunshine baked the ground, and the rising air was thick and humid. The physical traces of the storm were everywhere: enormous, lake-like puddles, downed branches, and the wind-scattered detritus of suburban life—shingles, garbage cans, lawn ornaments. But the ferocious weather was gone.

Lindsay showered and changed. The normalcy of the routine of cleaning her body soothed her frayed nerves. There was one more thing she wanted to take care of. Lindsay climbed into the Buick and dialed Fleet's number on her cell phone. She didn't relish the prospect of talking to him, but at least the idea no longer filled her with dread. "Hello. It's Lindsay Harding. I wanted to thank you for saving me yesterday."

"Yes," Fleet said, matter-of-factly.

Lindsay didn't know what she had expected. Maybe a brief moment of mutual understanding? Maybe a "you're welcome"? Anyway, nothing more seemed to be forthcoming, so she shifted the focus of the conversation. "Also, I need a favor," she continued.

"Oh?"

"Yes, I need Warren Satterwhite's address."

"I would have thought that you would already know it. Or perhaps he likes to keep his home life with his wife separate from his…activities with you."

"We don't have any activities. We are not dating. We are not a real couple and we never have been."

"I am heartened to hear you say it. I trust you are not

thinking of rekindling things with him. Married men make many promises, but in the end, that kind of thing can only bring unhappiness. To use your own words, you can never be a 'real couple' in a relationship like that."

Explanation was futile, so Lindsay said simply, "I'm sure you're right. I just want to return a few things of his."

Fleet gave her the address, but before closing the conversation said, "Sergeant Satterwhite told me how much you helped in solving this case." Lindsay thought for a half-second that he was going to offer his thanks. His voice took on a vinegary edge that made the hairs on the back of her neck stand up. "If I were you, I would keep any talk like that to yourself. The timely and competent assistance of the FBI solved this case. And this case is now closed. Opening it again might expose all sorts of unsavory details about personal lives, relationships, families, parents… All sorts of things best left buried."

"I understand completely," Lindsay said, pressing the 'End' button with the sincere hope that this would indeed be the end of her acquaintance with Special Agent Valentine Fleet.

##

Warren lived on the two-lane road that led out of Mount Moriah, past the Richards Homestead, under the expressway, and into the farms and forests beyond. It wasn't far from Lindsay's own house, but the journey—through the part of the county that had taken the hardest hit from the previous night's storm—was treacherous. At least half a dozen tornadoes had spun off from the hurricane, cutting huge swaths of devastation. Branches lay scattered in the road, and in one or two places, whole trees had toppled, blocking the way. When Lindsay tried to bypass them, the ground on the shoulder of the road was so sodden that the wheels of Jonah's Buick struggled to free themselves from the mire.

When she finally spotted the numbers of Warren's address hand-lettered on a battered aluminum mailbox, Lindsay exhaled deeply, grateful that her harrowing drive was over. Her sense of relief evaporated almost immediately, however. She pulled onto a dirt track that dead-ended into a cleared patch of ground and surveyed the scene before her. Two-by-fours, pieces of drywall, and other construction materials had been scattered by the winds of the storm. A decaying tobacco barn stood at one end of the clearing. Its wooden siding had, over many years, faded to a soft grey, and the edges of the building seemed to melt and mingle with the trees surrounding it. But it was what stood at the other end of the clearing that made Lindsay's heart jump. A small trailer home had been bent into a U-shape by an enormous shagbark hickory, which had fallen into the center of the trailer and crushed it.

The massive roots of the tree spread out like a sunburst, hanging just above a 5-foot deep crater in the ground where the tree had formerly been rooted. The only sounds were the chirping of birds and a muted creaking, like the hinge on a rusty door. Lindsay ran toward the decimated trailer. Peering inside the cracked windows, she could see the dim outline of what had once been a bedroom. Shafts of light shone through the jagged opening in the roof. Enormous branches crisscrossed the bed—Lindsay saw no movement in the leaf-obscured space beneath. She screamed Warren's name again and again as she pushed desperately at the window frame, trying to find some way of getting inside.

Her heart pounded so loudly in her ears that it took her several moments to realize that someone was shouting her name in response. She turned around to find Warren emerging from the decrepit tobacco barn. He wore boxers and a t-shirt and his face was puffy with sleep. He ran a hand through is sleep-tousled hair and said again, "I'm right here, Linds."

Before she had time to think about what she was doing, she ran to him. She jumped up and clung to him, wrapping her arms and legs around him like a child. When she climbed down, the two of them regarded one another with astonishment. Finally, Lindsay spoke, "Why didn't you answer your phone?"

"I don't have a signal. I think the tower might've blown down."

"Why didn't you go into work?"

Warren gestured to the other end of the driveway, where the fender of his police car was barely visible under the enormous trunk of another fallen tree. "The car is temporarily out of service. That happened yesterday afternoon. I stopped back here after dropping off a suspect. The wind was pretty crazy. I half expected to wake up in Munchkinland."

"When I saw the tree," Lindsay began, her eyes welling up with tears, "I thought you got squished."

"I nearly did. The trailer was shaking like a sinner in church all day and night. I spent most of the night hunkered down in the bathtub in there because I thought I'd be safer." He gestured to the tobacco barn behind him.

"There's a bathtub in there?"

"Two. I'll show you." Warren held Lindsay's hand and led her toward the building. Somehow, holding hands felt perfectly natural, as if this was the way things had always been between them. Lindsay now saw that the barn, which she had originally thought was derelict, was in fact a building site—windows had been installed and a new roof put on. Warren opened the solid oak front door to reveal the half-finished interior. He explained that he was living in the trailer while converting the barn into a house. Right now, he was adding a second story where the former loft of the barn had been. Through the open studwork interior walls, Lindsay see could the entire back wall of the building had been replaced with enormous windows, revealing a breath-taking view of the rolling hills beyond. The finished house wouldn't be large, but it would be beautifully in harmony with the surrounding land.

Warren gestured to the space that was laid out as the ground-floor bathroom. Sofa cushions and a down comforter filled the bathtub. "That's where I hunkered down last night. I tried to stay as far away from the windows as I could. They're insulated triple-thick glass, but I don't think that would have made much difference if a tree made its mind up to come inside. I guess I'll have to step up the pace of the work now that the trailer is gone."

"I love fixing up old buildings," Lindsay said.

"Is that an offer? Because I will put you to work."

"Well, I owe you. I can't thank you enough for what you did for Sara..." Lindsay corrected herself, "for my mother."

Warren sighed. "I'm not sure I did you or her any favors by letting her walk, you know."

"I know she's not going to change. But it makes me feel better to know that she's free, doing her thing. And I'm guessing that that suspect you brought over to the lock-up in Mount Moriah was Leander Swoopes?" Warren nodded. "Fleet also told me that you 'fessed up about me helping with the case."

"Since when do you and Fleet chitchat about me?" Warren said with a smile.

"Oh, we're best friends now. We braid each other's hair and do each other's nails."

"Maybe he can be maid of honor at our wedding," Warren said.

"Aren't you jumping the gun a little bit? You should probably divorce your Vegas wife first."

"I suppose. And we should probably go out on a date or two. What are you doing tomorrow night?"

"Shopping for a new car."

"I know where you can get a New Albany police cruiser for real cheap. It needs a little body work, but it comes with a free tree."

Lindsay smiled at him. "I really do appreciate you looking out for me, you know."

"Least I could do."

"Aren't you afraid of getting into trouble for lying to Fleet and then basically threatening to kill him at the hospital?"

"No. Fleet gets all the credit for solving the Young case. I also gave him Swoopes. Taking scalps is what he cares about, not whether some little no-account Barney Fife from the middle of nowhere gets his mistress to help him solve a murder case."

"I don't think you're Barney Fife," Lindsay said, putting her hand on his cheek. "Remember? You're Shaggy from Scooby Doo."

"I don't want to be Shaggy or Barney Fife or anybody. Let's just be Warren and Lindsay."

Lindsay nodded and smiled. "You're right. I think I'm ready for us to be Warren and Lindsay."

"Hey, I have a big surprise for you," Warren grew suddenly animated. "You're really going to like this." He led her outside to a little shed alongside the barn. "Sarabelle and Swoopes still had it hitched up to the back of their pickup." He flung open the door of the shed to reveal Lindsay's erstwhile jet ski, its metallic paint shining like a diamond in the sun.

Acknowledgements

I would like to thank all of the wonderful friends and family who read drafts and gave me encouragement, especially, Bethany Keenan, Elizabeth Enenbach, Margaret Reis, Tanya Boughtflower, Lori Williams, Julie Neef, Lori Hohenstein, Sandra Heyer, Claire Jacob, Barbara Quigley, Valerie Pate and Amy Feistel. My sister, Jaime Gagamov, deserves extra credit for providing me with an endless well of ideas and an unstinting source of support. Special thanks go to hospital chaplain Elizabeth Harding and ministers Allison Farnum, Maud Robinson and Kate Bradsen. If you ladies look closely, you will see flashes of your witty and wonderful selves in Lindsay Harding. Thanks also to the wacky folks in the Duke University Medical Center's Pastoral Services Department. You guys do an impossibly difficult job, and you do it well.

A giant, enormous, super-sized thank you to my husband, Paul Quigley. You are a better writer than me, and a better person, too. I heart you.